LES...
IS ALREADY DEAD

They shot across the last intervening distance, forward lasers firing in a converging pattern. As they broke through the ragged group of 528s, their after-weaponry searched and found targets.

"Way to go! Smoke the little—"

Jan heard the other sound, then blank hiss over the channel. "Gunny, you're hit. Talk to me."

Gunny's response was flat, leeched of its usual vitality. "Got you . . . "

"Are you hurt?"

"Negative. Targeting lead ship. We can't miss."

"Kill'm," Jan snarled. "Kill'm."

In this moment she was pure predator.

Other AvoNova Books by
Parke Godwin

BELOVED EXILE
FIRELORD
ROBIN AND THE KING
SHERWOOD

PARKE GODWIN

AVON BOOKS • NEW YORK

LIMBO SEARCH is an original publication of Avon Books. This work
has never before appeared in book form. This work is a novel. Any sim-
ilarity to actual persons or events is purely coincidental.

AVON BOOKS
A division of
The Hearst Corporation
1350 Avenue of the Americas
New York, New York 10019

Copyright © 1995 by Parke Godwin
Cover art by Vincent DiFate
Published by arrangement with the author
Library of Congress Catalog Card Number: 94-96867
ISBN: 0-380-77300-7

First AvoNova Printing: August 1995

AVONOVA TRADEMARK REG. U.S. PAT. OFF. AND IN OTHER COUNTRIES,
MARCA REGISTRADA, HECHO EN U.S.A.

Printed in the U.S.A.

RA 10 9 8 7 6 5 4 3 2 1

I am indebted for technical advice in the preparation of this book to Susan Shwartz, who co-authored the original version of this story in 1986; to Col. Clarence "Bud" Anderson, author of *To Fly And Fight*; and to Richard Herman, USAF (Ret.), author of *Dark Wing*.

Glossary of pilot/ search operator terms

all green—or "stay in the green." All systems on-line. Personally the equivalent of calm and cool.

cone—behind and within a "cone" of 30 degrees to left or right of target craft's tail. Optimal position for attack.

crits—critical reaction time for fighter pilots.

endees—NDs, adjusted new dollars.

five-by—radio signal strength, measured 1–5. Five-by is a loud, clear signal.

Have Quick—system enabling rapid frequency change for transmitters.

HUD—heads-up display of data and targeting on pilot's forward view screen.

Home/Warn—system enabling a craft to detect hostile radar scanning.

hushout—radio nets gone silent longer than usual.

kays—kilometers.

MOA—Morse Operator Analysis, electronic fingerprinting of individual operator's "fist" or touch on a key.

redline—status critical. In personnel, fitness below minimum standard.

rig or rack—operator's complex of receivers, recorders, etc.

six—as in "checking the six," pilot's six o'clock position behind the tail surface on 12-hour clock method.

tix—transmission or transmitter.

VOA—as MOA, electronic fingerprinting of an individual voice.

Limbo Search

—I—

UNIDENTIFIED
VOICE TRANSMISSION:
DESIGNATION SEARCH 528

Charley Stoner was originally posted for the Hydri IV Search mission, but Ed Reinecke took it for a hundred dollars and three packs of contraband cigarettes, which were as good as money anywhere. Reinecke regretted it now. He ached, squirming his fat buttocks on the position seat padded to take acceleration, though after ten hours the padding seemed to melt. His screen was divided into twenty-four squares at the moment, each a visual readout of an individual frequency as the auto-traverse receivers tuned, hovered back and forth and then slid by it. The unique alien signal he hunted first emanated from Hydri IV rolling five thousand kilometers below their small Sparrow listening craft. Since insertion between the barren planet and its two small moons days ago, Reinecke had heard zip, nothing, and twelve hours of each tedious day had been spent in this cramped position, listening for the unidentified entity designated by number alone: Search 528.

Come up, Reinecke thought as he watched the changing pictures on his matrixed screen. *I want to go home. I'm getting too old for this.*

Two more hours to go, then Rothberg, the Sparrow pilot, would ask for recall to the carrier *Moyers*, pacing them a few thousand kays farther out in space. Reinecke pressed the intercom switch on his seat arm. "Johnny, you got the carrier visible?"

"Negative. Just over horizon curve. Should have them in a minute. Let me know when your ass gets tired, Ed."

"Like now," Reinecke muttered irritably. Rothberg was only twenty-five. That was old as fighter pilots reckoned themselves if they lived that long, but only half his own age. "Just fly, Johnny. I got two dozen freqs to—"

Reinecke snapped alert. One of the squares on his screen jumped to life in two writhing, intertwining green lines. He wiped the screen and one receiver to the single frequency, listening. *Payday. There you are.*

The eerie double-throated voice sang in his ear.

"Johnny, he's up. 528. I got him but he's garbled and weak. Reverse course. I want to get a clean D/F cut on him."

"Not advisable," Rothberg came back. "I don't want to push if I don't have to."

Reinecke shot a frustrated glance forward at the cockpit. Rothberg had lived through a lot, but there was such a thing as being too careful. With 528 up and tixing, they could recall early, but Reinecke needed a clean directional cut. With the weak present signal his readouts were fluttering indeterminately, refusing to settle. "Come on, we're not that close. The carrier will pick us up with no sweat. Gimme surface coordinates. My D/F is nothing but hiccups."

Rothberg fed him the precise coordinates of the

terrain the Sparrow was passing over, adding: "Okay, I got *Moyers* on P-scan."

Reinecke called the carrier on operations channel. "Big John, this is Little Boy. I have Search 528 on 100.4 megs measured. Coordinate your D/F with me, over."

Excited now, Reinecke forgot his fatigue. "Johnny, carrier's backing us up. Give me a descending pass, close as you can. There's a glitch in his transmitter."

In the cockpit, Rothberg dubiously calculated orbital decay factor for their speed and mass. Skin temperature would rise as they dropped through atmosphere, but with *Moyers* visible they had an acceptable safety margin. But as Reinecke had sensed the alien about to transmit, Rothberg's instincts pulled his attention to the perimeter scan.

"Come on," Reinecke coaxed in the pilot's headset. "Take me *down*."

"Okay. You strapped?"

"Like a rupture in a tight truss. Let's *go*, I'm losing the signal."

"Firing ATs now."

The Sparrow lost velocity as the attitudinal thrusters reversed its course, descending at a shallow angle. The alien voice crooned in Reinecke's ears through the G-pull of the maneuver, still weak but with increasing signal strength as Reinecke's jittering D/F readouts began to settle. Search 528 was his find from the first, his and Stoner's, from the first tix recorded back on Limbo Station . . .

Fat Ed—Warrant Officer Edward Reinecke—was the first Search operator on Limbo to hear the alien double-voiced transmission from Beta Hydri IV.

He picked up the unidentified signal while searching out voice chatter from corporation pilots, thinking his antenna was oriented toward the Gamma Three System. Warrant Officer Charley Stoner, working at the next position, found that the previous operator at Reinecke's pos had forgotten to call Antenna Plot and cancel his program.

"But hey," Reinecke motioned Stoner to jack in his headset. "*Listen* to this sucker."

First Contact signals were a running joke with Limbo operators. None had yet been heard and there was a substantial bet pool on who would hear the first. The traffic analysts in TANAL didn't laugh; within a few minutes of Ed's intercept, they were elbowing for room around his pos. The alien entity was designated Search 528 and given top priority. Within seventy-two hours, the station Intelligence Officer, Major Nigel Pauley, received orders to insert an electronic surveillance Sparrow craft into the vicinity of Beta Hydri IV via the carrier *Moyers* for a probe.

"Great," Stoner predicted unhappily. "Guess who'll get the duty."

Eleanor Roven had it last time, Reinecke the time before that. Ed was getting too fat to cram his ass into a Sparrow pos for days on end. Stoner would be happy never to strap into one again.

"Tell you what," Reinecke conspired. "Make it worth my while, I'll take the mission."

"Serious?"

"Who found him first? Make me an offer," Reinecke tantalized.

"Hundred bucks," Stoner offered gratefully.

"And four packs of cigs."

"Bull*shit*."

"Take it or leave it," Ed concluded airily.

Stoner winced, wanting to leave it. Cigarettes were prohibited contraband on Limbo Station, heavily fined if discovered, and they cost fifteen endees a pack. "Three packs and deal."

"Done," Reinecke agreed—a little too quickly, Stoner recalled later. "I'll tell Pauley."

Before the mission they both haunted TANAL, comparing visual screen images, digital readouts and voice prints of the anomalous signal. No one discounted the possibility of a new corporation simulated voice code, but much more traffic was needed for any reliable construct. Corporations were not thought to be moving into the Beta Hydri System yet—not supposed to anyway, though that never stopped Corpses before.

"Somebody's out there," Stoner said, hovering over the playback, "and they ain't us."

Search 528 was officially tagged a first alien contact. Ed Reinecke collected the five hundred endee pool and lost most of it at poker.

The galaxy revolved. In permanent orbit around Beta Hydri I, Limbo Station turned lazily with it like a bright coin spinning in slow motion against black velvet.

Not the hubbed wheel of earlier concepts, Limbo's overall form resembled a mutated Tinkertoy or tic-tac-toe matrix with added doodles, each a complex of functions within the whole. Secured to airlocks by flexible umbilici, the FTL sister carriers, *Kennedy* and *Moyers*, turned with the mother station.

Built by Texas Mineral as a base for commercial exploration and exploitation, Limbo had been

ceded (more or less) peacefully to the United Earth
Space Authority twenty-five years ago before TM
had the muscle to argue in the running skirmish
between shifting administrations and shrinking
budgets on both sides of the public/private sectors.
Corporations being more accountable than governments in spending, Limbo was the result of low-
bid construction, functional and up to specs but a
reflection of no-frills planning, from the orbital attitude that required frequent adjustment to the environment simulators in the recreational, mess and
wardroom areas that rarely worked right. Intended
panoramas of Niagara Falls or the Bavarian Alps
projected on the bulkheads with all the reality of
antique computer simulation. TM workers nicknamed the station Limbo, being as far out as humans had traveled in space at the time. As a
UNESA listening station, the name became official.

Around the clock three shifts of operators fanned
sophisticated antennae to monitor electronic traffic
from giant corporations like TM, Allied Development, TransWorld or Myoshi Metals. Monitoring
the inter-system communications of the huge corporations, they copied electronic emissions of every
known type from high-level policy nets to voice
chatter of small-craft pilots. Limbo cryptographers
broke Corpse ciphers and read the traffic, scanning
cleartext messages for hidden codes and references.
Nothing was irrelevant; the type of supplies req-
uisitioned via low-level net could point to the nature of their eventual use.

Corpse operators, aware of being monitored,
played fox and hound up and down the spectrum
with have/quick transmitters. Search operators
learned to predict the changes without losing too

much traffic. Within Intercept, Search was a separate and almost hallowed sub-section charged with identifying and reestablishing known nets whenever they changed frequency, callsigns or cipher systems, to find and ident new nets when they appeared, and to record any unique transmission like Search 528.

Headed by Warrant Officer Stoner, Search reported to the Intelligence Officer, Nigel Pauley who answered directly to Intelligence Coordination (COORDINT) at UNESA's Earthside headquarters, with no interference from the station CO, Lt. Col. Hubert Dorfmann, a large and phlegmatic last-tour officer from Tennessee. On Limbo's T/O, Pauley was second in command; in practice Dorfmann left OPS alone and Pauley interfered as little as possible with the day to day maintenance of Limbo. Each was perfectly slotted for his function. On his sunset tour, Dorfmann wanted to make no waves to impede his retirement as a full bird colonel. Nigel Pauley's career and talents lay in sensing the wave before it rose.

His first daily concern was operational summary from Intercept, especially Stoner's Search picture, the cutting edge. Pauley considered Search the instinct and the flying Sparrow operators its sixth sense. Presently he had only three qualified Sparrow pilots and three flying warrant officers, Stoner, Reinecke and young Ellie Roven who was a prodigy even by Stoner's formidable standards. Both her flying peers were old enough to be her father. That did not hinder Reinecke's speculation.

"I'll say this. She ain't hard to look at."

"Yeah." Charley Stoner had passed through marriages like diseases, finally immune. "But I

won't screw up a good thing. Good lays are anywhere, but good Search ops? One in a hundred."

When Ellie qualified for flight duty they adopted
her as a kid sister in the elite Sparrow fraternity
dubbed the Claustro Club, where you had to be the
best just to endure the worst.

One in a hundred. If you were sharp enough to
graduate two years of concentrated total immer-
sion in the five major languages employed in
space—English, French, Russian, Chinese and
Hispanic Complex—interspersed with communications theory from the ground up, including component familiarization and all phases of intercept,
you could boast of being in the mere fifty percent
of your class that finished at all. Statistically half
the candidates buckled under the academic pressure reflected by a changing strategic picture in
space. As an international regulatory agency in
deep space, UNESA was struggling to maintain
control over corporate expansion, and losing.

Fifty years earlier electronic surveillance had
been a matter of monitoring automatically transmitted traffic on the same components as the intended terminal. As the free-wheeling Corpses saw
increased regulation pinching their profits, they developed more intricate ciphers, which required
more sophisticated decryption and, in escalating
turn, more evasive methods of communication.
Myoshi Metals, with a Japanese gift for augment-
ing the present with the past, implemented a simple but subtle method that astounded unbelieving
UNESA operators.

"Morse! I swear to God, they're sending *Morse*."

Older specialists were aware of it as antiquarians
recalled the process of sheepskin-to-parchment.

Other corporations followed suit, though so slowly that UNESA, while reviving Morse in their training schedules, wondered at the tardiness in gathering the harvest of conventional traffic. The answer became apparent in the dismal performance of their own students. The problem had nothing to do with intelligence. What you don't use, you lose. As humans from childhood became more visually oriented through generations of television, film and computer displays, they had become correspondingly less aural. Research showed discouragingly but unequivocally that even in the 20th century, Morse aptitude was fairly limited and closely related to sense of pitch and innate ear for music.

From sheer necessity, UNESA had to revive the obsolete skill, pushing their trainees toward high-speed proficiency and losing sixty percent of them. There was no choice. The high-level Corpse policy nets grew faster and more elusive every year; intercept must keep pace. When and if you made it through training, you were only a specialist corporal but a valuable commodity. Then, if you could adjust to Limbo's cramped quarters, monotonous food and recycled air, if you could unerringly follow Corpse operators trying to throw you off through a rapid and bewildering series of frequency changes and identify an individual operator or transmitter from memory, or hover on a frequency and feel a target net about to come up surely as Ahab sensed the presence of Moby Dick—then you might go to Search with a promotion to sergeant.

At last, if you attained operational sainthood, you might be good enough for Sparrow duty and the shoulder boards of a warrant officer. One in a hundred. Currently short of saints, Pauley considered carefully his choice of pilot and operator for the Hydri IV mission. The orders seemed a halfway measure, sending only one craft. It made as much sense as some of Dorfmann's fussy housekeeping fiats: *no*body bed-hopped on his station, bah gawd, so condoms were declared contraband as cigarettes and liquor, officially nonexistent.

Ellie Roven was twenty-three, the youngest officer on station. An over-achiever, Sparrow duty was still a challenge to her, if one rapidly molting its glamor as Ellie shed post-adolescent plumpness on flight diet. Spaceborn of a French Canadian mother and a colony mechanic, Ellie was still green enough to believe she couldn't die ever. Reinecke, the oldest, was still a cowboy from Kansas who would do anything for the fun of it—

"Sure, Sparrows get old after a coupla days, but you get in *close*."

—and avoided nothing except his former wives when he went Earthside on leave. But Ed was inching into the antique class now. If his pilot had to slam the Sparrow around out there, Ed's sedentary bulk would take a lot of Gs.

Right, then. Roven or Stoner. Ellie was good, but Stoner had the edge in experience and if there were trouble out there—well, he'd lived twice as long as Roven. His turn by roster anyway. Pauley would have preferred a wider choice, but instead of the three additional Sparrow-qualified warrants he'd requested, the last supply shuttle brought one replacement engineering officer for the *Kennedy*, fifty redundant manuals on personal hygiene in space, and a training holo-film on desert survival.

Your turn in the barrel, Stoney, and spare me the sad

songs about never wanting to be here in the first place.

Pauley knew the background on all key personnel in depth. When younger but no less indolent, Charley Stoner had been a civilian intercept specialist and Morse instructor at a UNESA listening station in California. As the story went, his second wife's alimony demands reflected her terminal disgust with a man who never thought to wash a dish or empty an ashtray, was rarely home and then left discarded undershirts about the house like clues in a paper chase. Cigarette sale was illegal anywhere in California—and Charley needed money. He plied back and forth between the Bay Area and Reno, going without sleep to bootleg cigarettes on-station by the pack. When they caught him, he'd put a dent in his alimony payments but faced seven years in a minimum security prison for possession with intent to sell.

Or (now pay attention, Stoner. This could save your ass, which is more trouble than it's worth) a change of status, transfer to refresher training, finally assignment and time equivalent to his full sentence at a deepspace listening station. At the age of forty, Stoner donned UNESA blues and became a reluctant minion in what pro-UNESA politicians, at budget appropriations time, dramatically referred to as the "ever-unfolding imperative of space."

But Stoner was the best. There wasn't an operator or analyst from Reinecke to the newest arrivals who would argue that. Pauley put the handwriting on the wall.

Mission alert 72 hours. Pilot: Lieutenant Rothberg, John K. Operator: W/O Stoner, Charles.

Forget it, Nije, Stoner thought as he turned away

from the posted alert and went to find Ed. He'd headed this one off at the pass for cash, cigarettes and the kid-cowboy in his roommate. A deal was a deal.

At T minus 48 hours the IO's assistant, Sgt. Kim Bok Thun, informed him that Mister Reinecke had presented himself as an alternate for the mission. Pauley sighed from experience as Ed lumbered through the office hatch. "Don't tell me. Stoner doesn't want to fly. What is it this time? Hangnail?"

"No, sir." The heavy parentheses of Reinecke's jowls broadened in a grin. "I wanted to go."

Pauley frowned. English genes and the profession of intelligence gathering had given him a habitually noncommittal countenance. Disapproval in his pale eyes differed barely from the preoccupation of a clerk. With Charley Stoner, comfort was everything and the pursuit of indolence a passion, but he had no authority to scrub himself from a mission. Pauley did not feel tolerant today. "You bought the duty?"

"Nah, he paid me. Hundred bucks," Ed snickered confidentially, omitting mention of the cigarettes. "He's a fish. I beat him at blackjack all the time. *I* found 528."

Pauley knew the money wouldn't matter to Stoner. UNESA scrip was just paper wadded in the man's coverall pockets amid shreds of contraband tobacco. "Sorry, that's right out. Stoner's posted."

"Come on, I got a first contact here."

"I don't plan a mission with tarot cards and couldn't foresee that Stoner would be indisposed. That's all, Ed."

Reinecke leaned his walrus bulk over Pauley's desk. "Look, Stoney's no burnout or redline like Tyne. She hates ejection pods so much, she don't even like to pre-flight them. Just Charley's gone claustro in Sparrows. He said it's like looking at the universe from a broom closet; that's his words."

"Spare me," Pauley said. "I know Stoner's qualifications. He's a bit untidy but on the other hand he demonstrates a numbing lack of motivation."

"Bullshit."

"What's that?"

"Sir."

"Pack it in," Pauley concluded. "Return the money to the hapless Stoner, bid him Godspeed and tell him he can fucking well suit up and fly."

And that was that—until Lt. Rothberg appeared in the hatchway less than an hour later. "Request, sir."

Like the other two Sparrow pilots, Willington and Tyne, John Rothberg was a recycled fighter pilot from the old carrier *Lincoln*. Twenty-five, with the bad skin of someone who had absorbed his sunlight from a lamp since offworld birth, Rothberg reminded Pauley of a ravaged boy scout with the chilly Lazarus stare combat pilots acquired if they lived that long, but at the moment Rothberg was live enough to be emphatic. He did *not* want to spend X number of twelve-hour shifts in a Sparrow with Charley Stoner.

"He talks to the receivers," Roth said plaintively. "He argues with the computer. He mumbles over intercom, then forgets to lower his gain going from headset to speakers and blows your ears out. When he eats from a tube, half of it ends up on the bulkhead velcro or floating around in zero G until there's gunk all over screens and readouts. Ask Tyne: You need a handvac ready all the time. Spatially the guy is still back in Texas or wherever."

"California, I think," Pauley said. "One of the larger states."

"It would have to be. What I'm saying, sir. I heard Reinecke volunteered."

"And I said no. Message ends, John. Out."

Rothberg persisted. "Major, this is my last tour. I have nervous twitches and I need pills to sleep. My insides feel like an old sponge from Gs and flight diet. There's a condo on Mars Station two thirds paid for, and I'd like to enjoy it without Stoner's one-more-time aggravation or his goddam food all over me. I don't *need* this crap. Reinecke wants to go. Please, sir."

Pauley considered. He had some slack after all, and if Rothberg was going to go ballistic over it . . . He stabbed at intercom buttons. "All right, John. You've got Ed. That's all until briefing."

When Reinecke came on the line from Billet A-27, Pauley said, "Ed? Make the 528 briefing. Stoner's scrubbed. You're on."

Stoner avoided the compulsory aerobic periods whenever possible, all the more diligently when MED Section insisted they were good for anyone in space and especially over-forty slugs like himself. They could kid themselves. Nothing out here was good for anyone. Anything that zapped you Earthside got you faster out here, from bad skin to cancer and accelerated aging, so the hell with it. In philosophic moments he seriously regretted avoiding the possession rap. By now he could have been paroled and back in Tahoe—broke, maybe, but happy.

He ducked aerobics this time by swearing he was late with his daily Search summary for the IO, and went to find Ed before the *Moyers* left for Hydri IV. Reinecke was at one of the Search positions at the far end of the Intercept bay, listening to his hundredth repeat of 528's single known transmission. Stoner jacked in a headset and listened, his head resting against the receiver rack. Below average height, neither particularly lean nor tending to weight, he could have been described as compact with better posture and the exercise he loathed. The fading brown hair was spiderwebbed with onsetting gray and the expression in his sad brown eyes hovered perpetually between disgust and disillusionment with a world, a culture and now a universe he never made—the whole of which Stoner called "Twilight of the Dogs." Listening now, his mouth hung slightly open, his eyes focused on nothing with the incongruous, vacant intensity of a man muting all other senses under that of sound.

The sample was a fascinating three minutes of something akin to two alto singers, rising and falling in a chromatic duet. On Reinecke's screen the two writhing snake lines and their digital readouts were too consistent in their intervals to be separate voices, though TANAL and CRYPT sections were still playing with the two-voice theory. Stoner didn't buy it.

"One, Ed."

"One something. One very weird little Somebody."

"What'd they get from VOA database?"

"TANAL tried," Reinecke said. "Nothing like it.

Closest was that TransWorld tone-code a few years back."

"One voice's not impossible." Stoner was sure. "Used to be tribes in Africa could voice two notes like that."

"Three minutes running? That's what's hanging up the analysts."

And would, Charley Stoner predicted, until human thinking expanded beyond Earthside parameters. Like learning Chinese Mandarin: First you accepted the fact that certain inflections changed the meaning of given syllables entirely. *Accept, don't fight.* Mandarin was not as difficult for an occidental to learn as English for a Chinese national. Where westerners would describe a man as balancing on his hands, Chinese said, "There's a man with his feet in the air." Until you wiped your preconceptions, you'd never understand. That would have to come first with 528, but where did you start?

Reinecke stripped off his headset, rising with the effort of his bulk. "Gotta go. First briefing in ten minutes."

"Who's your Ops control on *Kennedy*?" Stoner had already heard Pauley was not taking the mission himself.

"Headly. Carrier intelligence."

That made some sense, Stoner assessed, as 528's altos lilted in his ear. Lt. Headly was checked out on the procedures and equipment in the tiny Search cubicle within carrier operations compartment, with a Maximum Security clearance. They were shorthanded and Headly still green, but he had to learn sometime—

"Wait." The recorded signal had altered radically. He'd heard the altered sounds before but this time they pressed a button. "Run it back."

"I'm due in briefing."

"Play it over," Stoner insisted. "There's something . . ."

They listened again to the two-note chords as the intervals broadened, narrowed, dipped and rose and then went disconcertingly choppy.

"Wondered about that," Reinecke mumbled. "Almost like . . ."

"Words." What words Stoner couldn't say, but a grotesque approximation of human voiced sounds as if shouted to someone underwater, bracketed in hiccupy glottal stops. Reinecke swung away down the narrow bay aisle between the rows of positions. "Ride'm, Stoney. I'll send you some more—live and in person."

Stoner settled down to absorb the alien sounds, placing the pocket-sized personal data recorder on the desk before him. Most of the Search ops presently on shift were scanning for more 528 traffic and possible Corpse activity from the vicinity of Hydri IV. UNESA had red-flagged the planet and its two moons: no commercial exploration until they knew what was there, which was like posting NO TRESPASSING signs to keep ants away from a picnic. Hydri IV was hot. Automated UNESA probes had soup-tested the soil's proto-organisms, scraped at the polar ice and found limited terra-forming possibilities but high mining potential. But this far out, UNESA clout was only what it could back up with muscle and intelligence gathering. High-level Corpse traffic was already yielding new codenames which TANAL suspected referred to

Hydri IV. Only a matter of time before someone reached for the goodies.

And maybe got wasted by 528 as a very interested third party. If the Hydri System was frontier for humans, couldn't it be the same for someone coming the other way? Two eyes meeting through a keyhole.

That wouldn't stop Corpses with all those blue chips in the kitty. Instead of bootlegging butts, Stoner belatedly but often thought he should have signed on with Allied or Myoshi—except for the perverse, gleeful thrill he garnered at the thought of throwing the blocks to a quadrillion-dollar concern. All those fat contracts and kickbacks hung up while a few players like himself and Ed and Ellie put a lock on the game. Lots more money working for Corpses, but money didn't mean much out here, mostly electronic records in PERS. What UNESA scrip he did carry was left in coverall pockets, returning from the laundry a sodden wad in a pocket, like a hairball regurgitated by a cat.

Stoner strained now to detect any pattern in the singing, any readable element in the "word" fragments. The latter were too inconsistent with the rest to be part of the base language. *Two languages? Why not? We're using five out here.*

He and Reinecke met again in their quarters before Ed left to do component check aboard his Sparrow. He saluted Stoner jauntily. In his coveralls, Ed looked like an oversized bowling pin stuffed into a sock.

"Captain Ed of the space rejects! Go get 'em, hot rock," Stoner blessed him. "I'll be copying you."

"Now where?" Reinecke picked up his flight bag and glanced about the compartment vaguely. He snatched up a plastic sack from his bunk. "My luck."

"Your barf bag! You gonna be sick coming out of FTL, sweetheart?"

"Nah." From the sack Reinecke extracted an antique manual Morse key mounted on a wide clamp. "My old knee key. Twice as old as me. More."

"Nothing's twice as old as you."

"My grandfather—you know: he helped me build my first ham rig in Wichita?—he busted into a Shiite net with this very key. I ever tell you that?"

"Fifty times you told me that."

"Now *there* was a hot rock. Look around; have I got everything?"

"Cigarettes?"

"Jesus, thanks." Reinecke opened his locker, took three packs of cigarettes from various hiding places, and stuffed them into the flight bag. "Guess that's it."

He surveyed Stoner's littered floor and locker area which always reminded him of a hurricane path. "Stoney—stun me when I get back. Sweep the floor, okay? I'd do it for you."

Stoner watched him lumber down the corridor, pear-shaped backside jouncing in his coveralls. Don Quixote in search of alien windmills. Reinecke stopped at an intersection to hurl a raucous farewell to his friend. "Hey, Stoney? I robbed ya. I fuckin' robbed ya! I'da gone for nothing."

"Big deal. Better you than me."

Stoner hauled himself into his upper bunk and lay with hands laced behind his head, troubled in the moments before his nap. Maybe he should have gone himself after all. He took fewer chances than Ed, didn't cut it as fine. Old Ed and his family heirloom knee key, wouldn't part with it. His grandfather rode an armored recon vehicle through one of those three-week wars in the Middle East, banging away on that key. As Ed told the story, Grampa broke into an enemy net, mimicking one of their outstations with fake priority ciphered traffic. The fascinated endeavors of both sides failed to unmask the Desert Shark, though Baghdad and Tehran entertained dire suspicions when the messages broke out to recipes for roast pork. Perhaps it was genetic. The whole family down to Ed had a go-to-hell zest for life.

So did Ellie Roven who wanted to wallow in the colors of an Earth she'd never seen. The sort of girl who should have been born there.

Dark and chunky, with short legs and wide hips, Eleanor Roven possessed tremendous energy and what her French Canadian mother would call *joie de vivre*. She won her warrant boards after only a year as a sergeant on Limbo, cutting her intercept teeth on Corpse supply reports but advancing quickly to the fast priority nets. Ellie adapted to the claustrophobic conditions and diet of Sparrow duty better than most, regretting only that she moved to officer country a week before Sergeant Francis Hardesty arrived onstation, putting them mutually out of bounds for fraternization. A pity, Ellie thought. Frank was attractive, her physical opposite, gangling and red-haired with a quiet niceness about him Ellie found refreshing after ducking grabass enlisted tekkies and then carrier officers.

She confided to her confessor, Charley Stoner, "I would definitely love to fraternize the hell out of Frank Hardesty."

To Stoner she seemed much more openly emotional and sensual than most spaceborn women. He slid into the role of her confessor without thinking about it. He had two former wives Earthside, preferring not to know exactly where, and while a third was unlikely now, he enjoyed having some kind of family to take care of. When Ellie almost didn't make it back after tailing a Myoshi carrier for voice traffic, Stoner went through the first genuine cold-sweat terror of his life. The carrier was lurking on the rim of the Hydri System. Piloting the Sparrow, Gunny Willington scanned them moving toward Hydri II in violation of the UNESA ban. Ellie was getting voice and telemetry from them and wanted to keep contact to nail an ident on the ship. She thought it was Myoshi 117, the carrier *Iteki*, which had gone silent two weeks before and not yet reestablished.

Their Sparrow was detected and had to run from a swarm of Shrike fighters, dodging laser fire as Gunny ran for the *Kennedy* aligning to retrieve them. White-knuckled at her position and in physical misery, Ellie transmitted her copy to Pauley on the carrier already initiating primary FTL sequencing as they tractored the damaged Sparrow aboard.

At Limbo, hours later, Stoner was waiting at the airlock when Ellie emerged, raking savagely at the short, blue-black curls that covered her scalp, and streaming tears.

"Stoney . . ."

"It's okay, baby. You're home. You made it."

"I'm okay. Damn it, I'm okay." When Ellie wept, her eyes lost their tight tension-squint and went huge and soft. "B-bad enough almost getting killed, but doing it with PMS—but I got him, Stoney. I nailed 117."

"The *Iteki*? You got him back?"

"Yeah." Stoner could feel her shaking against him. "But God, it gets old. *I* feel old."

That was last year when Ellie was only twenty-two.

Ellie churned down the access way to Stoner's billet and banged on the hatch. "Stoney!"

"Yeah, it's open."

When she entered, a gray-blue swath of cigarette smoke swirled in the stale air. Stoner lay on his bunk with a book of crossword puzzles. Ellie closed the hatch quickly. "God, how many times has Dorfmann fined you for smoking? Use your neutralizers; eat this stuff up."

"I'll spray, I'll spray," he promised languidly. "Later. What's a four-letter word for 'strange'?"

Ellie snatched the odor neutralizer from a shelf and sprayed liberally. "Tyne."

"Not that strange."

"Reinecke's up. Got 528 coming in on Hardesty's pos."

The puzzle book sailed across the compartment. Stoner hit the deck, scattering wadded paper and tangling his foot in a discarded undershirt. "Come on."

In Intercept, he and Ellie elbowed and side-stepped down the narrow compartment to Search where Pauley, a clutch of analysts from TANAL, and Sparrow pilot Janice Tyne hovered over Frank Hardesty's position. Stoner edged in beside Tyne, nudging her. "Sit/rep?"

"Orbiting surface," she said. "No problems yet. Traffic coming in."

Standard Search procedure, the Sparrow coasting while Headly on *Moyers* relayed Reinecke's traffic and chatter through more powerful transmitters to Limbo on separate frequencies, Ed's chatter coming out onscreen and hard copy. Tyne said: "No problems yet," a pilot's wary judgment implying a lot of ifs. As a fighter craft, the Shrike had formidable armament. Converted and redesignated Sparrow for intercept, something had to go. Faster than a Shrike but with minimal weaponry, Sparrows were designed to streak in, get the traffic and be long gone. If crippled or destruction imminent, the crew ejected and prayed to be picked up.

Supposed to eject, Stoner amended with a sideways glance at Jan Tyne. Jan wouldn't go near an E-pod after what she went through in the Gamma Three System. She had a strong face, almost masculine in its features, though the hardness was more habitual tightness than caste: wide cheekbones and a mouth drawn tighter than its natural feminine curve. Her flat, compact pilot's body bent forward now over the hard copy curling out of the printer while 528 wailed from Hardesty's speakers and analysts made feverish notes.

The spine-shivering alto duet ceased abruptly, followed by the incongruous "word" sounds Stoner noted before. His eyes went vacant as he rode the signal with Ed, forgetting things like time difference . . .

Suppose they've been copying us longer than we've known about them, and that's likely. Suppose they have analysts who can match up the look and sound of our words and maybe some idea of meaning.

Stoner cocked his head sideways to read Ed's chatter. "He's got a clean D/F cut on 528. Planet surface."

Pauley looked doubtful. "Can't be."

On the carrier *Moyers*, Headly didn't buy it either—

> BIG JOHN: LITTLE BOY, DO A LINE CHECK ON YOUR D/F AND VERIFY. BRIDGE CAN'T READ ANYTHING ON SURFACE.
> LITTLE BOY: REPEAT PLANET SURFACE. PILOT VERIFIES COORDINATES.
> BIG JOHN: UNLIKELY, ED. OUR AUTO PROBES WOULD HAVE PICKED UP ANY ELECTRONIC INSTALLATION ON THE FIRST SURVEY.

If Ed says he's there, believe him, Stoner warned silently. *Ed, send the coordinates again.*

> LITTLE BOY: I DON'T WANT TO BREAK ANY HEARTS. HAVE THEM RUN ANOTHER CUT FROM THE BRIDGE. WE'RE IN AS CLOSE AS WE CAN GET. COULD BE NEW, MOBILE OR EVEN UNDERGROUND.
> BIG JOHN: ALREADY RAN IT AGAIN. NOTHING REPEAT NOTHING YOUR COORDINATES.
> LITTLE BOY: GET THE BIRDSHIT OFF YOUR RIG AND READ IT RIGHT. WAIT . . . WAIT ONE.

Chatter and traffic ceased. Seconds crawled by, then the printer stuttered softly again.

> BIG JOHN: LITTLE BOY, WHAT'S HAPPENING? ADVISE.

Now the twin voices sang again over the speakers, much stronger and audibly different from the earlier ones. Hardesty swiveled around to Stoner. "New signal, sir. I think it's the other end of 528."

LITTLE BOY: NEW TIX. REPEAT NEW TRANSMISSION. PILOT PERIMETER SCAN READS BOGEY. HOME/WARN SAYS WE'RE BEING SCANNED. SOMETHING BIG ALL OF A SUDDEN JUST THERE.
BIG JOHN: BRIDGE CONFIRMS HOME/WARN, SCANNING US TOO. SOMETHING BIG JUST CAME OUT OF JUMP. CRAZY SENSOR READINGS.

Stoner's stomach contracted.

BIG JOHN: BRIDGE TRYING DATABASE FOR CRAFT IDENT.
LITTLE BOY: COPY, PILOT LIKEWISE. DATABASE JANE'S HAS NO MATCH. WAIT . . . PILOT HAS THREE SMALLER BOGEYS INCOMING. OPEN THE DOOR, HEADLY, WE'RE (illegible on printer).
BIG JOHN: OH MY—IT'S—
LITTLE BOY: SAY AGAIN.
BIG JOHN:—HUGE. WE ARE MOVING TO RETRIEVE YOU.

Fists balled tight at her sides, Tyne muttered through her teeth: "Evade, Johnny. Push it. Go!"

Stoner looked at her. With a dry mouth, he asked: "What do you think?"

"Fighters," she said tonelessly. "From a carrier."

"They said a Jump ship."

The new alien voice went silent. The chatter roll hung unmoving from Hardesty's printer. He turned anxiously to Pauley. "Can't hear Big John or Little Boy, sir. Just gone."

A gabble of frustration burst from the analysts huddled about him, while silent Tyne looked to Stoner as if she were straining across space to Rothberg in the Sparrow with speed and evasion his only chance. If he had any chance at all.

"Mr. Stoner, Mr. Roven?" Hardesty beckoned them, one hand pressing the headset's tiny earpiece tight against his head. "I'm getting Morse on the 528 frequency. Very weak."

"Put it on speaker," Pauley snapped.

"No use, sir. Too faint."

Ellie and Stoner grabbed the nearest headsets and listened: It had to be Ed, but even with maximum gain and Hardesty muting out natural interference, the keyed signal was feeble, barely audible. They strained to follow it.

Pauley wondered, "Why is he on traffic channel?"

"Trying to reach us directly," Tyne guessed. "I'd say the carrier's been hit, probably losing power fast."

The faint signal faded out completely. Stoner put down the headset, collating what he'd read with Ellie and the copy Hardesty had tapped out onto his screen. "Ed used his hand key, hoping we could read him. The carrier must have lost main power all at once; not much auxiliary left from the sound of it. We got this much."

HIT . . . TRYING . . . COORD . . .

Reinecke had tried to send the D/F position on the surface transmitter before fading below readability.

"From the chatter, Headly already had the co-ordinates," one of the analysts reasoned. "We don't know for certain the ship's down. There'll be the bridge navigational log for backup."

Tyne turned to him, fierce and fatalistic. "Forget it."

"He's right. We don't know," Pauley put in with quiet authority. "Let's get back to work, people."

"They're gone." Jan Tyne's voice was a hammer nailing down a coffin lid.

Pauley glared at her. "I said pack it in. We don't know for certain. *Moyers* may still be FTL-capable."

Stoner glanced around aimlessly, avoiding eye contact with anyone, especially Ellie. Hydri IV was just under one light-day from Limbo. What they'd struggled to copy Ed had sent near twenty-two hours ago. Somehow, with 528 singing eerily over the speakers and Ed's chatter murmuring out of the printer, it had just happened.

Tyne strode out of Search down the long compartment. Pauley clapped his hands to break up what was turning into a funeral. "Hardesty's on the pos. The rest of you carry on . . . Mister Stoner?" The IO's tone softened perceptibly. "You're off duty now."

"Right."

Ellie Roven looked after Stoner as he shambled away, wondering if she should follow, but reading in the message of his slumped shoulders that she shouldn't. Not just now.

Stoner walked out of Intercept and along the access corridors, miserable. At his billet hatch, his eye fell on Ed's nameplate beside his own. He wouldn't take it down. Ed still lived here. He locked the hatch behind him and stood in the middle of the small compartment. There was Ed's bottom bunk with the blankets tucked neat and tight, desk and locker area squared away—and his own area, Disasterville. He never bothered to make his bed or pick up after himself, but Ed never hacked him about it. Ed was good to live with.

A hundred bucks. Because Stoner was lazy and hated Sparrow duty. Because it was claustro and scary out there and he was sick with the need to touch home again. Because Ed wanted to be the Desert Shark like Grampa, riding his Sparrow and a wailing double-voiced signal for a hundred dollars and three packs of cigarettes.

He needed to do something for Ed right now but didn't know what.

Stoner stood motionless, a man carefully considering what he should do next, what was most needed. He opened Ed's locker and groped behind the neatly hung uniforms for the small broom and dust pan. With more care than he'd ever spared the task, Stoner began to sweep his area clean.

After a week of no contact, the *Moyers* was written off and with it any hint of 528's surface location. Stoner packed Reinecke's gear, turned it over to PERS, and staggered Pauley by urging they expedite further probe on Search 528.

"Soonest, Nije. Intermediate, Proximity, the whole enchilada."

"Ye gods, Stoney. Are you actually volunteering?"

"I gotta go anyway." Stoner didn't punctuate

with his usual screw-it-all shrug but held Pauley's eyes. "I *want* that singing sister-act son of a bitch. End of message."

Orders to that effect would probably be cut soon by COORDINT, but Pauley now had only two qualified flight operators and two pilots. Stoner pressed him; any chance at all of bringing in flying warrants from other stations?

"Not so far. We can requisition a pilot from *Kennedy*. For an op we'll have to kick a rating upstairs. Who's your best in Search?"

Stoner answered with no hesitation. "Hardesty. That kid on the pos when—when the carrier got it."

Pauley considered rapidly. An endorsement from Stoner went without question. Hardesty's training and performance records were excellent, and he had been cleared already to Max/Sec level. The IO had only one reservation. "Awfully young and green."

"No more than Ellie, and I'm too old and ain't that a shame?" Stoner snorted, disgust tinging his tone like a chronic low-level infection as the subject veered close to his chief and long-standing complaint. "So screw it. If UNESA knew what we were up against, we'd have the big flying platforms we need and full shifts of ops to do the job right instead of three poor fish in Sparrows." He departed Pauley's presence, growling, "Fucking ridiculous . . ."

Pauley put Hardesty in for field promotion with emergency justification, rather touched by the young sergeant's uncertainty at the prospect. At twenty-three, Frank Hardesty looked no older than eighteen, the sort who would be estimated ten years younger than his actual age until middle life.

As for Stoner's bitch about Sparrows, Pauley would never argue the point. They were a halfway measure. Against the barely regulable, better funded corporations, with electronic intelligence vital, flying platforms—essentially carriers with full intercept/analysis/crypt capacity—were the obvious answer. To less single-minded men than Charley Stoner, the obstacles were as evident. UNESA was an international body whose influence and budget fluctuated with the fortunes and politics of the Earthside governments involved. There weren't enough line carriers in service yet; platforms would call for major redesign of function at enormous expense of money and time. These proposals had to be pushed through all authorities concerned, each with priorities of their own. Difficulty went head-on against need; temporary expedients were proposed. As UNESA and Corpse scout craft evolved to the formidable Shrike fighter, the Shrike begat the Sparrow as an economical compromise.

Considering the rigors of Sparrow duty, Pauley couldn't blame Stoner or anyone for hating it when a little more foresight and budget would have yielded exponentially better results. One carrier platform, just *one* . . .

UNESA wanted the alien 528 for more complex reasons. Pauley's new operational orders arrived by supply shuttle, hand delivered by COORDINT courier in a sealed pouch, his eyes only, shred and burn after reading. The orders were part one of two. Like a blind man sensing silent movement about him, Pauley felt vast gears begin to mesh.

Decisions had been made, meanings becoming clearer. Simply a matter of time.

More immediately disquieting was a Max/Sec memo in the same pouch—

REASON TO BELIEVE ALLIED DEV OR OTHER ENTITY HAS INSERTED SLEEPER YOUR STATION. NO PRESENT IDENT BUT ADVISE YOU SCAN ALL PERSONNEL FORM ONES.

Sleeper agents were easy to plant and difficult to find, usually inserted long before the specific tasks they would be ordered to carry out. Fingering such an agent would be a solitary, time-consuming task. PERS couldn't know, or Dorfmann, not even Pauley's assistant, Sgt. Kim Thun.

On top of the 528 orders—this. Bloody marvelous.

Thirty-nine, the spaceborn son of terrafarmers out from England, Nigel Pauley had entered UNESA as a COORDINT field agent before coming to Limbo. In appearance alone, he was the physical type no one would remember in a gathering of three or more men. Of average height, thinning light brown hair lay limply over his high forehead and plain, rather remote cast of features. Behind rimless reading glasses, his unremarkable pale blue eyes had an off-putting effect on glances that met them closely. Risking his life daily as a mole in a Corpse facility or holding down his present slot, Pauley had the efficient, preoccupied calm of a desk clerk logging invoices. Misleading, of course, in a personality as complex as the concerns Pauley dealt with. Stoner respected Pauley but could never feel any warmth toward him. Reinecke puzzled that he could never get a *handle* on the man. Ellie Roven, who drew and painted in her spare time, saw Pauley as a pen sketch in faded ink, the expression self-possessed and impenetrable as a 16th century Holbein.

After reading and burning the dispatches, Pauley tried to concentrate on the daily Intercept summary. He passionately wanted a drink, but the last of his hoarded contraband Scotch was gone. That had been a clandestine gift from Col. Tony Waites, his COORDINT superior. Like many in his profession, Pauley had become a solitary, controlled but hard and steady drinker. "Tweedle" Waites likely knew that as he knew intimately most of his people's habits, including the ass-paining station policies of Hubert Dorfmann who considered himself a weary pillar of strength doggedly holding his station's helm on course while, actually, he was no more than an administrative drone.

Pauley massaged his face with both hands, resting his eyes. There were orders he didn't want to carry out, and he needed a drink. He considered a half-liter of "Jesus Juice," the creation of enterprising bootleggers in HYDROPONICS, but decided against that for the time being. Officially, the still didn't exist. To contact the entrepreneurs directly would appear tacit approval on his part, but there were always connections in MAINTENANCE for the right price. So went humanity ever. Dorfmann was unaware of the operation; the clot would close it down instantly with fines and busts for all involved. Nothing for it but to stay dry for the time. Pauley opted for coffee in the officers' ward room.

The ward compartment was sparsely occupied by five officers from their remaining carrier, *Ken-*

nedy, three Russian armament officers laboring to comprehend an endless German joke as mangled by Lieutenant Willi Krug, and a Chinese bridge officer futilely endeavoring to activate the environment simulator, rewarded with a few seconds of verdant rain forest before the panels went blank.

Pauley punched a coffee order into the service panel, chose a seat far down the ward area from the carrier men, and settled to brood over the mediocre drink. Tea would have been his choice, real tea the way his parents brewed it when they could get it from Fortnum's or Harrod's back Earthside, but Limbo tea was more insipid than the coffee.

A few minutes later Colonel Hubert Dorfmann, two hundred and thirty sedentary pounds billowing under his blue dress uniform, lumbered down the ward room aisle toward Pauley, reminding the IO of an agitated water bed. Dorfmann grunted a hello and settled massively opposite him.

"Pauley—ah got a problem with your people." Dorfmann scratched at his undistinguished mustache. Pauley found his Tennessee accent abrasive. "I don't know, maybe you got a problem. Thought I'd clue you. Hey, Nigel? You with me?"

"Sorry." With the orders just received, Pauley wasn't disposed to conversation. "Actually, sir, I have a number of problems. Just wondering if I couldn't get an Earthside job playing piano in a posh bordello."

The reference sailed over Dorfmann's head. "What?"

"Old Joplin rags and that."

"Now that's what ah'm talking about," Dorfmann pronounced weightily. "You going weird as them Sparrow types? Lt. Wray . . . you know Carol Wray?"

"Carrier pilot, isn't she?"

That was her, and a good steady young officer. Did her job, no trouble. "But her billet mate, Tyne—she's one of yours."

As Wray pleaded to Dorfmann yesterday morning in terminal frustration, Jan Tyne never slept more than two hours at a stretch. Got up, sat in a chair and mumbled or lay in the top bunk and just shook. "I mean *shakes*. Wray says she gets the vibrations down the gawddam bunk frame. Tyne talks in her sleep. Cries in her sleep, know what I mean? Don't know what the med/profile term is."

Pauley did. The precise terms were on Tyne's Form One, and Willington's, for that matter, probably on Rothberg's before they closed his file. *Posttraumatic stress. Reaction time marginal. Recommend med/discharge at termination of present tour. Psych/ response to combat conditions considered unreliable.*

"Tyne sounds ready for the farm, know what I mean?"

And then, Dorfmann bore on, there was Willi Krug sitting over there, complained about *his* billet mate, Rufus Willington. Dorfmann leaned forward, speaking in what he considered a tone of authoritative significance. "Lutherans ain't flakey, Major."

"I beg your pardon?"

"Willi Krug is a good Lutheran like me, even if he was born in Germany, and Lutherans don't flap. Steady. Don't make waves for nothing."

For all of that, the unflappable Krug appeared in Dorfmann's office three days ago, urgently requesting reassignment of quarters with any other officer. Willington slept poorly as Tyne just sat there in the dark, twisting some silly toy cube this way and that all night, *rick-rick-rrrick.*

"It's an antique puzzle," Pauley explained. "I think they were called Rubik's Cubes. Object is to align all the colors evenly."

"Not Willington. Krug says he just works it into the worst mess he can, then starts all over. In the dark with Krug trying to sleep. Say something to him, he just stares at you."

Pauley knew that stare, as he'd seen it in Rothberg. Gunny Willington had almost colorless eyes and an overshot upper lip. His features were off kilter, partly from birth, the rest battle damaged, plus that disconcerting stare that reminded the IO of a preoccupied snake.

"Look," Dorfmann said. "I got Wray and Krug different billets, no problem since, you know, we lost the carrier. But what kind of basket cases you got working for you, Nigel? Your people online or not? Sounds like you got an epidemic of crazy."

Pauley gave up on his coffee and pushed it away. "Colonel, you're not dealing with cooks and clerks. The operators alone have to be exceptional just to finish training and far better than that to work in Sparrows. I've flown familiarization in them, they're not fun. My people are specifically trained and highly talented personnel, an interface of facility with instinct. You can't instill that level of talent, Colonel, you can only groom and care for it. Now and again, they . . . twitch a little."

"A little? Like an outhouse in a hurricane," Dorfmann opined. "I thought you ought t'know. Reinecke, rest his soul, he was normal, he was okay to be around—but Stoner? Twitch? He does puzzles all day long, then makes up more. And he's de-

structive, I know it, gah-dammit, I *know* it. You remember when MAINTENANCE ran short of toilet
paper? Somebody enciphered the requisition and
Supply couldn't break it in time for the shuttle
back, and I got my suspicions who did it. And he
smokes . . . Christ knows where he gets cigarettes,
'spensive as they are, or how many times I fined
him a hundred endees when we caught him. And
there's Roven. Nice kid, but she plays with colors
and paints—like my daughter when she was five.
Lavender cows. A purple tree with gray leaves.
Weird."

"Yes, Ellie gave me one," Pauley said. "She
never saw an Earthside cow or tree except in pho-
tos. But then brown tree trunks, green leaves and
umber cows are so usual, don't you think?" He
stood up to leave. "Excuse me, sir. Must run."

"But mind," Dorfmann said. "You better profile
those fruitcakes before one of 'em goes out an airlock without a suit, know what I mean?"

"Sensory deprivation," Pauley shrugged. "We
all have it to some degree. Come to that, Colonel,
you're not looking well yourself."

Before going off duty Pauley punched up PERS
records on Willington and Tyne. The Form 1 was
exhaustive: personal history, parents and grand-
parents, service record, fitness relative to combat
and/or sensitive operations. Nothing about
security-cleared personnel was too minor for inclu-
sion, from nicknames like "Gunny" for Rufus Willington, to scars or moles or the vaguest behavioral
idiosyncrasy. No individual of any rank even re-
motely vulnerable to blackmail or bribery, or
whose relatives for three generations past had been
in any way associated with space corporations, was

cleared for duty on UNESA listening stations. This led inevitably to a high discard and waste level, Stoner being an exception. His suspended sentence was public record and anyone attempting to bribe him would find the Californian avaricious as a toadstool. Besides, Corpses liked to get them young, paying high for the bright new talents and predators, though now and then an IO got a Stoner or Reinecke, or the old FTL carrier *Lincoln* was blessed with Shrike pilots like Rothberg, Willington and Tyne.

As Pauley sifted the records, the disquieting ghost-fact of the sleeper agent rose to nag at him. He wished Waites was here to answer questions, at least to clarify. What made Tweedle suspect in the first place, and how in hell was Pauley to find him/her? Someone bought and primed young, whitewashed and settled into the UNESA pipeline without a trace.

As virtual hostiles Corpses were always in flux, UNESA in constant regulatory hearings with one and deepspace firefights with others. COORDINT moles gathered information in a complex design to tangle the corporations in legal tax suits. This far out regulation was more difficult and corruption predictable. The megacorporations had more constant cash flow than UNESA whose funds had to be authorized by a dozen, sometimes impoverished, governments, all with their own priorities and agendas. Most real wealth lay in space development. Corpses could buy law through lobbyists at home. Out here they could hire hot young pilots to shoot it down while the companies increased their profits as much from imperative as greed. At this point in time, the opposing forces were locked in an undeclared war, using up people like disposable handiwipes.

Pauley punched up the further records he sought. Rothberg, Tyne and Willington came out of the crucible of Gamma Three.

Eighteen months earlier in the Gamma System, Allied Development was tolerating no interference from anyone. One of the worlds, a little larger than Earth but with a similar geological history, had ore-tested with so much potential that Allied laid claim and shipped in workers before UNESA could survey and certify surface conditions or life support standards. Allied fought off the main competitor, Myoshi Metals, in a two-day engagement that littered the planet with fighter wreckage, then put their miners to work in twelve-hour shifts at premium pay. And killed too many of them, Pauley remembered. The human heart was designed for so much gravity stress and no more. More than a few men died long before their year's contract ran out; others coldslept home to chronic coronary problems likened by cardiologists to those of a small combustion engine raced at top speed for a thousand hours.

Allied maintained that Gamma Three System was not covered by existing regs but open ex-and-ex: first explore, first exploit. UNESA argued, warned and finally intervened. To Allied that meant money lost while sub-standard conditions were investigated through the ponderous workings of UNESA. They committed the new carrier *Swift* with full fighter complement, afterward producing their carrier's logs and other evidence to the effect that the *Lincoln* had never identified herself and fired first in any case.

The old *Lincoln* lost sixteen craft in the first two days, the entire strength of 18 Squadron. Allied pilots flew newer Shrikes and took insane risks, their crits far faster than those of the UNESA pilots. The older carrier had to maneuver constantly to stay out of *Swift*'s better armed range. Launched fighters never knew if there would be a ship to return to. By the third day, pilots like Willington and Tyne went from briefing to their craft like mourners to their own wake. Briefing officers tried to be optimistic—

"We think their pilots are on some kind of stimulant. That's a short party, people. Hit them hard. Push them. They'll unravel."

But they didn't. Allied Shrikes continued to chew up the old Link's craft, inflicting damage on the carrier herself. A routine battle report provided part of the answer before the Link was forced to break off, calling for emergency repairs, two of her three squadrons lost.

The battle report was part of the Form 1 on Lieutenant Janice Tyne, 14 Squadron (UNESA Commendation Medal, Diamond Pendant for distinguished service, 19 confirmed victories).

He was all over me, just too fast. I couldn't shake him until Gunny closed and gave him a squirt. The Link was visual then, so I guess he decided to go for it, which was very dumb with two of us in the cone and targeting his six. I tried for his core complex but the hit was off, just aft of the cockpit. He began to wobble, skidded off to port, then Gunny hit him. The E-pod popped clear right away . . . funny, he wasn't that badly hit. We finished off the craft. The Link picked up

the pilot. Lucky little prick. Corpses just waste our pods.

The captured pilot was a pale, pimply boy named Leon Janek, no more than nineteen. Link pilots ogled him during interrogation like a rare zoo exhibit. With no trace of drugs in his system, Janek displayed all the classic symptoms of withdrawal: depression, irritability, lack of physical/ mental coordination. Then Tyne noticed his short-clipped hair was even scantier at the crown. Janek's scalp was scrutinized.

"He's MUX'd."

True then, the rumor intelligence had discounted. With a MUX implant Janek was interfaced through his Virtual Reality helmet with his ship's computers. Link pilots were literally up against human software. Subsequent intelligence evaluations were not of much immediate use.

There is indication the interface is addictive with possible long term systemic/psych damage.

Long term wasn't now. In the final engagement, a flight of Allied Shrikes tore up the remainder of 14 Squadron. The only craft to return to *Lincoln* was John Rothberg's. The pilot's report was limited as single-observer accounts always were, but grim enough.

I got the ship tailing me, but I was damaged and had to break off. We were way out, too far out. I opened the solar wings to recharge aux power, praying no one was scoping me because I couldn't do shit if they were. Shut down as many systems as possible to save power. They were . . . the E-pod beacons were all over distress channel. Seven, eight of them. Then they started to go silent. Not faded out, just gone. No way

those pods fail that soon. The Corpses were fin-
ishing them off one by one, had to be. Then there
were just two left on the channel. I kept listening
to them all the way back, wondering who they
were, knowing I couldn't do a damned thing for
them. Better to get hit clean. I don't give a shit
about us losing. I'm just glad to be out of it.

Appended to the report was an interrogator's
note that Rothberg wept during and after the session and was barely coherent. He was considered
a burnout thereafter, not to be returned to combat.

Four solar days later, a UNESA repair ship,
moving to rendezvous with the badly damaged
Lincoln, got a fix on one, then another weak distress signal. They tractored in Tyne and Willington, more or less alive. Tyne had the lethal
O-tablet clamped in one fist. Somehow Willington's pod had lacked one. He couldn't clearly say
why he hadn't offed himself with the pod's sidearm. Jan Tyne had already made the decision but
spent she didn't know how long trying to shake
loose of stubborn life even when most of her had
already accepted death. She and Willington were
redlined for further combat.

Pauley logged off the computer and sat back,
steepling fingers over his mouth. He'd have to request an FTL pilot to crew the third Sparrow. That
was easy enough, but there were intangibles to factor with Willington and Tyne. They'd flown, fought
and almost died together. Shared convalescent
leave in a Mars Station condo, briefly intimate at
the time. Emotional permanance was not a mark of
their breed, but all this would tend to bond them.

Pauley's job and nature asked the question: how

deeply bonded? In a crisis or terminal situation, would they follow orders or cover each other?

With yet no solid lead on the sleeper, other developments provided Pauley with a clearing intelligence picture. Traffic on Allied Development reflected increased orders for atomic fuel for Shrike fusion engines. One alert operator detected a deviation buried deep in a dummy message, which broke out to confirm WILDCARD as Allied's codename for Beta Hydri IV, and part of an operations order to their carrier *Swift*. Listening for Search 528, his antennas arrayed toward Hydri IV, Frank Hardesty caught a fragment of Allied voice chatter from that vicinity.

"They were Shrikes off the *Swift*," Stoner evaluated for Pauley. "That's the badass ship that chewed up *Lincoln*."

"And there's this from Allied's main supply net." Pauley handed him a message broken a few hours before. "They're getting smart as well as mean. Going in for intercept on their own. Interesting."

To Charley Stoner the decode was more ominous than interesting. Training and equipment would cost Allied time and money; in the meantime they'd be apt to pirate any Sparrows they could find. "Open season on people like us. I want to go home."

"*Pro Patria*, Stoney," the IO observed sardonically. "God and country."

"God and country don't fly Sparrows."

"Well anyway, here's what you've been waiting for."

Stoner read the hard copy order. Per operational

requirements noted/approved by COORDINT etcetera, Specialist Sgt. Francis J. Hardesty was promoted to the rank of warrant officer. Stoner jammed the message into his pocket. "For once they got off their asses in a hurry. As of now the kid's relieved, Nije. I'll start breaking him in today."

"Sooner the better," Pauley clipped. "IP coming up."

Stoner paused doubtfully in the hatchway. "Not too soon. He's got a lot to learn. Sparrow rig, all the procedures and drills and—"

Pauley's pale eyes flicked up at him. They, rather than his quiet voice, conveyed the imperative. "Mister Stoner—soon. He's got the rank; he carries the load. Expedite. Push him."

"Mah Gawd, Hardesty." Colonel Dorfmann inspected the new officer summoned to his office, from the boy's smooth face to his neat dress blues. "Are you shaving yet?"

"Yes, sir." The question no longer offended Hardesty. Everyone else had inquired the same since he came onstation.

"Well, that's Major Pauley's backyard, not mine. PERS'll have to find you some insignia. Here's a temporary ID for the ward room and that stuff. Congratulations."

Dorfmann offered a meaty paw by way of rite of passage, then prepared to deliver his usual speech on an officer's responsibilities, trying to decide how, paternal or brother-officer he should allow himself to be with the fledgling. Spaceborns always seemed a little alien to Dorfmann, spaceborn Catholics rare and vaguely suspect on Lutheran principle. "Now, boy—ah want to talk seriously about the conduct that goes with being an officer. Sit down."

Hardesty complied, sighing inwardly. Dorfmann's ponderous lectures to his troops were known neither for wit nor brevity.

"Used t'be they wrote in an officer's commission: 'reposing special faith and trust.' That still goes, boy. You have been picked out—"

For the next twenty minutes, Hubert Dorfmann shared the stored treasures of his wisdom with Frank Hardesty while refraining from any comment on the nest of Sparrow bugfucks the boy was to be part of. Frank pretended to listen and thought of Ellie Roven.

An hour later he showed the ID and mumbled his new status to the ward room attendant, spotted Ellie drinking coffee alone at a table close by and moved toward her, self-conscious and awkward to be in officer country with stripes on his sleeve. He hovered over the table with a tentative smile.

"Sir?"

She returned his smile generously. "Hi-i, Frank. Join me."

He felt happy, shy and very clumsy, aware of Ellie's sweet face and black curls for a long time across the separating gulf of rank. He always supposed she was officer property, like maybe some stud on the *Kennedy*, but the word around station (gleaned from oblique and elaborately casual queries) was neutral. Obstacles of rank removed, he could play his cards for what they were worth or forget it. Not very experienced and naturally shy, Hardesty was tempted to pass and not make a fool of himself. But something in her smile seemed to encourage him.

"I wanted to tell you my warrant came down. I'm in Sparrows with you."

"I heard. Good." When he sat down, Ellie pushed her coffee toward him. "Want to finish this? It's awful."

It was. Hardesty set the plastic cup aside. "What do they call me now, Mister?"

"Yeah, but I'm Ellie. You're Frank short for Francis, right?"

"Yes, sir."

"Ellie." She did a few strokes on the picture she was sketching. "I know; feels odd at first. I did too. Don't worry about it. Stoney's not what you'd call military."

He began to feel more at ease since she obviously tried to make him comfortable. He glanced at the picture she was doing with some sort of colored sticks. "Mister Stoner says you're a fine op."

"You too." She smiled again. There seemed an inner glow to Ellie Roven now that he could talk one to one, an openness in her round face. She was clearly glad he sat down and let him know it. Hardesty allowed himself to speculate that perhaps— just maybe—she'd been checking him out for a while herself.

"Stoney says you handled your pos—you know, when Ed was sending from Hydri—like a real rock," Ellie said.

"Thanks. Never thought I'd make it out of training." Except for the need. If you wanted to make a decent living or life out here, you cut it in the tough jobs or did shitwork for the rest of your days. He didn't want to talk about that, not yet. Hardesty looked at the picture Ellie had colored in on a flattened microwave carton. "Never saw anyone draw by hand before. Just with screens and light pens."

"Pastel and charcoal." Ellie showed him the colored sticks. "My mother sent them. She shouldn't have troubled."

"Why, are they expensive?"

"No, just hard to find. I know Mama; she prob'ly went all over Ville-Marie to find them, and she shouldn't. She's never been very strong."

She had sketched a bright blue cow with green udders, skillfully shaded to use the flat white of the carton for accent. "Like the colors?"

Hardesty tactfully allowed they were very original. "Never saw one live, but aren't they sort of brown or black?"

"Only to the naked eye," Ellie dismissed the notion airily. "My cows are creative. I did a great purple one for Pauley. Like to have this one?"

"Sure . . . thanks." More for the thought than the startlingly atypical bovine. "I'll put it up on my wall." Not knowing what to say next, he tasted the insipid contents of the plastic cup once more. "This is really sad stuff."

"Frank, you'll really know sad when you go on flight diet. Where's your new billet?"

"I think with Mister Stoner."

"Great. I'm down there all the time. He's my big brother." Though Ellie was morally bound to add a warning. "Don't ever play poker or blackjack with him. Reinecke was the only one who could beat him. And here comes the honcho himself."

Stoner ambled casually down the ward area to place the two warrant shoulder boards before Hardesty. "Only ones PERS could find. They were Ed's."

The cloth-covered boards with their single thin stripe, blue on a field of lighter blue, were faded and worn. Ellie jumped up quickly. "Stoney, let's christen him. You do one and I'll fix the other."

Together they fitted the insignia to the shoulders of Hardesty's tunic. So much for ceremony. Stoner jerked his head toward the hatch. "Class time, Mister Hardesty. Let's go."

Hardesty was then subjected to the most grueling cram session since training—pre-flight Sparrow familiarization done on a mock-up of the operator's pos with all rig components. Receivers, recorders, transmitters, D/F complex, MOA and VOA units. Manual and auto-controls for each and their backups—with the admonishment that, operating in a Sparrow, he was required to do by himself much of what traffic analysts did for him on Limbo.

Trust your banks, trust your components, but first trust your *instinct* and ear for sound. Analysis units would accurately search out ident or match, but not as fast as your own memory. Got that? Remember it good. Tomorrow Hardesty would do it all over again in Gunny Willington's ship.

When he could steal a minute, Hardesty made a solitary stop at the small PERS-area compartment used as an all-faith chapel. He genuflected to the plain altar, feeling groggy with all he'd tried to assimilate, and definitely inadequate.

"Christ Jesus and Saint John," he prayed in one of the pews. "You kept me from washing out when I needed to make the grade so much. Don't let me down now. Ellie's a wiz and Stoner's a genius."

Until today, Frank Hardesty thought he was pretty damned good, as hot a rock as anyone could find on Limbo. But the data for which he would rely on memory banks, Stoner kept in his *head*.

"So, please don't let it be I've bit off more than I can chew. Amen."

Hardesty's first breakfast in the officers' mess was literally as concentrated as the first indoctrination session. As regular station personnel, he was used to microwaved meals and processed concentrates, but this was unidentifiable. Two small lumps, reddish brown and a bilious green on his tray, and a plastic cup only half filled with a watery citrus drink. No coffee or tea.

"You know what this means?" Ellie greeted him as he sat down with her and Stoner.

He looked at the substance on his tray. "I don't even know what it is."

"Low fiber concentrates," Stoner said. His own tray held two identical lumps as did Ellie's. "Low liquid to start you dehydrating."

SOP before a prolonged mission for pilots and ops alike. Out on a ten- or twelve-hour stint in a Sparrow, you stayed empty or wore a diaper under the skintight undergarment.

"Which is uncomfortable enough," Stoner informed him, tapping his own tray with a spoon. "Diet makes you irritable after a few days. Longer, you get downright mean. Meet us at the FTL airlock in half an hour. Today you get to do dry runs. Eat up."

Hardesty obeyed without gusto.

Gunny Willington was waiting for the three operators on the hangar deck of the *Kennedy*, Jan Tyne already running line checks in her own cockpit. Willington shook hands perfunctorily with Hardesty. *I don't know if you can cut this*, the pilot's manner communicated to Hardesty. *Fly with me and you'd better*. He took the new officer through a walk-around of the Sparrow.

Waiting on the bay deck as maintenance crews passed back and forth, Stoner looked up at Tyne's head, visible through her forward view plates. "What do you think, Ellie? Are Gunny and Tyne making it?"

"I don't know. Who cares?"

"They always hang out together. Not much with anyone else."

"Tyne's not much for girl talk," said Ellie who had tried. "You want to be friendly, but she's got a personality like a paper cut. But . . . yeah. Maybe. Who else could stand her?"

"Gunny's okay." Stoner dropped the subject. The two pilots were not very sociable, but minds could suffer frostbite like any physical feature. They'd been bitten hard in Gamma Three, and maybe Ellie was still too green to read that.

Following in Willington's all-business wake, Frank Hardesty felt that the smallest forgotten detail about a Sparrow could and probably would kill him in space. As modified from the Shrike, the Sparrow looked like what it was, a hybrid: a blunt-nosed cylinder with ridiculously vestigial delta wings housing the solar panels for recharging auxiliary power.

". . . built for speed of evasion," Willington continued. "A Shrike's delta configuration is much wider and laser-mounted. That's the quickest way to ident between them, visual or imaging. Sparrows have only two lasers, one forward and one rear between the afterburners. Not enough, really.

What she does have is more power. You getting all this, Hardy?"

"Hardesty, sir. Yes, sir."

"Added length for you and your rig. This isn't hard, kid. This is basic. Hard is working in one. I guess you went through iso/dep in training."

Isolation/sensory deprivation tests had to be passed by anyone to qualify for deepspace assignment. Failure to adapt accounted for a large percentage of training washouts. "I stayed in the green, sir."

"You'll have to. And speaking of velocity . . ."

Hardesty dutifully recorded on his PDR unit everything commanded by Willington who seemed to know so much about the Sparrow he might have shepherded the craft from the first drawn sketch-concept through building. For the rest he tried to make his mind a memory bank while the pilot rattled through the relationship of launch and cruising speeds to orbital decay factors and the effect of the ship's ATs, attitudinal thrusters controlling maneuverability. Every system in the ship had redundancy, all systems and backups must be checked out before launch.

"Get this too," Willington told him. "If you fly with me, I never launch until every check is complete to my satisfaction. That means your checklist too. Learn it like your ID number, do it quick and right. And here"—Willington slapped at a section of the Sparrow's underbelly—"is your front door. Mine's forward."

"I know, sir."

Gunny Willington surveyed him coolly. "Do you?"

"I crammed the manual."

"I'm impressed. By the way, name's Gunny."
His first concession to informality. "I'll go in and
pop your hatch. Come mission, crews'll have it
open for you."

Hardesty started forward to the cockpit ladder. "I can do it, sir."

"No, you'd stick your big foot where it shouldn't
be and fuck something up." Willington climbed the
ladder assembly by the open cockpit hatch. With
one leg inside the dorsal opening, he added, "I said
my name's Gunny. We cut the sirs and the saluting
unless Dorfmann gets an attack of by-the-book.
When that happens, we all snap sharp for a day or
two and then forget it. What you never do is go
redline on your pilot. Lose your head. You stay in
the green and leveled out. Okay, let's work inside."

When the aft hatch was popped, Hardesty
climbed directly into the op's compartment, bumping his head against the pos seat. Willington completed the nomenclature session from the cockpit.
Access between op's pos and cockpit was a narrow
space between the computer complex and dorsal
bulkhead, no more, most easily negotiated in zero-
G. Aft of Hardesty's position rested the top of the
spherical ejection pod, behind that the fusion
shielding, engines, afterburners and rear laser assembly.

For E-pod familiarization, Willington ordered
Hardesty to take it from the inside, talking him
through from the cockpit. The pilot gazed bleakly
at the visible hemisphere of the pod, then called to
Hardesty buried in its interior. "One more thing. If
you fly with Ja—well, E-pod is usually pilot checklist, but make it yours. The pod can be prepped
and/or ejected from inside where you are or from

the cockpit. You're closer and the pilot's got enough to do. Learn everything that goes into that beast, and I mean everything."

"Learned it from the manual," Hardesty's voice came out of the depths. "Think I've got it."

"Outstanding," Gunny Willington sighed. "Sound off."

"Manual hatch lever. Explosive bolts, manual arming switch for same. Manual backup release. Eject charge enable, safety lock . . . on. Oxygen release regulator. Reserve O^2 cannisters, four. C-bars, fifteen. That's five more than specified."

"You can buy them. They're used in Corpse Shrike pods. Better than ours. More chocolate. Keep going."

"Sidearm." The voice from the pod went quizzical. "I wondered about this in the manual. Sidearm in a pod?"

"To repel boarders," Willington said drily, "what else?"

He waited. "And?"

The flame-red head of hair rose from the pod, reminding Gunny of a puzzled carrot. "No O-tablets. Should be two."

"Right." The pilot's damaged countenance crumpled in a sour grin. "That's what I meant by everything." He took a plastic packet from the breast pocket of his coveralls and tossed it to Hardesty. "Took them out to see if you'd forget. Put them back. In the right place."

Hardesty let the packet lay in his palm, foreign and repugnant. "How quick are these?"

"Quicker than you can change your mind if you bite into one. Don't think about it."

"I'm Catholic."

Willington started to answer, then suddenly couldn't look at the face a hundred years younger than his own, or the packet in his hand. *Not in a pod,* he wanted to say. *When your life support goes redline, you're just an animal that can't breathe. Tell Jesus you're sorry as hell and bite.* "Well, it gives you a choice, Frank. The piece or the pill."

He hooked one hand through the overhead hatch and raised up. "Stoner! He's all yours."

Soon, Pauley ordered. Have Hardesty ready ASAP. For the next three days, with Stoner leaning over from the cockpit and Ellie virtually in his lap, Frank Hardesty relearned his job in a small craft already cramped without personnel. Receivers, transmitters, computer screen, recorders and analysis components for every mode of transmission from Morse to computer-to-modem. The position seat, padded for G-pressure and with backup controls on its arms, was jammed too close to the inductance keyboard controlling all functions. Hardesty continually banged his long legs or an elbow—

"Damn! Hardly move in here."

"You get used to it," said Ellie.

"No, you don't," Stoner grumped. "What they need is midgets, but there ain't too many out here. Welcome to the Claustro Club."

Billeted with Stoner possibly as a good housekeeping influence, Hardesty was treated by his chief and Ellie Roven to a clandestine bash on Jesus Juice and pretzels long past their prime. The jayjay bootlegged by Hydroponics varied in taste from batch to batch but never in potency. Considering the cost and that there would be a few minutes of weightlessness in station orbital adjustment, they kept the container capped and covers handy for their cups. Ellie thoughtfully set a hand-vac ready, not sure how Frank's stomach reacted to zero-G. They were laughing over their drinks when the shift commenced ten minutes before schedule. The liquor drifted up out of their cups in globules—

"Caps! Caps!"

Like swimmers in a pool, they hung onto bunk-frames until the maneuver completed. Stoner righted his chair, grumbling. "Boy, I love this place. Party on, kids."

Frank was still unused to intimacy with officers and disappointed to find officer country no more commodious than his old pigeon-hole billet.

"I was a sergeant three years out here before my IO approved me for warrant," Stoner told him. "He said it was giving aid and comfort to the enemy." He reached for more pretzels, spilling some of his drink.

"*Sto*ney!" Ellie sucked up the spill in the hand-vac. "I'm from a colony like you, Frank, but Stoney's from California. Between a lake and a large desert which he needed for littering."

"You want me to take the top bunk, Mister Stoner?"

"No, you . . . you can have the bottom, it's okay." Stoner didn't feel right about taking Ed's bunk when he should have taken the mission, all the more like admitting his friend was dead. He sipped his drink while Ellie and Frank fantasized about Earthside leave. Neither of them had ever been there. Next to seeing Italy and painting in Florence with real pigments, Ellie Roven wanted to taste chocolate cake topped with something called cream cheese. "Then I'd like to be a debutante and dance all night."

Frank had never heard the term. "A what?"

"Debutantes were a long time ago. Girls wore gorgeous gowns at a party and . . . came out? Stoney, is that right?"

"Yeah."

"Out of what?"

"Just meant they could get engaged."

"Well, it sounded so nice, old things like that. Like courting. Did you court your wife, Stoney?"

He had to think for a moment. "Sort of, I guess. The first one. Second time around we just drove to Vegas and got married. For the divorce, she took a plane. She couldn't get there fast enough."

Ellie smiled tenderly at her mentor. "Miss her?"

Charley Stoner did not. "My last wet dream was about an hour in a hot bath."

"I tasted a real steak once," Hardesty put in. "Long as we're dreaming. Like to spend all night eating a steak."

"Eating anything user-friendly." Ellie's giggle ended in a hiccup.

Stoner slipped out of the conversation and let the young people talk. They liked each other immediately; that was good wherever it was meant to lead. He wouldn't disillusion them about anything Earthside. Beef in restaurants, or any good meat if available, was ninety endees a plate the last time he took home leave. If the place hadn't been ripped off by the street people or black market storebusters. Most restaurants and super-malls had armed security guards. You lined up and showed your cash or plastic just to get in, a few at a time. "Who wants a refill?"

Everyone did. Stoner poured all around. "Frank, gimme that again about the Allied traffic."

The boy hesitated; by rule they didn't discuss sensitive intercept outside secure operational areas.

Stoner jeered. "Where's a spy gonna go? Out an airlock?"

"We're all Search here," Ellie prompted. "And 528's our baby."

"Ed's baby," Stoner corrected pointedly. "Tell me, Frank."

Hardesty picked up the transmission by luck and confirmed the orientation. Hydri IV. That Allied or any Corpse would be near the planet at all . . .

"Figures." Stoner bit into a pretzel that limply refused to crunch. "Sooner or later."

Hardesty looked as eager as he was concerned. "That mean bogeys when we get in close?"

"Sure." Stoner snapped at him, wondering at the same time why he sounded so sharp. "Bring along a vidcorder and get a live record of all of us running like hell for the carrier. Anything you scan out there, if it's not us, it's a bogey. Equal-opportunity hostiles; they'll waste anyone. When your pilot tells you to strap and seal, do it, because he's going to slam out of there fast."

"So why didn't Mister Reinecke's pilot—?" Hardesty blurted the logical question without thinking, but choked if off short in the face of Stoner's sudden, forbidding glare that made him feel like an inferior specimen under glass. There was an awkward silence. "Sorry, sir. That was dumb."

Ellie rescued him smoothly. "Not at all, Frank. Stoney—level out. Be nice."

Stoner took a swallow of his drink while Ellie laid it out for the new Sparrow op. "We know Ed had a D/F cut on the 528 signal. It was from the surface, and none of us figured on an installation. ODF would tell Rothberg how close the Sparrow could descend. Tyne figured Ed cut it too fine. In the crunch Rothberg was fighting Gs and bogeys together. No dumb questions out here."

The intercom phone fluted softly in its wall cradle; Hardesty snatched at it gratefully. "Sergeant, uh." He cleared his throat and lowered his light voice toward an authoritative baritone. "Mister Hardesty here . . . yes, sir."

Stoner exchanged a prophetic glance with Ellie Roven. "Any bets?"

"Seventy-two hours. Right, Major. I'll be ready." Hardesty hung up and swung around to the others. "Hey, it's here."

"Mission," Ellie said.

"How'd you know?"

"Always seventy-two hours. Three extra days to let the delicious goodness of flight diet seep through you."

"It's a practice mission from the carrier tomorrow. Two Sparrows, me and Mister Stoner."

"Make it Stoney." The kid tried hard and learned fast; it wouldn't kill him to put the guy at ease. "Look, about Reinecke. Ed was a hot rock, sure, but always a cowboy. Real good but reckless. He liked taking chances. You be careful Frank. I don't need any more dead cowboys out here." He winked at Hardesty to change the subject and mood. "Listen, if I gotta fly tomorrow, let me get some sleep. You two go down to Ellie's."

She picked up the suggestion with light speed. "Come on, Frank. Got some great old music. We can dance or something."

Hardesty was as ready, jumping up quickly. "I never danced."

"Then we'll something. Grab the jayjay."

"Go easy, Frank. I don't want to have to nurse you on O^2 tomorrow."

"I promise." Frank and Ellie capped their liquor and tucked the cups inside their coveralls. The main container was too large to conceal. "You got a bunkie?" Frank asked Ellie as they departed.

"She's washing her underwear," she invented with swift determination. "I washed mine last week when she had a guest. For two hours. She was hung over, but I had the cleanest underwear on Limbo. 'Night, Stoney."

Stoner went to bed thinking about the two of them: that for all his bitching, things would be worse and lonelier without them now that Ed was gone. As he sank toward sleep, he thought again of Reinecke and 528, an alien voice that sang chords and waited, listening for his own kind on a ship far beyond anything humans could build, hovering over a cold planet with two moons on the edge of known space. Two eyes meeting through a keyhole . . .

Skin breached, life support hissing out. At dream speed, weightless and far too slow, she swam past the shattered computers and the smell of fried circuitry, flowing head first into the E-pod, sealed and pressurized, and the eject charge blew her clear of the crippled Shrike, a last live blossom flowering from a doomed stalk. She felt herself flung impossible distances through black space jeweled with a billion glittering eyes.

She lay shivering in the pod while breathing became more labored and pointless, while the O-tablet in her hand swelled large as a plate with eyes and a big smile-button grin. *Take me*, that smile urged with the tender concern of a true friend. *Bite me or drink me now, I'm all there is.*

The worst of it was, she knew she was dead. Lying there listening to the beacon bleat its futile lost-lamb call through an empty void. Except now it was talking too, saying her name over and over, as if trying to convince a jury who'd already condemned her. *I was Jan Tyne. Janice Tyne, really I was. Look at my ID when you find me.* And the smiling O-tablet waited while her life support went past red-line. She fought for air, anything in her lungs, already dead but her animal body denying—*when was I ever alive?*

Jan Tyne opened her eyes. Her mouth was buried in the dry pillow. She twisted on her back, sweaty against the sheets, dragging the stale, recycled air into her lungs. The sweat on her body was cold. She shivered.

She couldn't go through another night like this, not with a flight in the morning. The verol sedatives weren't cutting it alone anymore. She had to double up, do something. Tyne slid out of her bunk, fuzzy-minded, holding onto the upper bunk to steady herself. She'd taken the lower since Carol Wray moved out.

"Nothing personal, Jan, but let the medics look at you."

Look at what? Profile what? She'd sweat and shake wherever she went. Tyne groped in the small cabinet over her tiny sink for the plastic container of verol. Empty. She swore fretfully and reached for the intercom phone.

"Me," she murmured when Gunny picked up. "Did I wake you?"

"No, I wasn't asleep." Gunny Willington didn't have the sexiest voice in the world; flat like hers but it sounded reassuring, part of her. Something new since their convalescent leave. Giving assurance or needing it didn't go with either of them. "How about you?" he asked.

"It's bad tonight, and I'm out of verol."

"Come on down."

Gunny Willington shook two verols out of the container, placed them on the small fold-away desk and drew a cup of water. The recycled water tasted rotten as usual. He considered adding a touch of jayjay, then made it half liquor, poured a small one for himself and knocked it back. MED section warned about mixing sedatives with alcohol. What could it do, kill them? *Been there already, Doctor.* Willington smoothed his bedclothes and plumped the pillow. Jan would want to lie down. If she fell asleep, he'd take the top bunk or doze with his arms around her. If he could drop off at all.

He'd come to need Jan, and neither of them was ready for that. Didn't happen much to people like them, but the thing was there and scary. They talked around it, backed away, edged closer. Like what happened after this tour was up, their last for sure. Their crits were far too low. Reassignment to Shrikes was out of the question. Med/profiles would be bye-bye time. Then what? Where did you go when you were burned out at twenty-seven?

Rothberg thought he had it together, talked about tomorrow like it would actually come, buying shares in a condo complex. Johnny R. was going to get out at twenty-five with a whole ass and maybe an instructor's slot, and homestead his condo on Mars Station. Real nice.

Pretty late. Get Jan to sleep, maybe he could cop some himself. He was flying the new kid tomorrow. After hard-assing the guy through familiarization, he had to show some stuff himself.

Four and a half months, then he and Jan would be finished with this tour. Maybe they could go somewhere, put their money together. There wasn't all that much saved; that meant thinking tomorrow. They never used that word, scared of it. Sad way to be.

Willington sat down on his bunk. He didn't shake like Jan, not where it showed. They never really got out of those pods. For Jan it was a matter of biting the Big Off, but he hadn't checked the pod that thoroughly, so Jan held the pill, he gripped the sidearm and looked at the trigger switch, then the business end . . .

Almost did it . . . don't think about that. Jan's bad enough. She can't take care of you too.

They took convalescent leave in one of the condo units UNESA kept for R&R on Mars Station, even looked at the unit Rothberg bought into. There were two good-sized beds in their quarters, but after the first night they only used one. Blew two hundred endees on Earthside Scotch, got blind and jumped each other's bones. Willington wished he could remember more about that, but when he tried there was mostly Jan coming apart, screaming and sobbing until he got her into bed. They had sex but more often they cried or babbled compulsively at each other, far past drunk into sheer exhaustion.

"Normal," the fat little therapist told him before he and Jan were transferred to Limbo. "Nothing about you wants to die, Lieutenant. You came too close. Life compensates by affirming itself. One *Lincoln* pilot screwed himself silly for a week, an Olympian effort, cock so red and drippy the medics thought he had a world-class case of clap. Turned out to be just strain. Wrapped it in salve and a love-glove, told him to stay in bed and screen a good book. Life affirmation."

Life affirmation. Now there was a tidy, sterilized term for him and Jan. Very neat. You couldn't feel the sweat or hear the screaming in that.

In a pod when the Big Off is coming one way or another, you think very clearly about what you've done with twenty-seven years and how much or how little was personal quality time. When he crawled out of the pod like coming from his own tomb, it was like being born again, anything like fear plain worn away and from then on, every day—every minute—could be profit. Could be.

He and Jan were so much alike—same age, same off-world birth and background. Flight cadets in the same class at seventeen, graduated in the top four percent of their bunch, recruited into Shrikes. So cocksure and swaggering when their shoulder boards were new, but after a few months against Corpse fighters, they went mean and wary like the rest. Team loyalty but no close friends.

You got to be the best because anything less died. You could handle anything. Then all of a sudden you were alone with a woman strong as yourself, your female counterpart, and not ready when she fell apart, so you

*gave her the only thing you could and called it loving.
Slept back to back, not touching because closeness got
bred out long before the two of you hit the E-pods, the
part of ordinary people who touched and shared and took
tomorrow for granted. You looked at Jan's face on the
pillow, shut down tight even in sleep, and knew the only
difference between you was that she screamed and you
didn't. She broke with it and you learned from that how
done with it you were, whether Jan admitted that or not.*

Jan and himself. The idea was a sudden new display lighted in his cockpit of a mind. They'd never
said things like, "When I'm older, when I'm retired, when there's time . . ." The first night on
leave when they started drinking, the pathetic fact
struck them: neither could imagine being thirty.
The more Willington thought about that, the sad-
der it felt. You could always die. They accepted
that, but life was scarier because you started to care
and need. Much as that frightened him, he knew it
terrified Jan all the more.

He heard her light tap at the hatch.

Jan had put on the heavy red robe Gunny bought
for her on leave. Earthside cotton, expensive. She
loved the soft, sensual crush of the material against
her skin. He didn't hug her when she came in; that
was typical of them, neither used to touching. Jan
never thought of that until recently. Sex was like
laxatives: get it on, get it over, back to work. More
of a male attitude, but somehow she'd got that
way. Until their leave. One day, sharing the shower
ration, she came up out of scrubbing her face to see
Gunny standing there in the fallout from the noz-
zle, reaching for her. She wondered if he wanted
sex again when they'd just finished.

No, just . . . just you looked so thin. Why had she bristled then when she wanted to melt?

"Pills on the sink," Gunny said by way of hello.

"Take a couple now, I can have it together by briefing." Jan sniffed the drink. "Jayjay."

"Drink it slow."

She washed down the sedatives in water, noticing Gunny's old puzzle cube on the deck. "You couldn't sleep either?"

"Who sleeps?" He guided her to the lower bunk. "You're still shaky. Lie down. Give the pills a chance."

Jan stiffened instinctively. "I'm all right."

Did it again, goddammit. Why did she always get defensive when he tried to be gentle? To make up for it, Jan slid to one side of the narrow bunk, leaving room for him, hoping he'd hold her. That was new too. Sex was one thing but touching someone, reaching out, was a foreign language.

Gunny eased in beside her, cushioning her head on his arm. "Want to stay?"

"Maybe, I don't know."

They weren't too great as lovers, not that she had that much to compare with. Maybe in time—Jan pressed a mental button and deleted the thought. The sedatives began to untie the knots in her body and mind. Even her body seemed new and strange now, if nothing special in a mirror: narrow hips, flat belly and small breasts like fried eggs. Nothing to make any man look twice. She'd always been like software interacting with a ship's systems, strictly functional, went months sometimes without menstruating, but the period after that leave was heavy and somehow emotionally pleasurable. Jan spent two days in her billet at the reassignment station, wrapped up in her red robe, drinking the last of the leave Scotch and weeping frequently for no reason, or simply perhaps she wasn't used to feeling like a woman.

But the dreams still came and told her she wasn't anything of the sort, just a component blown out of a dead ship to float in a bubble with a monotonous piping beacon, an irrelevant smudge on infinity—

What if that happened again? Bad enough once, but to float there full of memories and futures, someone you lost, caring and feeling until you knew there was no chance and had to bite the Big Off? She didn't want to think about that.

"Know what I liked about leave, Gunny? Washing my hair with real shampoo and the hell with what it cost."

"Smelled good." He grazed fingertips through her close-cropped hair; soft on leave but now chemical-stiff as his own. "What's it like long?"

She'd honestly forgotten. Jan's hair hadn't been long since before she entered flight training. "Gunny? That lake Stoner's always talking about . . ."

"I'd like to see it sometime."

Maybe, Jan thought. When Stoner went on about Tahoe, Ellie Roven listened like a little girl at her father's knee. Jan never knew her own father. Her mother split the colony after Jan was born, cold-slept home and disappeared. No big thing; happened a lot out here, just sometimes Jan wished Stoner would sing a different song with less bullshit. Most Earthside lakes weren't that fresh or clean anywhere now, she heard. But stupid little Roven ate it up, couldn't get enough.

The pills were working at last; she heard the languor in her voice. "That place Rothberg was buying . . ."

"Yeah, nice. Wonder how much he still had to go on payments." Gunny shifted closer. "You leveling out?"

"Umhmm . . ." She was glad just to be held like this without having to ask. They were so clumsy with each other and didn't always know what the other meant or wanted. "Getting short, Gunny."

"Few months. Maybe we could go somewhere." After a moment he said, "I guess PERS is still holding Johnny's condo shares. Didn't have any family he ever talked about."

"No, Johnny R. was a leftover like me."

Like both of them. Gunny's parents had nothing Earthside but couldn't stand colony life. They left him in school and went back to nothing again; at least it was familiar.

They drowsed through a silence, but any mention of Rothberg always brought them back to the Question. "Johnny R. was good," Jan murmured. "He never went redline in combat."

Gunny finished the thought with the other inevitable question. "Why didn't he evade and run when there was a chance?"

Jan wouldn't say it aloud. If Rothberg ever had a chance against 528. They might be MUX'd or even cyborn, bred to interface with computers. To say nothing of the armament they might carry. Rothberg was good, but even the best Shrike pilot could go a second too long without checking his six. Jan was grateful the upcoming mission was to be only Intermediate Probe for the time, nothing close. She felt sudden tears sting at her eyes and flung an arm over her face to cover them from Gunny. "No win. Sooner or later."

"Hey," he soothed, bending over her. "It's nothing, Jan. We got it covered. I won't let you take any chances you don't have to, okay? Hell, it's a milk run, just driving the ops where they need to go."

Jan didn't know the term. "Milk?"

"Read it in an old book. Easy flights, routine, no sweat."

She nudged him to get up. "Guess I can sleep now."

"You can stay."

"I sleep better alone; so do you." That was pitiful of her, Jan seethed, tying the robe around her narrow waist. Not what she meant at all. But he said she *could* stay, not that he *wanted* her to. Some pair they were. Some female she was. Didn't know a damned thing about men or herself.

Gunny sat on the edge of the bunk, watching her. "Maybe we could go somewhere."

"Like where?"

"I thought I could ask about Johnny's condo."

Stop . . . will you stop? Jan begged out of bottom-line despair dulled only a little by verol and jayjay. If she needed a boost in the morning, she could cop some B1 and then oxygen in the Sparrow. That was as far ahead as she dared to think. You fell into a lot of dangerous habits, but hoping was the worst.

"Go where?" she flashed suddenly, one hand on the hatch lever. "Do what? Condo here, colony somewhere else? Stoner's lake, Reinecke's goddamned prairie—what? It's all dried up and dead now, has been for years. Bad food, bad air, hole in the ozone. Don't bullshit yourself like Roven.

There's no place to go anymore. Don't bullshit me, I take it straight."

Arms folded on his bare knees, Gunny just shook his head, sure of that much. "Not straight, just safe and scared. Whatever we do, alone or together, we better go for the condo. Know what I mean?"

"Look, when we were on leave, that's one thing, but don't make it more than it was."

"I was there," he said gently. "Remember? I held you when you cried and later when you were sick and needed me. I needed you. Maybe we ought to hang onto that—because in less than five months, that's all there is."

"You forget Hydri IV?" she threw back. She was shaking again. "That one of your milk runs, Gunny? How do we know the area's not crawling with Corpses right now? How do we know those little 528 fuckers won't blow us away? How do we know what else is out there? Don't talk about all there is. We don't even know where *there* is."

"But whatever," Gunny said softly, seeing the truth in her face, "Jan Tyne is scared as hell."

She hovered by the hatch, afraid of his truth and her own. "Damn right, Gunny. Because I can't cut it anymore."

"Cut what, for God's sake?"

"Anything."

Hardesty had logged a week in Sparrows when all Allied Development nets went suddenly silent. Their periodic freq/callsign change wasn't expected for another month; at such times Search usually found and idented most of them within twenty-four hours. The unexpected hushout signalled a major cipher change and possibly something imminent. Limbo Station went on alert. Completely in the dark until the nets were recovered, the tension flexed through the muscle of Search, TANAL and CRYPT sections. Off-duty operators hung around the working positions to stay current, analysts and cryptographers lived on coffee in their duty areas.

Circling the *Kennedy* at a thousand kays, ten thousand out from Limbo, Stoner made the Allied changeover part of Hardesty's flight indoctrination, vindicated when the kid nailed two high-level policy nets and an Allied Shrike squadron from memory.

From Tyne's ship a hundred kays away, Stoner's question rasped in Hardesty's ear, scratchy from hours on canned life support. "That squadron voice net confirmed on VOA?"

"Matching now, but I've copied this guy before. I know it's him."

VOA proved Hardesty right: Dieters Lieberman, a Bavarian fighter pilot who swore in Swabische when irritated. He had a slight speech defect, a kind of lisp. Hardesty had pegged him before the VOA matchup. Stoner's accolade was brief but sincere.

"You remembered where I'd forgotten. Way to go, Mister. Wrap it up and let's go home."

During the Allied hushout, jayjay sales had slacked off—with one rumored exception. Stoner got the word through his own connections that Major Pauley was buying it now. Not worth a second thought. Pauley held the hard stuff better than any three men. Meanwhile CRYPT was breaking the new Allied ciphers and Limbo relaxed from alert to routine.

Returning from flight, Stoner lurched through the airlock toward Intelligence to report Hardesty ready to go operational and the Sparrow complement prepared for Intermediate Probe on 528. No Pauley in his office, only the intelligence sergeant, Kim Bok Thun. The prim, precise little Korean operated at one speed: slow and methodical. Formal and always a little distant behind his glasses, today Thun glowered at Stoner and the crypter keyboard he worked over.

"Where's the IO, Kim?"

Thun stabbed at the keyboard. "I'm sure I don't know, sir," he said with an audible edge. "He has not been in."

"Down in CRYPT?"

Thun's response clearly resented the inconvenience caused through Pauley's absence. "You might try his quarters, sir."

The secure classified phone sang softly; Thun glared at it. "He's been late on duty these last two days," he volunteered, snatching the phone from its cradle. "Intelligence, Sergeant Thun . . . no. Major Pauley is still not in. 625? Please wait."

Thun stabbed rapid commands onto one of the office terminal screens. While he worked, Stoner's eye fell on the memo Thun was ciphering for transmission, reading it upside down and recognizing the hard copy from Pauley's own printer, date 0900 two days ago to UNESA Personnel, Mars Station.

REF YOUR MEMO 5326 ADVISING THREE PILOTS AVAILABLE, PLEASE CANCEL MY MEMO 1713 REQUEST FOR SAME. WILL FILL SPARROW POSITIONS FROM ONSTATION PERSONNEL.

Thun was back on the phone. "Yes, that's Allied 625. You're reading them again? Good. I'll inform the IO *when* he comes in." He replaced the phone. "Something else I can do for you, Mister Stoner?"

A clear farewell. "No, that's it."

They'd probably skip debrief today with Pauley out, but why did he cancel the request for Sparrow pilots? Tyne and Gunny were stressed to max and getting short anyway. Gunny even had an old-fashioned FIGMO chart on his billet wall (Fuck It, Got My Orders). Tyne was wound tight and looked it.

You expect us to IP and then go Proximity without replacements? It's scary out there, Nije. The life you're screwing with may be mine.

He'd put ten hours in the Sparrow but the three-minute shower ration wouldn't be turned on until morning. For now no more than a moist chem pad to wipe himself down. Beautiful.

At least Ellie and Frank could relax. The last supply shuttle had brought a windfall: seventy gallons of real ice cream and even some sugar cones to go with it. All one flavor, chocolate. The cones tasted like cardboard and crumbled, but Dorfmann, by his own lights, had scored a moral coup and a morale measure in one stroke, bartering for the ice cream a thousand superannuated condoms—

"Ah want those rubbers off station—off! Plain temptation, just asking for it. I didn't requisition them; where'd they come from anyhow?"

—and a VD holo seen so often by Limbo personnel that they mouthed the sentential dialogue along with the soundtrack. Female station personnel had mandatory subcutaneous contraceptive implants, though MED Section regretted the loss of

condoms which would have helped against the
mutated strains of chlamydia going around frontier
stations and the shuttles that serviced them.

Stoner locked his billet hatch and groped at the
lining of the dress tunic he almost never wore for
the tiny snaps that formed an accessible pocket between lining and outer fabric, his cigarette stash.
Time for a quick smoke before Frank got in. Still in
his pressure suit, the kid had run to get Ellie and
go off for ice cream. Neither of them had ever
tasted it before, real or synthetic.

But no pilots. *Why?*

Stoner sucked deep on the cigarette and jetted a
defiant cloud of smoke at the bulkhead and the
deadweight thought of Dorfmann. He grabbed for
the neutralizer spray, wielding it like a saber, cutting swaths of frustration through the smoke.

Lieutenant Willi Krug inspected himself in the
narrow strip mirror and passed glum approval on
the image he would present to Major Pauley in five
minutes. Blues pressed, hair regulation trimmed to
a precise inch and a half, the whole effect soldierly
as the day he won his wings in the Deutsche
Reichsluft ten years ago. Promotion there was slow,
though Willi Krug considered himself on the fast
track to high command when he transferred to carrier duty with UNESA.

He resented being drafted to pilot a toy Sparrow
because they would freeze him on the promotion
list while the duty lasted. From his mirror the
heavy-lidded, slightly protuberant blue eyes spoke
tacit truths that still rankled a man who could
never tolerate personal failure. He'd always had
the flying ability for fighter duty but never the crits

or aggressiveness required of Shrike pilots. FTL duty was ideal where older and more stable profiles were the rule. He was due for promotion. Captain Satin of the *Kennedy* had given him a high performance evaluation endorsed by Dorfmann—and now this.

Krug slammed the locker shut and went to report.

The Intelligence Officer was swallowing the first of three pills with water when the pilot entered his office. To Krug, Major Pauley's eyes looked definitely bloodshot as he flipped open the records jacket in front of him.

"Stand easy. Sit down, Willi." More weary suggestion than order. "I see you flew ME-30s and B-10 Stealths."

"Yes, sir. A beautiful ship, the B-10."

"Expensive at any rate, but not very stealthy as it turned out. You were decorated for . . . commended for . . . un hm. Hundred hours in Shrikes. Good. You won't be lost at the start."

Krug kept the stiffness out of his answer with a conscious effort. "I would not be lost in any case, *Herr Maior*."

"Really?" Pauley's head came up. Krug blinked: In the reddened eyes there was something merciless that chilled him. "Well, we'll find out, won't we? Right, you're mine as of today. Questions?"

"*Bitte*, for how long is the transfer?"

"Can't really say. Not too long, I should think."

"Sir," Krug couldn't help reminding him. "I have protested this assignment—"

"Yes, I know."

"—to Colonel Dorfmann in person."

"Noted in record, Willi. In point of fact, having

a taste for Milanese cuisine, I'd like to be in Tuscany, but my chances and yours are equally minute. Operational necessity. Anything else? Be in classified briefing at 1000 hours prepared to board the carrier directly we finish."

"Sir." Krug rose and saluted smartly, turning to exit just as Stoner entered. The German concealed his disapproval; the warrant officer's coveralls looked as old as he was, and the man smelled of tobacco. The salute he rendered the IO was a languid bending of his elbow; Pauley's was as vague.

Stoner glanced after Krug as the pilot departed. "Hope he flies sharp as he dresses."

"Might be someone to emulate, Stoney." Pauley massaged his aching temples. " 'Go thou and do likewise.' Need something?"

"About those replacement pilots—"

"Sorry, none to be had," Pauley cut him off. "Have to make do with Krug for now."

The surprised answer was on his tongue when something made Stoner bite it back. There *were* replacements available; he'd seen the memo canceling them. What the hell was going on? "You don't look good, Nije."

"Who does? Recycled air," Pauley mumbled, swallowing the last pill. "Sorry about the replacements."

"Yeah . . . see you at briefing."

Not the air. Stoner was sure of that as he headed for TANAL to get any last minute data on the Allied carriers *Swift* and *Condor*. No, none of the usual complaints. Pauley had a Force Ten hangover, drinking for days by the look of him—or a lot over a short time. And he deliberately lied about the replacements. Stoner had the unpleasant vision of a large bucket of toxic waste poised for intimate relations with a high-speed fan.

An accessway speaker blared suddenly and made him jump—

"Attention all personnel. Because Station Maintenance is still detecting nicotine in the filtering system, the fine for smoking onstation is now a hundred and fifty endees. This is a special reminder to previous offenders—"

The Grey Eminence of Dorfmann was evident in the warning. *Watch it, Stoner, or your ass is mine.*

"—Colonel Dorfmann and staff wish to extend to everyone a very Merry Christmas."

Stoner moved on as the announcement began to repeat tediously in French, which would be followed by the same in Russian, Chinese and Spanish. *"Avis a tous le personnel. Le Service d'Entretien de la station—"*

"Yeah, yeah, fuck off." Stoner had solid and ingenious supply connections for cigarettes, almost a hundred and fifty in scrip and close to a thousand in the PERS electronic records. They could fine him six or seven times before he went broke. There would be cramped and smokeless days on IP with 528 and probably Corpses to scare him. Culpable but unreformed, Charley Stoner headed on toward TANAL.

The classified briefing compartment lay just off the airlock to the carrier, with molded plastic seats in rows, a holograph projector and a small microwave station for heating snacks, coffee and tea. An easel stood ready for the red security classification placards stamped in white in the five working station languages.

Pauley set the MAXIMUM SECURITY placard on the easel. One degree beyond TOP SECRET: Not even Thun would be present, nor any other individual without a direct need to know. From his cubicle in *Kennedy* Operations, Pauley would control the Sparrow IP mission and, in effect, the carrier itself in all but emergency or combat situations.

He endured stoically the punishing jayjay hangover, his first of such epic masochism since retrieval from a Texas Mineral installation in Gamma Three. Pauley grimaced at the pale euphemism, "retrieval." He got out with forged travel orders an hour before his cover would have been blown, informed later by Waites that there was now a substantial TM bounty on his head. Now, for all practical purposes, Allied Development was offering the same for his Sparrows.

Willi Krug entered at precisely 1000 hours. The German's unconcealed dislike of this duty irritated Pauley. The man thought it beneath him. That would be wrung out straightaway. Stoner ambled in and poured coffee, managing to spill some as usual. He squinted at the Max/Sec classification and took a seat as the other two pilots entered.

"Hi, Willi," Gunny greeted him. "Sleeping better since we parted?"

Pauley frowned at the digital wall clock. Roven and Hardesty were late. He ducked out into the corridor; they were just coming, each with a half consumed ice cream cone. "Mister Hardesty. *Miz*ter Roven, you're holding up history. If you fey little tykes will get inside, we may board in time."

"Sorry, sir." Hardesty stood aside for Ellie, managing to touch her hand as she passed him with a wink not lost on Pauley. He locked the hatch and briefly considered the two of them while calling up his notes on the PDR. There was a subtle flush of happiness to Roven now. As he knew everything else that transpired onstation, Pauley was aware they were sleeping together whenever possible, and couldn't care less so long as the two of them functioned. Gunny and Jan had the same arrangement. Pauley saw no need to inform the Lion of Rectitude, Dorfmann.

"Right, people. Listen up, put all this on your PDRs. We're Max/Sec from here out. Board carrier in exactly . . . twenty-three minutes. Data follows. Willington and Stoner are pilot/ops control. Frequencies to be assigned when you're dropped."

Gunny tapped the data into his hand-held PDR, sighing. "Watch the food tubes, Stoney."

As command Sparrow, their callsign on both channels would be Venture 1. Tyne and Roven, Venture 2. Krug and Hardesty, Venture 3. Pauley as control would be Nestegg.

They entered the data while Pauley outlined Sparrow operational policy to Krug. By-the-book Willi found it difficult to conceive that the pilot was not craft commander at all times.

"Only in emergencies," Gunny quoted their own book. "Imminent attack, craft malfunction or decision to eject."

At all other times in a Search mission, they were simply drivers delivering ops where they needed to go. Krug clearly didn't like being commanded by an officer of lower and very recent commission who came to briefing with his flight bag in one hand and an ice cream cone in the other.

Pauley succinctly set him straight, his tone polite but straight from the Ice Age. "Willi, Mister Hardesty is one of the three best operators on Limbo. The other two are here with him. May we in time be able to say the same of you—in your presence rather than posthumously."

Willi subsided, mumbling to himself. "Ice cream . . ."

To no one's surprise, primary mission was any emanation from Search 528; second, any Allied voice traffic, particularly from carriers. "We have reason to believe that Allied's *Swift* and *Condor* are operating between the IP area and Hydri IV."

Tyne did a passable imitation of the IO. "Splendid. We can lay tea for them."

"Merry Christmas, Jan." Gunny grinned at her. She tried to smile back.

"Operators: Listen for codeword WILDCARD which our cryptographers confirm is Allied's codename for Hydri IV, also for RESTHOME, their rather derisive designation for Limbo Station. Pilots be advised that Allied is actively commencing radio intercept on their own, clever little shits that they are, and we know they've approached the Lund Corporation, which has an exclusive contract with UNESA to manufacture Sparrow intercept components, with an ironclad rider that none of these parts or their schematics may be sold to or even accessed by anyone else. So far as we can tell, Lund has not been tempted to adultery."

Developments therefore indicated that Allied would attempt to acquire this equipment intact by any expedient means.

"There may be no encounters, though in a worst-case scenario, pilots can set their destruct charges, ops crash their systems, and we'll pick up ejected pods. But *no* components or sensitive material will be compromised, clear?"

Jan Tyne said flatly, "You know what they did to our pods in Gamma Three."

"Minimal chance of that," Pauley assured her. "Pilots and ops, note this too. All ship to ship tix on scrambler, nothing in the clear, got that? Anyone comes down our chimney, let it be Saint Nick and not some grotty little Corpse pilot looking for a salvage bonus."

Stoner swiveled around to Ellie and Frank. "And keep the chatter *down*. Last couple of days, you two've been a regular coffee klatsch on ops channel. And no personal names. That's how we get files on them; they can do it to us."

Willie Krug commented weightily, "The Sparrow is too lightly armed."

"No kidding?" Tyne shrugged. "I wondered why I feel so nude out there."

Pauley checked the time; a few minutes to go before airlock. "Now the good news. We're not going FTL to insert you. IP destination is Hydri II, and that means a few days aboard the carrier, including Christmas."

There would be further onboard familiarization for Krug in transit, but rest and comparative comfort meantime. Flight diet was suspended twenty-four hours over Christmas. The experienced crews took this with a mixture of pleasure and resignation. Carriers managed better rations than stations and the *Kennedy* mess officer, Captain Adrienne Ferrier, through Gallic feminine charm and world-class scrounging, usually managed the extras that made life more human. The downside would be the laxatives to flush them out before mission, but what the hell.

"Captain Ferrier has roast goose for us proper folk and turkey for unreformed Yanks like Stoney. And a good Chardonnay and cognac, I'm informed."

Tyne snickered. "Who'd she fuck for the booze?"

"Hey, chill down," Gunny frowned at her. "Who cares, okay?" Jan's tension was giving her an increasingly unpleasant edge. More than one officer had mentioned it in the ward room.

"Yeah, what's with you, Scumgums?" Ellie challenged. "You're getting a real garbage mouth."

"Pauley?" Tyne slid her eyes contemptuously over the younger woman. "Can I have a new op? Like a grownup?"

Pauley brought them up short. "Knock it off! Dorfmann's already torn a strip off me about all of you. Time to go. Happy Christmas, everyone."

They jammed PDRs into their pockets, picked up their flight bags and filed out of the compartment toward the airlock.

— ‖ —

GETTING CLOSER

In his small, poorly ventilated cubicle aboard the carrier, Pauley made his hourly entry into the mission log.

IP DAY 4. IN WIDE ORBIT ABOUT HYDRI II, SIM-ULATION TO TRAIN NEW PILOT BEFORE PROX-IMITY HYDRI IV. NEGATIVE SEARCH 528 SINCE INSERTION. NEGATIVE ALLIED. TIME 1800.

Because of a sudden solar flare, ops channel was ragged with sunspot noise, more readable on head-set than speakers now. Stoner had tried different freqs for better communication, but the whole spec-trum was souped by the flare, so he and his ops had switched to Morse, their converted chatter curling now out of Pauley's printer as Stoner re-quested sit/rep from Roven and Hardesty.

VENTURE 2: AUTO/SCANNING 50-100 MEGS, 40-50 MANUAL. NEGATIVE.
VENTURE 3: ON AUTO 20-50, MANUAL 15-20. READABILITY NEAR ZERO. HOW ABOUT RE-CALL?
VENTURE 1: NOT YET, LITTLE LONGER.

Then Pauley read Ellie's light, swift rhythm on the automatic key:

VENTURE 1 AND 3, WAIT ONE . . . CHECK 47 MEGS QUICK.

Coasting four thousand kays above Hydri II, restricted to voice on the ops channel, the tired pilots sounded flat and strained after four days of twelve-hour shifts. Gunny was riding tight rein on Willi Krug.

"Venture 3, you're drifting out of glide path."

"It is instrument error then. They are reading strange."

Gunny didn't buy that. "If your cockpit checks were green, trust the instruments. Correct."

"There must be error," Willi maintained obstinately.

"You're over-controlling," Tyne advised acerbically. "Drive it or sell it, Willi, but don't beat it to death."

Pauley made a mental note for briefing: security. Tyne used a personal name. She was usually tight about that. They were all getting frazzled; better bring them in. No, better to let Stoner call it. Pauley switched to ops channel where Ellie was sending again. She had a fast fist on a key. He read the chatter as it emerged from the printer, admiring the efficiency of his operators. They never noted down each other's chatter, simply copied it in their heads at well over 30 wpm.

. . . 47 MEGS, VOICE TIX, POSSIBLE ALLIED 3256.

Then the rapid staccato of Stoner's key—

AFFIRMATIVE, 3256. GET D/F AND VOA CON-
FIRM IF POSSIBLE.
VENTURE 2: 47 MEGS IS ALLIED DISTRESS
FREQ. SOUNDS LIKE A SHRIKE IN TROUBLE.

Good girl, Pauley admired. 3256 was a *Condor*
squadron, operating where they shouldn't be. He
wiped one of his screens, hailing the bridge to
patch in their long range scans. The distance was
too great, but there was *something* of considerable
size out there. Pauley opened up on pilot channel,
speaking slowly, repeating each phrase through the
storm of static.

"Nestegg to Venture. Bridge has a bogey at extreme scan limit. Carrier class or larger. Stand by
for recall."

In Venture 2, Jan Tyne armed her lasers and sta-
tused all systems before calling the carrier. "Nestegg, are they moving toward us?"

When Pauley didn't respond immediately, Jan
passed through a fear-shot heartbeat, darting her
eyes to the solid red dot of *Kennedy* on her P-scan.
She went suddenly cold as her Hull Integrity
flashed red. The breach was small, a pinhole just forward of fusion shielding, but heat sensors read a
minute O^2 loss. What the hell was wrong with her,
losing it like this? Tyne took a ragged breath and
willed herself to control as Pauley came back on.

"Nestegg to Venture, bogey is off our screens.
Recall, recall. Match course, we are aligning. Nestegg out."

But Tyne could feel her pores exuding cold
sweat. *I am not in control. Dumping on Krug when I*

shouldn't be here myself, and now I'm freaking out over a pinhole.

She ascertained that Roven was strapped down, firing the ATs to bring her into retrieval line behind Gunny.

Last ship in the lineup, Frank Hardesty unstrapped after Krug's attitude change and floated forward to hang over the pilot's shoulder. "Gets real old, doesn't it?"

Willi's blonde head chopped up and down shortly. "Damn, but I need a wash."

"Me too. Like a bag of laundry." He glanced at the pilot's readouts. "Your armament's not online. Something wrong?"

"Who needs? We're going in."

"Should arm your lasers the minute a bogey is reported anywhere."

Krug ignored the statement, still rankling from Tyne's insolent remark. Among the FTL pilots it was common knowledge that she and Willington were burnouts; to have her snipe at him like an instructor flaming a cadet . . . "You see that?" he pointed to the blob of Tyne's ship on his heat sensor. "A leak. Not much but still. She is careless. That should have been caught before launch."

"Unless the breach occurred during this sweep," Hardesty said. "Speck-sized hunk of meteor. It happens."

"Should *not* happen," Krug insisted dogmatically. "I have flown Shrikes. This? This is a toy. *Kinderspielen.*"

Hardesty grinned as he pulled himself back to his pos, hooking one weightless leg over the seat back. *You said it. I didn't.*

Willi was far from incompetent in a Sparrow but

had a bad attitude from the start, noted by all of them. He condescended to the job, thought himself overqualified and undervalued, taking correction with bad grace. That led to mistakes like the one he'd just made and could get him (and Hardesty) wasted in a critical situation. Gunny had been patient with the German, Tyne less so. Tyne had a mean streak and did not suffer fools—or Ellie, for some reason—gladly. She'd made the laconic suggestion to Pauley in Hardesty's hearing.

"Long time since we had an obit. Might help."

Pauley's brief, chill smile could have been read as assent. "Up to Gunny."

Thoughtfully, Frank Hardesty fingered his autokey, sending to Stoner.

VENTURE 1 FROM 3: ADVISE UR PILOT MINE IS NOT ARMED. OBIT?

Stoner responded after a short wait:

VENTURE 3 FROM 1: PILOT ADVISES EASIER FOR CAMEL THRU EYE OF NEEDLE THAN FOOL TO STAY OUT OF TROUBLE. HERE WE COME.

Hardesty lay back in his straps and waited, grinning, for Judgment Day. *Child's play, Willi? Confucius say fool and his Sparrow soon parted.*

Willi came on com, sounding puzzled. "Hardesty, did you hear on ops channel any change in retrieval order?"

"No, why?"

"Willington and Tyne are turning out of line."

"Didn't hear a peep," the operator came back innocently. "Where are they going?"

"Not going." Willi couldn't believe it. "Coming at us. Full thrusters."

In the cockpit, Willi's logical mind rejected what he saw: two Sparrows coming head on, bright, growing jewels against dark space. "Venture 1 and 2, *vass ist*? Please advise your—"

The words died in his throat as the two laser bursts lanced out at him in very near misses that must have passed not more than a meter from his ship's skin. "Ven . . . Venture 1 and 2, what are you, crazy? Explain! What are you doing? Acknowledge."

His body jerked reflexively as the two ships flashed past and two more lances of light, silent and deadly, flashed across his view plates in an elongated X of light, like God crossing him off existence.

"Venture 1, you fucking *ezel*! I will report this."

"You can't," Gunny's voice broke in, husky but graphic. "You might have had a chance if your armament was online, but right now you're in free fall toward Hydri II in the remains of your suit. For further information, check your armament status and the IO."

Listening in on pilot channel, Hardesty grinned at the prank, which had a serious purpose. Willi had been caught with his systems down and would definitely be under glass at debrief. The operator checked 47 megs again for Allied 3256 but the distress frequency was silent. He refrained from any comment to his pilot as Krug maneuvered the Sparrow once more into third position for retrieval. When G pull lightened, Hardesty squirmed this way and that under the straps to stretch the cramp out of his lower back and butt. Four days of twelve-hour shifts had taken their toll. He tried to relax, wiping the strained day out of his mind and replacing it with the image of Ellie.

The whole thing between them had happened so fast, such a lot to encompass and believe. The night back at Limbo when they'd gone to her quarters, that was the beginning. They listened to old guitar music and danced frantically to something Ellie called "metal."

"It's sort of an heirloom." She displayed the microdisc proudly. "Belonged to my great-great grandmother. Or maybe *her* mother, I forget."

"Different from colony pop. Who're they mad at?"

They drank a little more and gradually opened up to each other, and the excitement grew between them as they discovered all they felt in common. Both were colony orphans, left to be raised in the Gamma Two System by parents unsuited for space and homesick. The children were left, less heartless than sacrifice. Career opportunities for bright children were all out here, few at home unless you were born rich.

So, Hardesty sighed in his soul: Here they were, both aware of being the youngest kids in officer country while the novelty of each other turned them to playful and then feverish kittens. When *the* time came, they were confronted with the problem of privacy. They could giggle nervously over the dilemma up till then. Now it had become a pain in the ass. Every meeting in Ellie's quarters had to be coordinated with her billet mate, a tekky officer in Hydroponics. No sweat when that could be man-

aged, but when not, Hardesty found himself awkward and shy about asking Charley to butt out of
their billet at odd hours. They dreamed always
about going home on leave—really home—to the
Earth neither had ever seen; first to Quebec, where
Ellie's folks still lived, and then to Italy where she
could paint.

"Flo-rence," she dreamed, drawing out the
sound. "I've read what the light does to colors
there. Florence, Frank."

In their first days before IP, with the sharp physical need for each other, the situation called for in-
genuity. They improvised, snatching a furtive and
unsatisfactory half hour in the Hydro lab, another
on the conference table in Col. Dorfmann's staff
briefing room. The key to the room, Hardesty was
gratified to learn, was available from a profit-
minded sergeant in Maintenance. Frank bought
key and time with his last twenty-five endees until
payday. To Frank, panting over Ellie on the conference table, the image of Dorfmann calling a sudden conference *now* was both grotesque and oddly
stimulating.

Their most desperate but innovative expedient
was the E-pod in Tyne's Sparrow, Ellie on top and
his legs without room to stretch and getting
cramped. When it was over and they nestled together in the pod like twin yolks in an egg, Ellie's
breath was warm against his chest.

"I kept banging my head on the hatch," she said.

"God, it's—I heard Tyne was in one of these for
days."

"Don't mention it to her; she's enough of a bitch
already."

Neither of them could say for sure when the idea

of permanence began to color their thinking. Ellie just told him she'd have no problem bearing children, but wanted to have them on Earth where she could get better food and prenatal care during pregnancy. She needed time in real sunlight with natural food. Like most people born and raised out here, her skin wasn't that healthy or smooth. But . . . she was Ellie. Eleanor. They'd go home, sure enough, but after that time in the pod, Hardesty determined to take the bull and Stoner by the horns. Charley looked after Ellie like sort of a father/big brother thing, and that somehow made it embarrassing. He wondered how to broach the subject delicately. ("Look, things have kind of changed between me and Ellie, and . . .")

But then Stoney had been around and knew how things were. Man to Man? ("Hey, Ellie and I have really got it on, got something going, but there's this problem. Privacy. What I was thinking . . .")

His actual request had been hardly that coherent. "Uh—Stoney? Ellie thought she might come down tonight, maybe around 2000."

Lounging in his upper bunk, Stoner grunted. "Yeah, she told me."

She did? Almost that time now. "What'd she say?"

"Just she was coming down." Stoner swung out of his bunk, grabbing the wallet from his locker shelf. "Think I'll play some poker in the ward room."

Frank wished him effusive good luck.

"Thanks. See you around 2200."

Two whole hours. "Right, Stoney."

"Not before then, I guess. Oh, by the way." Stoner paused in the open hatchway. "You know that numb-nuts in Maintenance who rents out the conference room key? He usually charges forty bucks. You and Ellie owe me a bottle of jayjay."

Hardesty was startled, having until now thought himself a master of deception. "Oh? Yeah. Well ... who told you?"

"Ellie, who else? I've made it with some big women in some real small cars—but an *E*-pod? E for effort, Frank."

After that, until IP, Stoner felt a nightly urge for poker and coffee. Hardesty foresaw no problems while his chief's luck and kidneys held out. He and Ellie luxuriated in privacy and each other—and had the inevitable first spat that came out of nowhere.

"Over *noth*ing," he anguished to Stoner. "All of a sudden she's more static than signal."

" 'Bout says it," Stoner philosophized from the upper bunk and two warzone marriages. He tossed the crossword book on the deck as Hardesty cut the lights and slid into bed, still grieving.

"She just blew up. We could always talk before—you know, like friends. Not last night."

"Let her cool down, then tell her you're sorry."

"That's the thing: I don't know what for." Not completely true, Hardesty reflected honestly. He remembered what he said but not why it should light her fuse.

"Tell her anyway," Stoner counseled from a thousand similar skirmishes. "Friends is one thing. A woman gets to be a girlfriend or wife, that's a major changeover." Following this pearl of wisdom, he went silent so long, Hardesty thought he'd gone down for the night. But Stoner came up again.

"This ain't a natural place for anyone, maybe women more than us. Look at Tyne."

Hardesty flopped over on his stomach and pummeled his pillow. "You look."

"That's what I mean. Out here it's real easy to forget you're anything but a job. Difference is, Ellie wants to remember and maybe Tyne never knew in the first place."

"You were married a lot, weren't you?"

"Not so's you'd notice," Stoner chuckled to the darkness overhead. "Marriage . . . someone talks, the other's gotta listen. Me and the wives, we were always on different freqs. Bring Ellie down tomorrow night. It could be just PMS or something. She gets rough periods. And maybe you're a major change for her, too."

Maybe, Hardesty allowed unhappily, staring up at the bottom of Stoner's bunk. *I know what I said.* And when he said it. Lying right here, close in his narrow bed, resting after love, drowsing a little, he'd said he wished she were Catholic. Not a big prejudice thing; he wasn't that serious about it. Just that Ellie would better understand the way he thought and the values he grew up with. God, he wasn't fanatical about church, but he felt Ellie's body stiffen against him and then draw away.

"That didn't bother you five minutes ago, did it? Is it such a big deal? My parents go to church twice a week back in Ville-Marie and they're *still* losers who won't speak English because they hate the Anglos and won't watch the news because they hate their own politicians and they hated it out here where they couldn't make it, and they dropped me off at a colony school like give-away furniture and went home to hate some more. You want a Catholic, there's one other in PERS, but he's not your type. *Damn* it, Frank. Sure, I love old things . . . some old things, but that stuff, there isn't time for that anymore."

She was angry, weeping, he remembered. Somehow he'd tapped into a fury in Ellie that went years back.

They did make it up, he being gentle and repentant as possible because, hell, it *was* a stupid thing to say, particularly just then. But they were revving up for IP, and there was the miracle of ice cream on the shuttle and a vid-disc only six months old, and Stoner went on regular and gallant ward room watch again. Frank Hardesty guessed he'd grown up a little more. Not everyone had the same values like a beacon to home on. There was a wound in Ellie Roven where her parents had chopped her off. She'd worked through that, tried to, and got past taking the fault on herself somehow, but never the habits that went with the problem. Was his own case so different? Some colony leftovers descended to trash; others like himself and Ellie overcompensated by rising through sheer clear awareness of the bottom line. You made the grade or went into the garbage.

"Okay," he reasoned to Ellie, "you're not the same religion. Then I thought: God, what if you simply were *not* anymore. Like Reinecke—"

"I know. That's it, and I get so scared, Frank. What if you—"

"Hey." He stopped her with a kiss. "So what if? C'mere. I'm here now and I can hold you."

And that was them. They had no problems. If Ellie wanted, they'd make up their own ceremony, do it civil with a clerk, any way she wanted it, with poetry and music thrown in.

Krug broke in on his reverie. "T-beam in ten seconds." Hardesty closed his eyes, tired and gritty, but at peace, idly marking off the seconds before the tractor beam caught and lifted them toward the ship.

Still in their pressure suits, seedy and stale, the crews filed into debrief and slumped into seats. The classification easel had been draped with black plastic wrapping for a pall, and Pauley wore a black armband improvised from an old sock. Willi Krug accepted what was coming with gritted teeth. When a UNESA cadet screwed up seriously in real or simulated flight, a gruesomely detailed "obituary" was read out to his class to salt the lesson in. Today's services had been Tyne's method of teaching Willi that handling Sparrows was not so negligible a job as he'd thought.

Pauley stood before them, hands folded, head slightly bowed, speaking in funereal tones. "We deeply mourn the loss of Lieutenant Willi Krug and W/O Francis J. Hardesty. Lt. Krug was cut off in his twenty-ninth year and the full flower of his career promise. Mister Hardesty was no more than twenty-three but equally gifted. 'In the midst of life . . .' "

Two seats away from Tyne, Roven hissed fiercely: "Not funny!"

"Shut up," Tyne squelched her. "It's needed."

"*Not.*"

"Cause of death, tragic pilot error. On being advised of an unidentified bogey on scan, Lt. Krug failed to arm his lasers immediately. When subsequently attacked—"

"*Sheisdrech*," Willi grumbled. "There was no bogeys on me. I knew who they were."

"Suppose we weren't," Gunny challenged.

"So? Arming takes only seconds."

"Which you spent dying," Tyne reminded him.

"The pilot took a direct forward burst from two enemy craft," Pauley explained meticulously, "neatly severing his head and upper torso from the lower body. He could not have suffered long. As for Mister Hardesty, the second burst, converging from the enemy craft, ruptured the core complex and fusion shielding and penetrated the E-pod. Unable to eject, Mister Hardesty died from massive radiation exposure."

Tyne threw a sardonic kiss to Willi. "*Auf wiedersehen*, bye-bye."

Willi Krug shifted in his seat, seething inwardly. He'd gone through the same twice as a cadet for much the same reason, slow reaction or faulty judgment, scored both times for being too dogmatic in the face of the situation at hand. Stubborn or hesitant. Yes, that could kill him and his crew mate. He'd forgotten over the years, where the feral ones like Tyne never did.

"All right, *ja*. Pilot error. My fault." He managed to laugh; it sounded forced. "*Bitte*, Major, how did I look at my funeral?"

"They salvaged your legs, nicely frozen, for bone transplant and the like. What was left looked quite serene. Mister Hardesty could not be viewed. Well, then." Pauley changed the subject at a sharp right angle, turning to business. Roven's ident and D/F on the *Condor* squadron signal confirmed the carrier's presence, and possibly why it had vanished so quickly from bridge screens.

"They've detected metal debris. Some of it is drifting our way. Something hit them fatally. We don't know what, but Captain Satin has ordered an intercept course."

"Guys," Ellie reminded them. "That was a pilot distress call I picked up. He hadn't ejected yet."

They absorbed the fact in silence. With no one to retrieve them, the Shrike pilots had nowhere to go but their pods and likely nowhere after that. Satin would approach the debris at sub-light and with caution considering what else might be out there. Only the pods drifting toward *Kennedy* would have any chance.

"Bad news first," Pauley caught them up again. "Water recycling has malfunctioned again. They're working on it, but showers are out."

"We're so cruddy we're gonna get quarantined," Gunny predicted.

"Back to the chem-pads, all of us. A small reserve ration has been allocated for brushing teeth and washing personal items like underwear. However, for a ray of sunlight through our gloom, Captain Ferrier, who must have been the Good Fairy in another life, has donated a tot of her personal Scotch for each of you tonight after mess. See her in her office. Crew breakfast 0500, briefing 0600, stations 0630. That's it, people."

Pauley watched them as they straggled out silently. Frank and Ellie walked apart, sagging stuffed dolls in their pressure suits. Flight diet muck for breakfast, something from a tube on mission, more muck tonight, tomorrow nothing to look forward to but danger added to the strain. *Condor*

might have come for them if Something hadn't
blown her away. Something might do it to them
tomorrow. They'd likely take the Scotch with verol
sedatives to anesthetize themselves before sleep.
The Claustro Club was in long session now.

Day five 0930. Five hundred kays in advance of
the *Kennedy* pacing them, the three Sparrows
neared the debris that grew on their scans from
bright scattered sand to imageable objects. With
Venture 1 as axis on match course with their carrier, Tyne and Krug were angled out from Willington's ship to provide maximum spread.

At 0935 Willington reported to Nestegg that the
closest object was drifting across him toward
Tyne's sector. "Venture 2, see it? Small metal debris . . . and what looks like a pod."

"Affirmative on imaging. It's a pod." Tyne cut
to com. "Roven, tune to beacon distress frequency,
cut it in on speakers."

In three seconds, the lusty bleep of a pod beacon
filled Tyne's cockpit. "Nestegg from Venture 2: you
hear that?"

"Grab it!" Pauley came back. "Pilot should be
alive. I want him. Pick up and advise."

Maybe alive. Tyne read residual heat emission
from the object. She didn't want to look at it.

At her position, Ellie smiled at Frank's voice on
ops channel, urgent and excited. "Nestegg from
Venture 3. Pilot has more wreckage to starboard.
Extreme range but big stuff. Too big for a Shrike.
We are closing."

Ellie felt the Gs as Tyne cut in ATs to match
course and velocity with the pod. As the maneuver
completed, the pilot came on com again. She

sounded different to Ellie, strangely subdued. "Roven, you ever eject in one of those things?"

"Just drills."

"Come up and have a look. See how the other half lives."

An actual invitation. Tyne must be going prematurely senile. She never small-talked on com or treated Ellie as anything but a chronic annoyance. Ellie unstrapped and floated upwards, using her gloved fingertips for traction on the dorsal bulkhead velcro to pull herself forward and hang over the computers behind Tyne. She was enormously curious about the occupant of the pod who was suddenly no longer the enemy or a disembodied sound she copied, but a human being. Her counterpart in a way, living his life in a tiny ship, sucking nourishment like cold soup out of a tube. Somebody who came from someplace, maybe Earthside. Someone real with a life.

The pod floated fifty meters below them, rising now into the gravitational pull of the Sparrow's mass.

"So small," Ellie said.

"Shrike pod." Tyne switched off the beacon's wail and cut in command channel. "Nestegg, Venture 2: We got him. Coming home, over."

"Good *on* you," Pauley responded heartily. "Adjust course fifteen, one-five degrees. T-beam standing by."

Fascinated by the occupant of the pod now only a few meters from the viewplates, Ellie got the distinct impression that Tyne didn't want to see the thing. Long before the sphere slid out of view and bumped along their belly, the pilot busied herself needlessly with instruments. But the pod's silvery skin was set with four large viewplates like their own.

"I could see the top of his head," Ellie chirped excitedly. "Wonder who he is."

"Someone real lucky. Strap down. I'm going to align with the carrier."

Secured again, Ellie waited impatiently through the tractor lift. When she felt the tripod thump on hangar deck, she cut all power to her systems, wriggled out of her pos and cracked the belly hatch. Tyne yelled impatiently for the ladder, snaked her thin body through the forward hatch and walked away without looking back.

"Hey, guys!" Ellie sang out to the duty teks coming to run postflight checks. "We got a live one!"

Resting on the deck only a few feet away, the small pod appeared undamaged. Eager and curious, Ellie skittered around it, jubilantly rapping on the hatch in welcome. "Hey, in there! You are one lucky son of a—"

She pressed her face to one of the viewplates, then quickly averted her eyes as her skin crawled.

The pilot was a woman; Ellie's stomach knew it before her mind, the obscene fact of death like a kick in her gut. The corpse was curled in a fetal position, mouth agape, the eyes wide open, blank as glass looking straight into her own.

Pauley trotted across the deck with Major Fuselli, the carrier's chief surgeon, an armed security rating and a little butterball med/tek behind them. Ellie stood back from the pod, managing a pitiful little mew. "She's dead."

Pauley gave her a disbelieving grimace and bent to peer through the viewplates. "Shit. Pop the hatch."

Both he and Fuselli were baffled at first by the time element. Barely fourteen hours since Roven intercepted the distress tix. Barring serious malfunction the woman could have lasted up to ten days. Fuselli's swarthy head and his right arm disappeared through the hatch. "Dead as they get."

Pauley touched Ellie's arm. "No need to stay."

Not clearly knowing why, she heard herself say, "I want to."

Fuselli fumbled about the corpse, his voice hollow from the pod interior. "Has to be dead five, six hours at least. I'd say closer to ten. Rigor is complete. Wait a sec . . ."

He straightened up and looked at Pauley. "Tongue and fingernails have a bluish discoloration. She bit the Big O."

Took the pod's lethal tablet. When her brain hammered in her skull, starved of oxygen in seconds, when her body convulsed in death, she never felt it. Ellie knew now why Tyne avoided the sight. She went through this. *And it could be Frank or me. Maybe I'm stronger than you, Jan. I want to look and remember.*

Between Fuselli and his medic, they knew they couldn't lift her out twisted up like that.

"Get a torch," Pauley barked at the hangar teks lounging in a group at some distance from the pod. "We have to cut her out."

The laser torch made quick work around the hatch rim and plating. The medic and security guard hauled the stiff, twisted thing out and set it on the deck. Pauley conferred quickly with the doctor who nodded and ordered his medic into the pod. The tek didn't take long, emerging with a reserve oxygen container attached to a breathing apparatus. "Sir? Primary O² exhausted, one reserve container empty. She was down to this."

The fact still made no sense to Fuselli. Even allowing for a minor leak, life support should not have run out so quickly.

"Not minor," Pauley said. "I'd say defective from the start. They're keen on low-bid contracts. Probably the interface sealing between viewplates and skin. Careless walk-around inspections, neglected pod drill, who knows? Doesn't matter now. Can you straighten her out?"

"Not easily for a while." Fuselli gripped the thin shoulders and pulled while the fat medic held her legs and finally had to sit on them because the body wanted to gnarl up again.

Ellie had seen the dead nicely prepared and laid out before cremation, but never this naked, obscene reality. *I can look at it because this is not going to happen to Frank or me. We're going home.*

Security would have checked the utility pockets of the suit, but Ellie motioned him away and knelt by the body. "I'll do it. I want to."

The last thing she wanted, but she made herself do it. Looked into the glazed eyes and willed her gauntleted fingers to reach out and close them. The pilot had been very young, but death had washed the youth away. Nothing dead looked young, Ellie discovered, not till they got made up and laid out neatly. Until then, they just looked dead. The girl was slightly built and thin as a slat, hair trimmed too short to comb but freshly washed. Ellie tried to match the dead features, the open mouth and protruding, discolored tongue with a personality. The thin cheeks and narrow lips might have indicated character once but no longer.

The pressure suit pockets were empty. "Give me something to cut with."

"Ellie, you don't have to—"

"Yes, I do. Tekky, you got a blade in your belt?"

"Scissors."

With surgical scissors, Ellie cut away the pressure suit front, revealing a light one-piece pajama of some synthetic material in bright vermillion. In one pocket she found papers, a partially consumed candy bar and two thousand dollars in Allied scrip currency. She passed the finds to Pauley and cut away the pajama to the skintight, stripping away the ID tags. "Tekky, unfasten the collar."

Under the skintight, the pilot had small breasts, but something bulged and bunched peculiarly. When the metal collar was lifted away, Ellie slit the skintight from chest to neck. "Thought so. Look at this."

Pauley knelt beside her, fingers brushing at the bloodless skin. "Not logical, is it?"

Beneath her skintight, the woman wore a French bra, obviously expensive and with wire foundations. Ridiculous; the damned thing would—had—cut into her in any kind of Gs. The marks, once red but now gone blue on the toneless skin as the blood ceased to pump and settled toward the lowest part of the body, stood out starkly on the rigor-firm flesh.

Ellie couldn't fathom the sheer masochism of the wired bra. "It's crazy."

After a quick inspection of the head, Fuselli found a MUX implant in the crown. "One of the hot-wired ones."

Pauley examined the ID tags and papers, nodding and mumbling little um-hms of approval.

"There must be a God after all. These tell us quite a bit about Liza Beth Ross, blood type A-negative, no allergies, Pentecostal Baptist, in-case-of-death-notify . . . etcetera. Doctor, I'll need that MUX implant and whatever you can get from autopsy."

"Need a few hours until rigor passes."

"Right, but soonest. And let me see . . . scissors, Ellie." Pauley cut away the pressure suit sleeve, then slit the sleeve of the skintight lengthwise to the elbow, baring the thin forearm. Beginning at the wrist, the skin was decorated with five neat tattoos in a line, four Xs and, obviously the newest, an O.

"Vanities, Ellie. Like her silly bra. They keep score on the arm. Sort of predator-chic. A short but very profitable life."

Ellie stared at the tattoos. "You mean kills? Shrikes?"

"All but the O, Mister Roven. That's a Sparrow."

Something went cold in Ellie Roven, freezing the last of pity out of her as the implication sank in. Somewhere, wherever the *Condor* took this bitch to hunt, there'd been a UNESA Sparrow unable to evade, its crew captured or more likely dead. She hoped out of long habit the operator had time to crash systems and sensitive data. *And they paid you good, didn't they?*

She rose, standing away from the thing. "Screw her," she heard herself say. "I'm glad she didn't get a chance to spend her loot."

Pauley slid the money and other effects into a glassine bag. "Earthside American from her tags. Just a nice girl trying to get along. I don't expect any of you ever heard the phrase, but they used to call it the American Dream. Someone else said, 'this too shall pass.' Doctor Fuselli, learn what you can, bag the rest and blow it out a utility lock, and flights of angels sing dear Liza to her rest."

No one moved immediately. Suddenly Ellie wanted the obscenity gone. "You heard him," she spat at the security man and Fuselli's fat tekky. "Get it out of here!"

She strode away, as Tyne had, without looking back.

Venture 3 was recalled shortly after Tyne and Roven, having salvaged several large fragments of hull skin. Frank Hardesty dropped out of the Sparrow hatch and stumped across the hangar deck feeling gritty and grim. He climbed the ladder to an access corridor. Just beyond the companionway, Ellie sat hunched against a bulkhead, arms locked tight around her knees, still in her pressure suit. Above the detachable metal collar, her round face was pale and tight-lipped.

"Ellie? What are you doing here?"

She didn't respond, just jammed white-knuckled hands over her mouth. Frank slid down beside her. "You okay?"

She shook her head listlessly. "She was dead."

"Who?"

"The pilot. In the pod. She took the O." In short, spastic bursts, Ellie told him about the tattoos and what they meant. How much money they found on the woman.

Frank whistled in cool appreciation. "Think we're working for the wrong side?"

"No!" Ellie hissed through her clasped fingers. "Don't make a joke."

He put his arm around her shoulders. Inside the

bulky suit she was trembling, not hard but steadily. "Sorry."

"Frank . . ."

"It's okay, I'm here."

"That's not going to happen to us. Promise me. We won't die like that or . . . live like that."

"Not us." He closed his eyes, trying to relax his body against the bulkhead.

"Are *you* all right?" Ellie asked.

He wasn't really, no better than Ellie. He needed to sleep, drink, anything to blot out the last two hours. Thank God they were recalled early. Willi in the cockpit saw more of it than he did, but Frank caught enough through the forward viewplates when they got close. "Not so bad," he lied. "We brought in some hull pieces, stuff like that." There were other objects drifting with the debris, but she didn't have to hear that. "Willi said they can tell us a lot."

Pieces of *Condor*. Whatever hit them was like a pin in a balloon, very quick.

"Work hard . . . work your buns off . . ."

Drained, eyes closed, Frank had started drifting toward sleep, distantly aware of Ellie murmuring in a low, compulsive monotone.

". . . work to be the best because it's that or go down the tubes, and you feel enough like a loser every day. Get to *be* the best, one in a hundred like Stoney said. All so you can end up . . ." Ellie wiped the rest of the thought, burrowing deep into his protective shoulder. "Stay with me tonight."

"Maybe we ought to skip it. I'm wiped out."

"I didn't say—we don't have to have sex *all* the time. I just meant—oh, forget it."

His own fuse was a lot shorter these days. "Hey,

chill out, okay? I'm out there too, and just as beat
as—" Frank caught himself and cut it off. The
whole thing got under your skin and left a mount-
ing residue of irritation, flying twelve-hour shifts
for days and doing it scared. He felt grubby all the
time, never really rested, unreasonably irked at the
smallest annoyances. "Sure, I'll stay with you. Even
if we have to sit up in the ward room."

"Don't want to be alone."

"No. Neither do I."

"We ought to go home soon, really home. Earthside. Stop talking and just do it."

"We will." That was better than thinking about
today, tomorrow or next week. Back Earthside
someplace where the air was still halfway clean.
Stoney could tell them where, maybe near where
he lived. Hardesty got up stiffly, feeling cranky.
Feeling old. He held out his hand to Ellie. "You
want to get something to eat? I'm hungry."

Most of all he wanted to sleep for a week, but
he would sit up with Ellie as long as he could keep
his eyes open.

Pauley could read the strain in his crews as they
filed into the next morning's briefing already suited
up, faces drawn and leached of everything but fatigue. He sighed and waited politely while Krug
finished and then redundantly explained to Gunny
a tedious joke about a circus elephant with stomach
trouble. Willington had very likely never seen an
elephant. Willi could be a Teutonic bore, but at
least his attitude and performance were improving,
and his finds yesterday were valuable.

"Right, let's get started. First off." Pauley displayed a small glassine bag. "The late Ms. Ross was

encyclopedic for our purposes. This is her MUX implant. New and improved since Gamma Three."

From her papers and ID, cross-checked with Allied personnel rosters in the IO's memory banks, Liza Ross was born in Clinton, Mississippi, just past her twenty-first birthday, assigned ten months ago to the *Swift*. Autopsy showed traces of the standard contraceptive implant removed some time ago and more recent traces of at least one first-trimester chemical abortion.

"Scratch the implant and then abort?" Ellie wondered. "It's crazy."

"But it fits," Pauley maintained. The general body condition yielded more than an active sex life without precautions. Fuselli reported a borderline malnutrition, and from the scanty contents of the stomach and lower intestine, Ross's last meal aside from candy was mostly other junk food. This combined with other clues strengthened the COORDINT theory that prolonged MUX exposure was not only addictive but shifted appetites and triggered cravings for quick energy foods. More seriously, the MUX very likely influenced behavior and judgment.

"I've been in Clinton, passed through it," Stoner remembered. "Mostly low income trailer parks. Welfare people. Kid probably never had a decent meal until Allied recruited her."

And a Pentecostal Baptist, Ellie recalled with a granite bitterness. Probably said, "Thank you, Jesus" when she scored the Sparrow tattooed on her arm.

"And here is the grand prize." Pauley held up the papers found on the body. "Ross was paid December 20th aboard the *Swift*, transferred to *Condor* the following day. No travel orders because no travel was involved. The ships must have rendez-voused near where we first scanned *Condor*."

The *Swift* could be and very likely was still out there.

"That's Allied 3251 for Shrike squadrons, 325 for carrier to their command," Stoner reminded Ellie and Frank. "Listen sharp. Use your filters on the solar noise, specially on carrier to command. They love to hide under it like a trout under a rock. Don't try to guess on ident. Patch in Voice Operator Analysis soon's you hear them."

"The late Ross is now part of Hydri II's atmosphere," Pauley said, "but we learned a few more interesting things about her. Ellie?"

She rose to face her fellow crew members, displaying the bra stripped from the body. "Any of you guys interested in measurements, she was a 34A cup. Not much for boobs."

But a French bra with wire foundations was as practical for a Shrike pilot as wearing razor blades under her skintight. "With the contra implant removed, the MUX and the rest of it, I'd say Ross was going redline fast, deliberately making self-destructive choices. A marginal crazy getting off on dangerous chances."

Stoner blew out his cheeks. "Go figure."

"I did, Stoney. Two thousand bucks on her. Her transfer orders described a thousand of that as salvage bonus for zapping a Sparrow."

"That's all my ass is worth? I knew they only wanted my body," Tyne commented. "Who carries that much scrip around loose anyway?"

Stoner could psych out that much of it. "Told

you she was a redneck from Clinton. They don't trust banks."

"More immediate than that." Pauley stood up next to Ellie. "Corpses don't usually fly with more than personal ID, same as you people. Wearing that expensive pajama thing over her skintight, so she must have known she had to suit up soon. But we think *Condor* was surprised and she had to scramble, no time to stash anything personal. Willi has something to tell us about that. Any speculations or insights on what we've covered?"

"Yeah." Ellie Roven daggered a glare at Jan Tyne. "Who stole my blue panties out of the wash cycle?"

"Had to be Pauley," Stoner deadpanned.

"What?" The surprise broke Pauley up. "You incredible clowns—"

"You can tell us, Nije," Stoner sympathized. "We understand. It's time you worked through the problem."

"I think it was Tyne," Ellie declared. "I got a pair of yours in my load."

Tyne's head came up truculently. "How do you know it was me?"

"You got wash ration in the same unit just before me. Mine don't have holes and I get them cleaner. And who stole the yellow acrylic out of my paint set, huh?"

"Me, why not? I wanted to paint flowers on my vibrator." Not an admission but a clear challenge from Jan Tyne. "I didn't steal your ratty pants or your fucking paints, little girl. Drop it."

"Sure." Ellie's lips disappeared in a thin line. She hurled the bra at Tyne. "Here, wear something upscale. She had fried egg tits just like you."

Tyne caught and snapped the bra back at her too hard. "What's the matter, Roven? Can't get laid this week?"

"Pack it in, you two," Pauley held up his hand. "That's not what I meant by comments."

"Sure as hell isn't." Frank Hardesty was on his feet, glaring at Tyne, fair complexion darkened with suppressed anger. "Do the whole ship a favor, Tyne. Next wash ration, use it on your mouth."

"Hold it." Now Gunny was up facing Frank. Jesus, Stoner growled to himself; this shit was getting deep. He planted himself between the two men. "All of you get back in the green. You too, Gunny. Rank be damned, chill down *now*. Frank, sit down."

When Hardesty hung fire, Pauley stepped in again. "That's an order, Frank. Gunny—sit. And you . . . ladies, put a lid on it. We're not finished."

They all subsided with injured looks at each other, their tension corked but still quivering. The IO was grateful when Krug stood up, holding a largish object wrapped in the same black material used to pall-drape his "obituary."

"Major?"

The phlegmatic Willi had ignored the outburst among the others, stolid and unruffled. Something of a blessing at the moment, Pauley thought, even if in twenty years he'd be another Dorfmann in FTL Command. "Go ahead, Willi."

Krug came forward, unveiling the hull fragment, a rough square about half a meter in diameter with a large clean hole in the center. Willi's Bavarian accent and thoughtful, pedantic manner softened the icy import of his words. "Repair bay cut this out from one of the pieces we salvaged. Standard heat-resistant alloy. Everyone uses it. This hole was made by something like a laser but not—*bitte,* what is the English word?—not usual?"

"Conventional?"

"*Ja, danke.* Not conventional. No burn marks, but you see the whole piece looks strange. Notice that it does not the light reflect so much. They did in repair a molecular analysis. You see?"

Willi broke off a piece easily as crumbling a biscuit. Powdery crumbs of rotted metal sifted to the deck. "The whole molecular composition, the *character* of the metal has altered. Metal fatigue abnormally accelerated. This weaponry is radical. I would say it is your Search 528. A Jump ship; that is my guess. If so, we have now no way of dealing with such technology."

Nothing but a large white flag, Stoner suggested to himself. "Say it was 528. Couldn't bridge sensors read anything?"

Willi tried to reconstruct events from the evidence. Their own bridge read *Condor* at extreme range; the unknown ship must have been farther out. Then how was it possible to surprise a Corpse carrier with state of the art sensors?

"We know *Condor* scrambled her Shrikes," Ellie reasoned. "Some of them anyway. I don't think they had much time."

"No, I agree, Eleanor. I will try to explain what I can." Willi laid his exhibit aside and chose his words carefully. "While a ship is in Jump, they are not in real space/time." In that state, they would not read on conventional sensors, nor, during their re-entry into the normal continuum, could anyone guess how they would register beyond sudden, lunatic readings. The ship would just be there. The crews absorbed the implications in silence until Gunny broke it.

"If that's what got Johnny R. I'd like to profile out on the grounds of severe cowardice and only four months till discharge."

Pauley laughed sourly with the rest of them, glancing at the digital clock. "Fly time, people. Remember priorities, 528 and allied 3251—oh, wait. I forgot."

He moved to Jan and peeled the Allied scrip bills into her hand. "You found Ross. Call it salvage bonus."

She shrugged. "Sure, that's what she called it."

"And your share, Ellie."

She wouldn't look at the money. "No, I—"

"Take it," Frank said softly. "Hell, it's only fair."

"Fair? It's bloody poetic." Pauley pressed the money into her hand. Back on Limbo she could turn in the scrip and PERS accounting memory banks would credit to her on payday. Ellie looked at Frank, then wadded the bills tight in her fist.

"Yeah. Why the hell not?"

Day six. In the Ops cubicle, Pauley listened to the ship to ship chatter between his operators, the roll of intercepted hard copy lengthening from his voice printer: as they suspected, Allied 3251, a Shrike squadron on patrol from *Swift*. His Sparrow crews sounded flat and strained over their channels. Pauley had decided to terminate IP and pull them back to Limbo for a good rest before Proximity around Hydri IV—where, like it or not, he would carry out his Max/Sec orders.

COORDINT rated him high for dependability and low on vanity, highly developed superego and a mind more analytical than synthetic in its processes. He accepted the imperative to regulate corporations in a reality where concepts like national politics and patriotism were obsolete and meaningless. Earthside countries were quaint conventions on maps now. There were no countries anymore in strategic thinking, only commodities, financial resources and the need to exploit them, power and the need to control it. The convention of national borders was untraceable through the myriad interconnected webs of electronic information networks. For over a hundred years now the precedent and lesson of the preemptive strike were paramount. Making the first move before someone else did.

For Nigel Pauley, there was also addiction to the game, as MUX implants affected Corpse pilots. With Jump capability, UNESA would ultimately bring the corporations to heel. At this middle-game stage, the *Swift* was only a pawn thrust forward on the board, dangerous but not significant in the long run. Pauley's nature was so integrated with function that it precluded real intimacy with his crews or any real trust. Humanly he paid for that in deep, private and savage drinking. The three-day binge before IP, when he wept and cursed and trashed his quarters, showed him how thin a line he walked and the price his conscience extracted from the disciplined rest of him.

Nevertheless, after all these years of penetrating deception and deceiving in turn, he wouldn't be much good at anything else. *Form follows function. I have evolved along necessary lines like a tool specifically shaped to its task.*

Pauley rubbed at his eyes and checked the position of his Sparrows fanned out in advance of the carrier, Tyne and Roven farthest out but closest by D/F determination to the transmissions from Allied 3251.

In Venture 2, Ellie sucked on a tube of something that might have begun life as pea soup, and hoped they'd pull back to Limbo soon. Fear of Corpses was enough to hassle. Scared and feeling like she'd been born in her pressure suit was added misery. She must look frazzled to Frank. They could shuffle their deck back onstation, get clean, relax, make love.

Gs tugged at her as Tyne made a slight attitudinal adjustment. Talk about attitude. Tyne was not and never had been very human, Ellie decided. She must have come with the ship as a component. How could you get to be twenty-seven without ever being young or even female? Beyond that, Ellie's resentment grew in response to Tyne's hostility toward her, especially the woman's raunchy mouth. The bitch wasn't jealous where Frank was concerned; Ellie didn't get that signal from her pilot. Then what? Everything the woman said was sharp or nasty.

Will I get like her? Am I already less than human? I've never seen natural earth colors except in pictures. Harder and harder to imagine them.

She tried to visualize brown and green together. The words came but she needed seconds to *see* the different hues clearly, but then they shifted and ran...

Tyne came over intercom, cutting as ever. "Roven, you want to mumble, cut your com switch."

"Sorry."

"We can't raise Venture 3 on command freq. Call 'em on ops, see what's up."

"Will do." *God, is there trouble?* "Venture 3 from 2, over."

"Hel-lo, Venture 2."

Ellie let out the breath she was holding when she heard Frank's voice, calm, nothing wrong. "Can't hear your pilot on command. Advise."

"Just about to report it. Pilot transmitter down, got a glitch. Nestegg, you copy?"

Pauley did, querying: "Does he want recall now?"

Hardesty informed his pilot declined. "But he requests you close up on us."

"Acknowledge, wait one." A few seconds later, Pauley was back on. "Venture 3, we are closing up and you will be first on T-beam."

"Acknowledge, Nestegg." Ellie heard the wink and kiss in Frank's voice. "And many thanks, Venture 2."

"My pleasure. Try to stay out of trouble."

"Will do, but I'm hungry."

"You're always hungry nowadays."

"Knock it off," Stoner cut in from Venture 1. "Still an hour to go. Venture 2, you're on 3251. Venture 3, we're still looking for 528. Let's do what they underpay us for."

Yes, Daddy. Allied 3251 was up again on one of Ellie's receivers, yakking too much the way they always did. If *Swift* had a radio chief half as sharp as Stoney, he'd rack ass with the pilots for all their unnecessary transmission. Cocky little bastards didn't know how much they gave away. Ellie had nailed an ident easily after a few seconds. Carrier control was BATON, flight leader BANJO. The others were PIANO, BASS and DRUMS. All male except DRUMS, all very young from the sound of them, and *Swift* and their own carrier possibly edging into each other's sensor range.

Us too. They'll scan me first. We're closest. She was glad Frank would be safe, gathered up first in order. She'd be happier if Tyne were coasting toward their own carrier instead of widening the distance.

From their chatter, the Shrike pilots might be checking radio glitches themselves—

BANJO: SAY AGAIN, PIANO.
PIANO: . . . CAN'T . . .
BASS: YOU READ ME NOW, BANJO?
BANJO: LOUD AND CLEAR. DRUMS, AC-
KNOWLEDGE. DRUMS? HEY, STEPANOVITCH,
WAKE UP!

Ellie caught the name; most likely Pauley did too. Since squadrons tended to stay together, the IO could nail other pilot names on the flight. She tipped a sardonic salute to BANJO. *Thanks, dipshit. While you're chatting, tell me what you and Stepanovitch had for breakfast. Had to be better than mine.*

DRUMS: NO PROBLEM. I WAS READING P-
SCAN. THERE'S SOMETHING—
BATON: BANJO, BANJO! STAND BY FOR POS-
SIBLE RECALL!

Seconds of silence crawled by, turning into minutes, broken only by static on 3251's frequency. DRUMS broke silence first.

DRUMS: ANY WORD ON CONDOR?
PIANO: BRIDGE SCANS PICKED UP PIECES.

PODS ON DISTRESS CHANNEL AT FIRST.
NOTHING NOW.
BASS: TALK ABOUT A BAD TIME TO TRANS-
FER.
DRUMS: I OWED ROSS A HUNDRED.
BANJO: NOT ANYMORE, I GUESS.

No, not anymore, Ellie longed to tell them. Ross
went out a utility lock and got jiffy-cooked when
she hit Hydri II's atmosphere. Anyone want to cry?

BANJO: NO SWEAT, DRUMS. I WAS RIGHT BE-
HIND HER IN THE PAYLINE. SHE PICKED UP
A BUNDLE.

Keep talking, Junior. Paylists were alphabetical.
Banjo would have a name beginning with *R* or *S*.

BATON: BANJO, BANJO. RECALL! WE HAVE
CONTACT.
BANJO: JACKPOT! RESTHOME ANNEX?

RESTHOME. That was Allied's codename for
Limbo—but ANNEX?
Ellie had no time to speculate. Pauley's crisp
command whipped over both channels. "Venture,
Venture. This is a recall. Break off for retrieval,
Venture 3 first."
Then Tyne on com: "Roven, strap and seal."
Still intent on following 3251, Ellie made sure her
harness was secure. She could seal the helmet later.

BATON: GOT A FIX ON RESTHOME ANNEX.
USING SCRAMBLER. GOT TO BE THE SPAR-
ROWS.

Ellie's stomach twitched inside her skintight. *It's us. We're Annex.* Instinctively she wanted to call Frank and Krug, urge them to accelerate, but that would only give the Corpses a better fix on them. The sudden Gs crushed her deeper into the pos seat as Tyne's ATs veered them up and around in a course toward their carrier, then a harder jolt as the afterburners cut in. Acceleration weighted Ellie's hand as she fingered the seat controls, shutting down as many components as possible. On 3251, BATON ordered pilots to strap down in the hangar bay as soon as they were aboard, preparatory to acceleration, and Ellie could guess where. *Lovely,* she mouthed in silence with a tongue going dry. "Tyne, how we doing?"

"I said seal. Get into your helmet. I can tell the difference on com."

Ellie twist-locked the helmet onto her collar. "Sealed. You read?"

"Yeah. Sit/rep: We're farthest out. We'll be last in and I'm reading *Swift* on my scans. Home/Warn says they're scoping us now."

"Are they moving away?" Pleasepleaseplease, Ellie prayed, let it be that. "Are they?"

"Negative, their retrieval course matches ours. You know how much we're worth. Scared, Roven?"

Damn right. Scared enough to hate Tyne then. She didn't have to say that, like she enjoyed the idea. The Gs increased as they streaked for the *Kennedy*. "Just move it, Lieutenant. I'm not crashing any systems until I have to."

Not until the last moment; not until Ellie knew there was no other way out. One more O marked on some armament tekky's arm. Bastards.

* * *

With Krug's Sparrow only two minutes from beam, Pauley checked position on the other two ships and the growing configuration of *Swift* on his imaging screen. Going for a salvage shot on Tyne and Roven. Not today, gentlemen. In some ways Corpses were too easy to predict. Silly sods should have developed search/intercept years ago. Now they tried to catch up with bash-and-grab in the teeth of a UNESA carrier.

The Russian-accented voice of Captain Satin punctuated Pauley's thoughts from the hailer. "Pauley? Captain here."

"Ops aye. Go ahead, sir."

"My status board has Venture 3 entering T-beam. We're now on retrieval course for Venture 2."

"Thank you." Pauley called Gunny on command channel. "Venture 1, you look close. We should be visual."

"Affirmative, aligning now."

"We're moving for Venture 2," Pauley advised, eye on the screen and the narrowing distance between *Swift* and Tyne, knowing she copied him as she fled the hostile. "Venture 3, sound off!"

Hardesty checked in with very audible relief. "Coming down the chimney now."

"Welcome home." Pauley smiled thinly, monitoring Tyne on the screen and the larger blip closing on her. A Sparrow's velocity in normal cruise was its launch speed from the carrier. Any AT adjustment decreased that base and had to be compensated, if necessary, with thruster. Tyne had spent much of her base in reversing course. Accelerating now, but the *Swift* would be in laser range momentarily, likely targeting right now. He called the bridge again. "Ops to captain: Venture 2 may not make it. Can you accelerate and lay down deterrent fire to cover them?"

"Armament crews waiting the order," Satin reported calmly. "And Drive Section standing by for FTL sequencing. We will give them a bloody nose and then, as the Americans say, be long gone."

"Very good, Captain. Venture 2, Venture 2, take evasive action. We are closing to cover and retrieve. Nestegg out."

Pauley lunged out of the cubicle toward the hangar deck.

"Sixty seconds to beam," Gunny advised Stoner over com. "Tyne's running like hell, using her AT's to evade targeting. She'll make it."

Hoped she would. Gunny wanted to talk to her now but Jan needed all her concentration. He restricted his tix to three seconds. "Venture 2, come straight home and don't stop to talk to strangers. Out."

He turned the ship with ATs, aligning smoothly with the tractor beam.

Aft of the cockpit Stoner glowered savagely at his receivers with a heartbreaking mix of triumph and frustration. *Now* Search 528 comes up!—*Nice to hear from you. Where the hell've you been?* —singing his alto duet on 100.4 megs. After days of search through the whole spectrum and a cacophony of sunspot noise, two minutes from beam and Stoner caught the familiar double snakes writhing in one square of his matrixed screen. Feverishly he wiped all other freqs and started to record what he could before the tractor beam blanketed the transmission.

The two tones broke off into the familiar glottals and a series of "words." Stoner felt like a man discovering a lost gold mine just as the whole mountain came down on him. He'd cut in D/F but needed backup, but Frank was already landed and Ellie had problems of her own, and there was no response from Pauley. Had to be Ellie; she could handle it. Just as he pressed his tix switch, the Sparrow jerked with the pull of the tractor beam and 100.4 megs mushed out under the maddening buzz of interference—

"*Shit!*"

That didn't help but it felt good.

When the tripod clunked down on solid deck, Hardesty popped the belly hatch and pushed through hurrying teks toward the bay's status board as the hailers blared over the hangar space.

"Attention: all personnel except armament crews secure for FTL."

Hell with that. Hardesty stared up at the status board. T-beam on but no craft on the board yet. *Make it, Ellie. Please make it.*

Pauley loomed up beside him, grabbing his shoulder. "Come on, get to a G-pad and strap down. Gunny's next on the beam."

"Wait." Hardesty twisted back toward the board, hating its blankness. "Where's Tyne?"

"Coming in. Come on." Pauley pulled him toward the row of reclining G-pads where other teks were strapping down. "We're firing on the *Swift* to cover them. They'll make it."

Secured, helpless now, glancing anxiously at the empty pad beside him, nothing to do but wait and sweat, Hardesty tried to feel the Christopher medal under his suit and skintight. On the next pad Pauley signed him a thumbs up. "Piece of cake, Frank. Ellie's done this before."

Sure. Running from Myoshi Shrikes. She told him how scared she was then. She ought to have a Christopher; he'd give her his. Might not help much but certainly wouldn't hurt. Just let God get her back this one time more. Pray to God, pray to luck, pray to anything—

"Attention: all personnel except armament crews—"

"All right!" Hardesty screamed at the hailer. "We fucking hear you!"

Pauley nodded toward the status board. "Gunny and Stoner coming in."

Hardesty lay back and closed his eyes, trying to pull Ellie in with the sheer force of his will.

Ellie stared forward, straining for a glimpse of *Kennedy* through the forward view plates. She never got used to this. Like Tyne or not, she had to trust the bitch now. Ellie jumped at the sudden needles of light whipping out too close before them in the black void. "They're firing at us."

"Sure ain't starbow," Tyne confirmed dryly. "ETA to beam three minutes."

Three minutes. One hundred and eighty seconds of hell. "Can you use rear laser?"

"Not yet. We're in their range, they're not in mine. Like boxing a guy with longer arms. I've got the carrier visual. See those flashes through the forward? They're firing on *Swift*."

Going to be tight, Tyne thought. Satin would be moving away into his FTL course while the beam pulled them in, already accelerating when Tyne cleared onto the hangar deck.

Ellie's heart missed a beat as the Sparrow lurched, yawing away from the laser burst glancing along their skin. Her voice was a squeak on the com. "Are we breached?"

"No, don't wet yourself. We're whole."

Damn you, Ellie swore to herself. "I'll crash my systems when I have to, not before."

"Your call, kid."

The carrier was giving Tyne what help they could, laying down a formidable cover of medium-range fire against *Swift*, now huge on Tyne's imaging. She flicked her glance to rear targeting on the HUD. Feasible for a shot. For what it was worth, she could add her pitiful rear laser—now.

She read the hit on heat sensor, a minute emission from the Allied forward superstructure. *Like I got 'em worried. But I'm okay, Gunny. Still got some of what it takes. Thirty seconds to beam and they're still on my six; must really want our rig.*

The adrenaline of combat cleared and speeded her thinking as her fingers hovered over the control board. *Swift* would have standard Lectra torpedoes, missiles that home on electronic systems as well as heat, but there wouldn't be anything left to salvage.

So what? Maybe they'll shoot if they can't loot and then haul ass.

Jinking the Sparrow port and starboard in a series of evasive turns, Tyne activated the E-pod outer hatch, the beacon and all pod controls operable from the cockpit, one eye on rear imaging. If they went for destruct, the pod might divert it. Maybe they won't. Only a few seconds to T-beam, maybe—

A hair slow, a fraction of a second late on her

AT controls. The laser bolt struck the dorsal bulk-head amidships, punching a large hole in the Spar-row. Like a football impelled from an immense toe, the ship tumbled out of control while small objects not secured whirled up and out through the wound, Ellie's sidearm with them.

"My weapon's gone," she jittered over the com. "Can't crash. Gonna wipe. Off mainframe now."

She punched the commands into her seat con-trols, feeling her body strain cruelly against the straps as the last life support rushed from the ship. The blessed, beautiful image of their carrier spun crazily in the forward plates as Tyne fought to re-gain control of the wounded craft.

"Roven, you hurt?"

"No." She clamped her teeth together to deny their chattering. "I wiped before the controls froze up." All sensitive data from her banks filed in obliv-ion before the killing cold froze her rig at absolute zero. Around the insulated fingers of her gauntlets, Ellie felt the frost-ghosts hovering, waiting for her as the underbelly of the carrier slid past them and the T-beam caught them up.

"More good news," Tyne reported. "Got a NO LOCK on the tripod. Must be . . ." Her voice fal-tered to silence.

"Talk to me, Tyne. You hit?"

". . . must be damaged. Hang on, we're going to belly on the deck. Use the forward hatch to get out. Roven . . ."

No, not Ellie's imagination or nerves. Something was wrong; Tyne was scared and sounded like it. Her voice was a forced whisper. "Don't pop your helmet. So cold in here you could freeze an ear off before you got out."

When the beam cut, the Sparrow slammed down jarringly on the hangar deck with a scream of lacerated metal. Ellie unstrapped and lurched up on unsteady legs as Tyne cracked her hatch. The deck tekkys were already hurrying a ladder toward them. As Ellie hauled herself out the cockpit hatch after Tyne, a crewman urgently pointed them toward the G-pads.

Muffled through her helmet, Ellie heard the acceleration warning repeat as she and Tyne stumbled toward the line of secured crews on the pads, four of them in pressure suits. Already battered and rawed with fear, Ellie called out to Frank, voice drowned in her helmet. "Made it, Frank!" She dove onto a pad, clawing at the straps. She didn't know if he heard her, but Ellie read the answered prayer in his eyes.

Satin's fire punished the *Swift* soundly enough to make them reconsider trading blows with him. The crews kept firing until all three Sparrows were in, then Satin went FTL for the few minutes necessary to shake off the Allied ship.

Just as well, Pauley reflected as he neared the mess officer's duty compartment just off the *Kennedy* ward room. If a fight were part of Satin's mission, he would have stood as stubbornly as his ancestors at old Stalingrad. That time was coming, already on the plotting boards at COORDINT, the resolution to the far-reaching question of who would control human expansion into deep space, and nothing honorable on either side, but when was it ever?

And you, old son? How honorable are you?

In the passageway outside Ferrier's compartment, he experienced a moment of severe dizziness and blurred vision. Pauley waited until it passed, then buzzed and opened the hatch. Captain Adrienne Ferrier sat at her desk as he remembered her from many more intimate evenings, cheek resting on one palm over supply inventories spread before her. A small woman, chunky as Roven, the Parisienne Ferrier carried it with much more grace. She sipped at a mug of coffee and set it aside.

"*Bon soir, mon cher.* Coffee?"

"No thanks, love."

"That is best," she counseled. "I do not recommend our coffee today. We are out of the fresh and down to concentrate. There is something wrong?"

Pauley settled in the tiny booth that served the mess officer as an extra desk. "Just the usual."

"You are not well, Nigel."

Adrienne always could read his moods and state through their brief affair two years ago when his too-taut nature would become blackly infuriated because she could never wake up without coffee, cigarettes and an hour of foggy mumbling. Her heavy-lidded eyes studied him closely now.

"Ah. Hold up your palms. So. Very red and dry. You drink too much. I hope not the Jesus Juice."

"I came in feeling fine," Pauley lied. "Now you've got me wondering if I'll live. Need a favor, love."

She shrugged with a smile. "But to ask—but the liquor locker is empty."

"My crews have had it. Took a real pounding today. I'd like to get them off bloody ops diet for a few days. What can you scare up for them?"

"*Bien*, let us see. Shall we have a cigarette on it?"

"Darling, that's a hundred and fifty fine nowadays."

"Ah, *zut!*" Adrienne took the magnetic placard from a drawer, slid open her hatch and slapped the announcement on the outside. CLASSIFIED CONFERENCE. NO ADMITTANCE. She locked the hatch, smiling impishly at Pauley. "In our time we have been more abandoned."

She delved into the depths of a small medical kit, lit and inhaled deeply before offering the smoke to Pauley.

"No, thanks."

"You are reformed?"

"One bad habit's enough."

"I remember when you could not open your eyes without a cigarette and gin."

"The drink still helps. I'm standing my people down. Krug's ship needs systems overhaul, Tyne's is in major repair. I was hoping you could manage them something decent the next few meals. Something special perhaps?"

He knew he was right to cut the IP short. After that hairy recall with deacceleration from FTL laid on, crew efficiency would be redline without solid rest.

The cigarette moved in Adrienne's lips as she spoke. "It is inhuman how they live."

"Yes." There were more than requests he wanted to put to Adrienne, feelings he wanted to share with her, but he would have felt foolish and naked. *I can't put it all on Stoner and Willington; they've done more than enough, and one ship won't make that much difference. I want to do more myself, Adrienne—do you understand that? —before it all comes down, and nobody out here but me knows just how soon it's coming. All of a sudden there's the same perverse, self-destructive urge in me as there was in Ross with her silly French bra, a need to do the needless, put one bullet in a revolver, point it at my head and play You Bet Your Life. And I can't tell you, can't tell anyone.* "Doesn't make any sense."

"Comment?"

"Nothing. Just wool gathering."

"Nigel, really," Adrienne urged. "See Fuselli or the doctors on Limbo. Get a profile."

"What about the goodies for my people?"

"I will try." Adrienne doused her cigarette at the wall sink, shredded the soggy butt and swaddled it in a tissue. Pauley spritzed the air with neutralizer. "Bridge officers have a private fund for extras. I may be able to requisition from those."

Meaning an outright steal in a good cause. "How much? I don't expect it free."

Adrienne dismissed the offer with a wave. "Who knows? I may have made an error onloading stores. Possibly there is a surplus."

"You are dear, love."

"That was long ago, and even then you did not deserve me."

True. Adrienne had paid some dues on his working for Col. Waites, who looked like an affable pub keeper with the soul of an assassin. After his last mole mission, between the binges and that horrible night when he came out of dead sleep and found himself pointing a gun at Adrienne . . . no, she was right to leave him. Pauley slid open the hatch and removed the classified sign. "Here. The only secret about your job is how you manage actually edible rations."

Adrienne shuffled her inventories. "It is like the

rabbit in the magician's hat. One admires the miracle, not the method."

Pauley started violently as a hailer blared overhead. "Major Pauley to Operations. Major Pauley."

"Jesus, what now? *Merci*, Adrienne." He mouthed her a kiss both reminiscent and sincere as the hatch slid closed.

The Search cubicle within carrier Operations was usually dim, lit only by screens and crammed with equipment. Stoner occupied the one seat, intent on a screen displaying what might be a drift of meteor rubble.

Pauley leaned over his shoulder. "You ought to be resting. What's up?"

His chief operator only grunted. "This is piped from bridge. Satin wants you on the bitch box."

Pauley slid into the seat Stoner vacated. "Bridge? Pauley here."

One of the other screens filled with the head and shoulders of Captain Alexi Satin, trim-bearded, square features creased in a pall of concern and suspicion, as if Satin already suspected Adrienne's piratical intentions toward his private stores. "Major, stay on this screen."

The screen wiped to a simulation of star chart. "Here is Hydri IV. Here we retrieved the E-pod, and this is our present position."

From retrieval point a green line arrowed lower left to upper right, fifty-five degrees off a direct course toward Hydri IV. "I did not think it wise to approach the planet directly in the present circumstances," Satin said. "But we are lucky. That is not meteor rubble you see. I think it is wreckage, possibly from *Condor*. We are on course to overtake, but the mission decision is yours. Bridge out."

At full magnification the largest object was still too distant for accurate imaging. Pauley squinted at the screen. "Could be . . ."

Stoner scratched vigorously at his scalp. "Could be. No one else got wasted recently that we know. Maybe today wasn't all shit."

Maybe not. There were those few precious moments of 528 before the tractor blanked it out. At least they knew their priority target was up. "Bridge scanning anything else?"

"Some very weird readings long range from the vicinity of the planet itself," Stoner said. "Remember what Willi said about a Jump ship."

"Someone guarding the henhouse." Pauley's fingers drummed on the side of the screen, waiting for the objects to be readable on imaging. "Such a thing as being too careful."

"Not in my book," Stoner said decisively. "Not with my kids on the line, beat as they are. Not to mention my own ass."

The objects onscreen drifted ahead of them toward the gravitational field of Hydri IV. Pauley's decision was needed quickly. He made it, excited now as a hunter on a warm trail. "Pauley to bridge scan: At present velocity, what's our time to that wreckage?"

"As she goes, forty-seven minutes, sir."

Pauley estimated rapidly. Perfect. "Thanks. Stand by."

At the longest effective range, Pauley punched in imaging and ENHANCE. The largest object went transparent, then webbed with configuration lines. One surface was jagged, but as it tumbled lazily on the screen, the shape was unmistakable.

"Bingo," Stoner breathed.

The sheared-off bridge section of *Condor* spun amid smaller debris toward the expanding sphere of Hydri IV. Pauley hailed bridge again. "My thanks to Captain Satin. It is *Condor*. How long before it hits the gravitational well?"

The technician laughed in easy reassurance. "At least eighteen hours, sir. Plenty of time to salvage."

"Good on ya, laddy!" the IO saluted jauntily. "Request a volunteer from External Systems Maintenance report to me at the utility lock, ESM bay. Ops out." Pauley shot out of the seat, buzzing the hatch open, swiveling about to Stoner. "If the bridge computers are intact, I want everything we can salvage."

"Only got one cut on that 528 tix, but it was strong," Stoner told him. "If that's the Jump ship, he could be closer than we think."

"Calculated risk. We'll overhaul the wreck close."

"We? I hope you're not ordering me out there, Major. That ain't in my job description."

"Not you, don't be wet. One backup man from ESM and myself. I'm the only one knows what I'm after anyway. What time is it?"

Stoner stared at him. "Nije, this is not you I'm hearing. This is some cowboy named Ed Reinecke. You don't have to do this."

"Mister Stoner, I want what those systems can tell me. *I* want it. We'll check in from the airlock when we're suited up. You're my com link. Don't let us get lonely out there." Pauley grinned suddenly. "Besides, why should you Sparrows have all the fun?"

"Fun he calls it."

"My turn in the barrel. By the way, don't miss breakfast. Should be smashing."

The closing hatch wiped Pauley from Stoner's sight.

The black crewman clumped up to Pauley in pressure suit and magnetic boots, flourishing a sharp salute. A dazzling array of white teeth flashed in the mahogany face. "Sir. Specialist Sergeant Maraibo Preston reporting."

Pauley discerned the undiluted Earthside accent, distinct as Stoner's from the flat sound of spaceborns like himself. Refreshing, he thought. Like well-seasoned whole food after a month of concentrates. Preston's British speech was underlaid with the merry jingle of the Caribbean. "You're my volunteer, then."

"They felt you'd want the best, sir."

"You're a Brit. My own people came from Surrey. We're a long way from home, Sergeant."

"Mon, I don't complain. Worth your life to get a job in England or British West now."

Before they sealed helmets, Pauley outlined his procedure. They would boost over and attach to the derelict hull well clear of the wound. Once secured, they'd get minimum T-beam to stabilize the wreck while they worked toward the interior. Two ESM teks twist-locked the helmets, handed a portable bank to Pauley and a test unit to Preston.

"Commo check, Major," Preston's voice jingled in his ear. "You read?"

"Right. Me?"

"Copy. You do much of this outside work, sir?"

"Not for years, actually."

"Okay, mon, here is the drill." Preston demonstrated with the chest panel on his own suit. "Red knob is your oxygen regulator. You're getting enough now. Don't turn it up unless you have to. Could make you silly high."

The thruster packs were strapped over their shoulders and secured at the waist, control handles elbowing out under the contours of their arms. "These buttons on your right arm do all the work. Radio, helmet light. And this—" Preston touched it—"is the panic button. Lights up red on any malfunction and the LED square next to it tells you what is wrong."

"Understood. Stoner, do you read us both?"

"Gotcha," Stoner responded. "I'm patched into bridge screens and external camera."

"Something wrong, Stoner? You sound odd."

"Like in nervous. You'll get heavy mush on this channel when the tractor comes on, so speak up. Take care out there."

"Ta, Stoney. Going out now."

As the inner lock door sealed, Preston's white teeth flashed again behind his helmet plate. "Since we're Brits, maybe we should run up the old Union Jack."

Pauley kept his attention on the decompression light. "None on board. Anyway, Captain Satin would object; we're supposed to be international. You want to claim part of the *Condor* for king and country, go ahead for old times' sake."

When the outer doors opened, Pauley lifted his boots from the deck and followed Preston into nothing, using minimum thruster to propel him toward the wreck. "Okay, we're out."

"Copy. You're visual and five-by. Preston?"

"Roger-dodger!"

Stoner's surprised splutter of laughter filled their helmet phones. "What the hell is that?"

"Real old-time radio talk, sir. I love it out here. Better than swimming. You ticking right, Major?"

"Stay sharp," Pauley ordered. "We're going to be like goldfish in a leaky bowl."

He shut himself up so Preston and Stoner wouldn't hear the tension in his voice. He asked for this but couldn't suppress the natural fear of this unnatural place. *That was what I couldn't share with Adrienne. Part of me wants to die, daring the rest to take the long odds. Is it guilt, Pauley?*

"Only one big thing to worry about," Preston counseled, floating ahead of him. "Can't touch down too near the wound. Puncture your suit and it's goodbye time."

Pauley concentrated on his thruster controls and the nearing hulk ahead of him like half of a dull gray eggshell spinning in the void. No more than fifteen meters from touchdown now, but the wound cavity was coming down at them. "Port, sir! Keep clear!"

Preston veered expertly to the left, extending a hand clamp toward the surface. Pauley followed. He stretched out his legs, felt them make contact . . .

Just like goldfish, Stoner agreed, watching the two doll figures dwindle on his screen. His own body tensed in empathy. The floating bridge section looked like a broken tombstone.

Sparrows are bad enough. You couldn't pay me to go out there.

Reinecke had more nerve than luck. Stoner figured himself for the opposite, and out here you didn't push either one. Nerve might last, but luck was a checking account against your odds. You could write just so many before one bounced. Pauley had rocks in his locks going out for kicks when he didn't have to, but he was always hard to figure. Something about him you couldn't get hold of comfortably, like you could with Ed. *But I'll give him this: He's got serious balls.*

Onscreen the derelict rolled as the two tiny figures neared its surface. Then Pauley's voice was sharp in Stoner's ear. "Touchdown!"

A hundred and fifty meters out, Pauley and Preston slapped hand clamps to the hull. With their magnetic boots, the purchase felt secure. They were only a dozen meters from the gaping hull wound.

"Secure, Stoney. Give us minimum tractor to stabilize the roll."

He'd barely ended the tix when he saw Preston's magnetic soles slip on the surface; as they did, Pauley's own clamp slipped. *Christ, we're not secure at all.* As he shouted to cancel the order—

"Negative beam, Stoner! No beam!"

—a riot of sound exploded in Pauley's ears. Preston's warning was drowned on com as beam interference washed it out. Pauley gasped as five Gs wrenched at his spine and insides, tearing him from the hull, twisting out of control in the beam's pull. He tried to scream at Stoner but could only grunt.

"Sto—"

Preston somersaulted before him, trying to fight the pull with his thrusters. Like a swimmer caught in deadly undertow, Pauley struggled to reach his arm controls as the beam cut suddenly. Tumbling midway between *Kennedy* and the hulk, Pauley cut in power to slow and turn him, immensely grateful for Stoner's voice in his ear.

"Saw you were in trouble. Want to go back to the drawing board on this?"

Pauley gasped for breath, battered and shaken. "God bless, Stoney. Preston?"

"Okay, sir."

"Right." Pauley took several deep breaths. "Right. Stoner, there's almost no magnetism in the skin. We'll have to get inside on our own."

Preston passed him, returning to the derelict; Pauley maneuvered in his wake. "Stoner, no beam until we're inside. Acknowledge."

"Copy."

"Maybe no beam at all, mon," Preston advised. "The skin, she feels wrong."

"We'll get it right this time." Pummeled by the beam stress, disoriented by unaccustomed weightlessness, all told on Pauley's inner ear. Nausea took him briefly. He increased oxygen for several more deep breaths.

Monitoring intently on camera, Stoner saw the leading figure make contact, bounce a little and come down again, flattening out along the skin for the meager hold his clamp afforded. The second doll shape touched down.

"Made it. Working toward the breach."

The derelict's ponderous roll took them out of sight. Retarded by the brief pull of the beam, the revolution was maddeningly slow. When the opening came into camera view, Stoner couldn't see either man. "Talk to me, you guys. Where are you?"

"We're inside; not to worry."

Stoner let out his breath. "Okay, wait one.

Checking with Bridge and beam control down in Launch.''

"I said we're *in*," Pauley shot back, testy with his own strain. "What's your problem?"

Jesus. The man was drifting in a hull fragment with no more tensile strength than a toothpick, and he asks what problem? What was Pauley doing out where he had no sensible business and didn't have to be in the first place? Trying to prove something?

"Major," he transmitted pointedly. "Acknowledge."

"Copy. We're proceeding."

Stoner received assurance from Satin that the carrier's mass pull would keep the hull section in their wake, but intermittent tractor might be needed to maintain constant distance and prevent drifting. Beam would not be activated until Pauley and Preston were alerted and secured.

"So far okay," Stoner relayed, "but Satin says get back ASAP. As a health measure, that's advisable. Standing by."

He switched from external camera to computer imaging. As the gridded shape of the derelict filled out on his screen, he requested Bridge to patch in and overlay their heat sensors on the grid. Exhaust from the two helmets read as faint orange blobs.

"Got your heat trails."

From Pauley: "We're at the helm/navigational positions."

"How's it look in there?"

A pause; then Preston answered quietly, "Sir, you don't want to know."

They floated like fish in a pool of ink, their helmet lights cutting around the stygian interior, until they found the helmsman and navigator, who must have been the only two strapped down. The navigator's head was turned, mouth frozen open in what might have been a command or scream. The hair on both their scalps stood up like fright wigs, bent toward the wound as the life support had sucked out in a lethal rush. When Pauley touched the navigator's hair, it simply powdered away from the head.

Preston touched his arm. "There." His helmet light swung forward. "Other side of the helmsman."

Two steps up to a small half-bridge: the communications position and to the right of it, the computer complex. They swam toward it between the overhead bulkhead and the wound, open to a billion kilometers of cold-starred space.

"Talk to me," Stoner fretted in their ears. "Lost your heat trails. No, there you are. Don't read much in that cold."

"Rough on hair, too," said Pauley.

"Say again?"

"We're at the modules. They seem intact." Hopefully with every byte of information bridge staff needed for ready access. Codebooks and callsigns, certainly their flight orders, possibly *Condor*'s specific orders relative to Hydri IV. "Running a line test."

"Was," Preston corrected. Powered by the test unit, functional circuits should have lit his display like a neon tree. The image barely flickered. "Forget download, sir."

Damn it! "Stoner, you copy that? Systems are hardened. I'll have to pull memory with a Burglar."

"Grab what you need and come back now," Stoner advised urgently. "Bridge has some freaky readings."

"Took that into account, Stoney. This won't take long. They're Denneline-Crays. I've hacked into enough of them."

"So it boils down to pulling memory, which any ESM tekky could've done."

"Oh, I needed an outing. Not much for scenery, but having wonderful time. Wish you were here."

That'll be the day.

A few minutes later, Pauley casually inquired, "Still reading our trails?"

"Yeah, yeah. You're Son of Tinker Bell. What's happening?"

"Got the memory. Preston's scooping up anything else we can use."

Before Stoner could reply, Krug was on the hailer, urgent. "Ops, those readings? We have a bogey. Long range but large. We are patching our scan to you. Captain says recall Pauley STAT."

"Yo! Patch to my number two screen." A gray sensation spread through Stoner's middle as the anomalous lunatic readings sprayed across the screen like mathematical stuttering, flickering, unsettled. "What the hell is that?"

"As simply as I can describe, something which is halfway between being there and not there," Willi attempted in his precise lecture-at-Heidelberg manner. "You are observing a craft emerging from Jump into real space. Very likely your 528."

Translation: deep trouble. "When you get a solid blip, pipe it to me. Recalling salvage now. Ops out. Nije! Bogey, bogey, possible 528. Satin may have to maneuver, orders you out *now*."

Pauley acknowledged as the Ops hailer exploded with a battle alert, all personnel to suit and seal. Satin would take no chances with the alien. There were no suits in the cubicle and none closer than the locker outside carrier Operations.

"Nigel, battle alert! I have to suit up but I'll be back."

Stoner sidled through the cubicle hatch before it was fully open, dashed the length of Operations toward the emergency locker where a dozen men were shedding clothes and squirming into skin-tights and pressure suits. Stoner had hoped to grab a suit and helmet and skin back to the cubicle to suit up, but the locker rack was stripped. No more suits. He started to bolt for the next closest locker—but stopped. Without him on the link, Pauley and Preston were blind out there. Stoner lifted his eyes to whatever foul-up fates planned this day—

"Why *me*?"

—and dashed back to the Search cubicle as the battle alert repeated in Russian and Chinese. He dropped into the pos seat, calling Launch Control. "Who's on T-beam down there?"

"Me, sir." the young voice answered. "Gosnell."

Stoner gave rapid, terse instructions and then checked the two faint heat trails within the dere-lict's gridded shape. "Major, don't acknowledge, just listen good, 'cause it's getting hairy and I got a personal interest in staying alive. You'll hear the buzz on channel when beam comes on. They'll pull that sucker in close as possible. Grab something and hang on. Advise when secure."

On his second screen, the fluttering numerals and symbols dissolved to plot as Willi patched in from Bridge. In the lower right corner, the clean dot of their own position. Upper left, large and amber, flickering in and out between ghost and substance, but coming closer. Stoner gaped at the size of it.

That's what got Ed?

"Secure! Secure!" Pauley barked over the speakers. "Give us beam."

"Right. Outer ESM lock is open, go for it flat out when I give you the word. Gosnell, Gosnell. Beam *now.*"

With a fearful glance at the ethereal Something creeping down the screen toward *Kennedy*, Stoner switched to external camera, reading the range in meters as Gosnell drew them in. One hundred . . . seventy-five . . . fifty.

Gosnell cut the beam at forty-five meters. "Tractor's off, Nije. Go for it, move!"

Willi on hailer again: "Captain is standing by. Let him know when they're in."

"Trust me, Willi. I certainly will." On camera the two figures cleared the wound, boosting for the ESM lock. "Two minutes."

"They may not have two. Stand by."

The bogey was no longer approaching, or else slowed to a relative crawl, hovering hugely on the screen. Stoner could no longer see Pauley or Preston, about to call when Pauley came on, disgustingly chipper. "Got the goods, Stoney. We're in the lock, pressurizing now."

"Right." Stoner flashed the word to Bridge; the two men would be out of the lock in less than a minute. He felt his body relax and sag down from tension.

"A bit grim taking ID off the Corpsicles," Pauley

reflected coolly over the speakers. "They tend to be fragile, but we did it."

"So glad." Christ, Pauley sounded more like a winning captain in a cricket match than a man who might have been marooned a few seconds ago. "Major Pauley, FYI, we got a bogey the size of fucking Texas sitting out there waiting to jump our bones and I'm not suited up—but what the hell, I've still got some fingernails left. Unless I'm vital to the big picture right now, I'd like to find a suit."

No answer. Stoner sat in semi-darkness. He should get suited but was too wrung out to move. Onscreen, 528 still hovered at the same distance. They'd cut it too close this time, just like *Condor*, and here was 528, very big and bad, able to waste them any time, like a bulldog in his own backyard, so sure of himself he didn't even have to growl.

What are they waiting for?

He blinked in the harsh light as the hatch slid open to reveal Pauley, still suited and carrying his helmet like a trophy. The man actually looked gleeful. "Stand down, Mr. Stoner. Debrief at 0900. Top marks for everyone today."

He squeezed in behind Stoner to squint at the unmoving blip on the screen. "God, he can't be that big."

"Stay suited, Major. We're at battle alert and I feel kind of naked." Stoner slid by Pauley in the narrow space. Pauley took the pos seat, sniffing distastefully at the air. "God, it's ripe in here. Don't you wish you could just open a window?"

On the bridge, Willi Krug and Alexi Satin watched the insane readings and flickering amber blip as they gradually steadied up on the screens.

"Not moving closer," Satin said. "Any response to hail?"

"None, sir," Krug told him. "But we are recording these readouts, for what can be determined from them. Very soupy."

"The soup is all we have. We will deliver them to Research and Development."

If they could, Satin amended privately. The alien ship had been moving inexorably on them and then, with an upsurge of turbulence in the readings on his screen, virtually frozen in position. His carrier was on multi-frequency hailing in five languages, intergalactic tone codes and visual color sequences. No response. They must know his ship was signalling.

Satin's exec officer was at his elbow. "Sir? Acceleration order?"

Satin considered before answering. "No. Remain at battle stations until he's off our plot. Helm, reverse course at present dead slow." He would make no sudden maneuver with the ship, nothing that might be construed as hostile. "We will let them see we are leaving."

Helm reported the maneuver complete. "On course for Hydri II, dead slow, sir, and the derelict is still in our pull."

"*Horosho.* Good. We will destroy it when we are clear of any threat." Satin kept his attention on the amber blip. "Hailer, send goodbye, tone and visual, whether they understand or not." He spoke softly to Krug next to him. "You look as astonished as I feel. Possibly you ask the same question?"

"Yes, Captain. Why are we still alive?"

What they had witnessed in fact was still only speculation on UNESA drawing boards and think tanks: the theoretical possibility of folding space, and its equally formidable dangers. From the fate of *Condor* there was no reason to assume merciful intentions on the alien's part. Something prevented them from closing for the kill.

"I don't think they could close, sir. I think they are damaged."

To their stunned surprise and enormous pleasure, the Sparrow crews were served an excellent breakfast of canned Polish ham, powdered eggs in cheese souffle and a mixture of salmon and lumpfish caviar. Pauley forked up the delicacies in tacit appreciation: The resourceful Adrienne had struck again.

To their relief, the crews learned that they were homeward bound at sublight, ETA Limbo just under three days. Until then they were to rest while they could. Mission stood down. Debrief at 0900 would be for Krug and the operators, Gunny and Jan excused.

"Whatever it is, I don't need to know," Tyne mumbled over her food. "Going back to bed."

No more than logic to cut IP short. Tyne's ship was badly damaged, Krug's in need of systems check and possible component replacement. After yesterday's hairy retrieval, the deacceleration from FTL and the battle alert that tore them out of exhausted sleep to fumble into suits, they all felt redline.

Ellie patted her stomach as she and Frank walked to debrief. "I can't believe breakfast was that good."

"My stomach feels weird," he diagnosed. "Happy but weird."

"Why not? First time it's been full since Christmas."

Pauley opened debrief with an evaluation of the previous day's activity, typically minimizing his part in it, then gave over the rest of the time to Krug and Stoner. When the pilot rose to speak, the thought struck Charley Stoner that the Claustro Club was soaking into Willi Krug. Heretofore always in pressed blues when he didn't have to fly, now the pilot was dressed in coveralls like the rest of them, his manner wilted somewhat from starched Prussian toward something more human.

"We are very lucky," Willi began. "We may be the first Earthers to obtain hard data on a Jump ship and live to learn from it. We cannot overestimate what it will tell us, because Jump technology is now the prize and the deciding factor in space, what Stoner would call the large enchilada. We must assume Corpses are working also on it."

Pausing to marshall his thoughts, Willi rubbed absently at his chin. Ellie noticed he'd forgotten to shave or just didn't bother. "A lot of ships and crews are going to be lost, but whoever accomplishes first this technology will be master for the next hundred years. No other outcome is realistic."

"They just sat out there and did nothing to us?" Ellie managed in an awed whisper. "That is luck to the tenth power."

"True, Eleanor. Also my point," Willi said. "When this data is evaluated, it may bear me out. I think they made a bad reentry."

As he attempted to explain, the others were quietly impressed. If Jump technology was beyond humans at the moment, its theory known but undemonstrable, its hazard obvious and grisly,

Willi Krug's grasp was sufficient to provide lucid illustration. Pauley had him pegged; the man was a teacher at heart and potentially a good one, a natural for FTL high command someday. Since a ship in Jump was actually outside of space/time, they were literally nowhere and no when. Any miscalculation or malfunction in drive, a minute error in navigational coordinates, and one could be trapped nowhere forever—or, as Willi believed the present case, make an imperfect reentry into the normal continuum. Everyone present knew the physical side effects of transition from simple FTL to sublight.

"Rotten," Frank agreed. "Don't remind me."

"Just so. A bad reentry from Jump"—Willi spread his hands—"could be a nightmare. For a physical body: agony. For a sentient mind . . ." He let the thought linger in their imagination. "So. That is all I had to say, Major."

"Thank you, Willi. The rest is for the ops. Go get some rest." Pauley saw Krug out while Stoner set his small pocket recorder on the side table used for making tea and coffee.

"Okay, gather round. Some real fascinating stuff here. From the 528 tix I caught yesterday."

He played the short sample through and then rewound the microspool. "I was too keyed up to sleep last night, so I played with this beast. Our cryptographers got zip out of the singing and hiccups so far, but the word sounds—well, listen."

DOWOO . . . DOWOO.

"Like dogs howling," Pauley remarked.

"Gets better." Stoner rewound a short section and increased playback speed.

DOW . . . DOW.

"Wa-ait a *min*ute." Frank put his ear close to the small speaker. "I think—"

"Me too," Stoner said. "Now even faster."

DA . . . DA.

Frank recognized the simple Russian word for *yes*. "Think it's coincidence?"

"No." Stoner fast-forwarded through more singing. "Now."

BOOLDOWAH.

And faster: BOOLDAH.

Finally: BALDA.

Ellie yipped, clapping enthusiastically. "Like a good meal and a long bath for every time I copied that on Morse or voice."

Balda: The Russian word for stupid or blockhead, sent by notoriously irascible Russian radio operators when they got mad at each other. To remove any lingering doubt, the next sample resolved to *horosho*, a common Russian term for assent or okay. "I knew there was something bugging me about these sounds. Now get this one."

CAWWPAYEE accelerated to COPY. At four or five times recorded speed, Ellie, Frank and Pauley recognized English words mangled by a voice musculature never designed to pronounce them.

AFFIRMATIVE . . . BATON . . . PIANO . . . BASS . . . DRUMS.

"Allied 3251," Ellie gulped. "I rode them yesterday."

Stoner nodded. "So did these guys." He switched the recorder off and pocketed it. "Listen, you did good yesterday. Frank, take Ellie and play some cards or something. Everyone's down until we get home."

"For once Tyne made sense," Ellie yawned. "I'm going back to bed."

When the hatch slid shut behind them, Stoner observed, "When kids that young are dead beat, you know it's a rough gig."

Pauley asked to hear some of the 528 tix again. "I may not like what I'm thinking."

"Me neither, but I didn't want to worry the kids."

"Kids? You're sounding very paternal these days."

"I was right about 528. If they won't talk to us, they're sure as hell listening. We're copying them, they're copying us. A listening station just like Limbo. And that Jump ship is a flying platform, Nije. I'd swear to that. Our exact counterpart with a real wide edge on hardware."

Pauley listened to the recordings again, then poured some tea from the ready urn. "We're so pitifully obsolete. The depressing truth is, whatever we develop for the next X number of years—or decades—will be antique to them."

"This *is* their space, Major."

The uncharacteristic gravity of Stoner's tone arrested the IO.

"They didn't ask us to come out here, so why should they give us any breaks?"

"No reason at all, I guess, except we have orders."

"Orders," Stoner grimaced. "And so we go back."

"Orders generated by necessity."

Stoner regarded him steadily. "When I was a kid in high school, they passed over that Manifest Destiny crap for laughs. But that's what this is."

"More complex this time," Pauley said. "More necessary, more desperate."

Stoner drank his coffee, measuring what he wanted to say. "I'm not a hero, Nije. You couldn't pay me to do what you did yesterday. Yeah, sure, I want to nail 'em for Ed's sake, because I should have been there in the first place, galloping survivor guilt and all that. But I'm scared for the kids. Hell, I'm scared enough for all of us. UNESA doesn't know what it's doing or where it's going, but this time Custer better get real, because the Indians got the whole game wired."

—III—

TO TOUCH THE EARTH

Back on Limbo the Sparrow crews felt security tighten around them in a reassignment of quarters and mess schedules that effectively isolated them from station personnel except in general recreation areas where nothing classified was discussed anyway. Over her own misgivings and Tyne's silent disgust, Ellie was billeted with her pilot, Willi Krug with Willington again. They messed together at a reserved table half an hour earlier than the rest of the station. To Frank Hardesty it all signified what no one else wanted to say openly.

"We're going back."

Proximity: in close to Hydri IV with 528 waiting for them. The better food and thirty extra seconds of shower time didn't sweeten Frank's opinion that working for Pauley was like ejecting in a faulty pod; there wasn't much future either way. From Ellie's silence, he knew the joke was lame. "Future" was her kick now, all she spoke of, sometimes feverishly, as if she were putting up a shield against

Now. She glowed with the idea of Earthside leave, talking of Tahoe with Stoner, a place for herself and Frank, who let himself be caught up and warmed by her need. The IP had changed and blooded them in its gritty way, bonding them on a deeper level since the business of *Swift* and *Condor* and the grisly incident of the dead Shrike pilot. No matter how the others viewed them, they weren't kids anymore. Nobody lived forever and no lives were charmed. Hardesty put his Christopher around Ellie's neck, a Catholic from lifelong habit but no longer the boy scout of Tyne's dismissive contempt. Stoner heard the bitterness in Frank's pungent opinion of the IO.

"Fucking Pauley won't be happy until he gets us all wasted. And for what, Stoney? *Why* do we have to go back?"

There were no second chances out there. Hardesty put that at the head of his Ten Commandments to make eleven. Pauley had long ago added a twelfth, counterintelligence, where you were lucky to get a first chance. You exploited that luck when it came or lost out, and people died either way. Planted in distrust, nourished on deception, fed to necessity with the nutritional result permanent paranoia. You are what you eat. Within that context Pauley would not have been offended or even surprised by Hardesty's sentiment.

He reported to COORDINT good results on the IP. In addition to the 528 traffic, the "Burglar" had yielded partial success on the memory salvaged. The tiny black-box unit got its nickname from the ability to strip-download any system not completely obliterated, beside the handy secondary function of seeding viruses in a system to make future access difficult if not impossible. From the salvaged intelligence, CRYPT and TANAL recovered standing *Condor* orders, personnel rosters, next-of-kin lists (invaluable toward future investigations and security clearances) frequency and contact schedules for Shrike squadrons and the carrier command net, most importantly that these skeds had been revised in view of the recent solar flare and for Allied's planned task force to Hydri IV, date unknown but imminent. *Kennedy* readouts on the Jump ship went to Research & Development with Stoner's evaluation of Hydri IV as a listening station, the Jump ship quite possibly a flying platform boosting monitored human traffic to an unknown destination.

Pauley forwarded a commendation for Preston, refusing one himself on cool professional consideration—"The Corpses know me. Don't want to tell them where I am"—and included in his report the phrase "advise pull the plug," significant only to Col. Waites and COORDINT. At that rarefied Earthside level, in the teak-paneled board rooms where UNESA chairmen met with corporate heads to drink thirty-year-old Scotch before cutting each other's throats in deep space, Operation Plug was about to hit Allied Development like a legal nuclear missile.

A tax evasion case, built on five years' patient work and at the expense of a few lives less fortunate than Pauley's, was now ready for trial. Allied claimed huge tax writeoffs for legitimate research and an endless list of charities, traced by COORDINT through a maze of cash laundries to their destination in illegal exploitation. Allied might claim and submit convincing proof *Swift* was nowhere near Hydri System, but the chatter from un-disciplined pilots would belie them.

Operation Plug called for giving Allied enough time to prepare defense, handsomely allowing for delays and appeals for continuance from their tax counsels whose retainers ran into millions. In actual trial, UNESA would present Pauley's evidence from the *Condor* to crucify Allied with staggering fines and costs and open the door to another case on exploitation. The weakness in this chain was that biddable, buyable senators and ministers from a dozen countries had to be forced into more effective legislation at the same time suave, tailored men were urging them for the good of commerce and their own pockets to reconsider and delay. No one in COORDINT deluded themselves as to the outcome. There would be no clear "feel good" happy ending. A few top-level Allied heads would roll, a motley clutch of middle-management types would go to minimum security prisons where some would write self-exonerating memoirs and the less imaginative claim to have found God, but for the time, UNESA would have an unobstructed hand in the Hydri System. In the small, locked box where he kept pride and personal ego, Pauley was vastly pleased to learn that the Allied price on his head had doubled. That this bounty kept rising five years after his death would be a tribute to the efficiency and protective coloration of a man whose face was difficult to remember at the best of times. And that, as the IO would say, was how the thing was done.

Other matters worked through Pauley's fine-grinding mill. He still had no concrete lead toward the suspected sleeper agent beyond logic and the

X factor of instinct. The agent would likely be one of the later replacements assigned to Limbo and *Kennedy*. For his own reasons Pauley tentatively fingered Lieutenant Philip Beaudry of the carrier's FTL drive section.

The regular supply and courier shuttle arrived on Limbo three days after Pauley's return. The IO was surprised to greet his superior, Colonel Anthony Waites, who requested they confer in a secure area. Pauley chose the classified briefing compartment.

Coming toward one, Waites resembled a generous pair of parentheses. Hence his rotund resemblance to a Tenniel drawing from *Through the Looking Glass*, whereby he was nicknamed Tweedle, though never to his face. Pauley respected the affable little man while keeping his distance. Their relations were cordial, though Pauley always allowed Waites to choose the time for informality. He indicated the sealed pouch the colonel carried. Waites flipped a button on the seal. A red light glowed. Pauley held the light at eye level until it went green. Retinal scan complete, the bag unlocked automatically. The contents were a 9 x 12 envelope marked YOUR EYES ONLY and a two-pound tin of genuine Earthside tea. Pauley opened it and inhaled luxuriously.

"Real Earl Grey. God, sir, d'you know how long it's been since I had a decent cuppa?"

"Managed it from Harrods just before leaving," Waites said. "Let's have some later. Got a good tin kettle?"

"Sergeant Thun has one for warming his rice wine."

"Yes. By coincidence." Waites tapped the envelope. In the ineffable English way, he had become *Colonel* Waites again. "Orders and justification. You're to acknowledge in my presence."

When Pauley read the order he was not shaken but momentarily thrown off balance. He hadn't expected this at all. His self-esteem dropped a peg.

PER ENCLOSED, SGT. KIM BOK THUN CON-
FIRMED ALLIED SLEEPER AGENT. URDIS/ER.
ACKNOWLEDGE, SHRED AND BURN.

URDIS/ER was COORDINT shorthand for "at your discretion, effect resolution." At Pauley's convenience and by the most expedient method to hand, his Korean assistant would cease to exist. Confused, Pauley could only blurt the obvious professional question: "Don't they want to interrogate him?"

"Shouldn't think it necessary," Waites denied crisply. "With the Plug case airtight, Allied's effectively out of your immediate picture. This is just cleaning up. Can you ER soon?"

"I'd think so."

"Good." The congenial twinkle in Waites' eyes went utilitarian as a laser beam. "Acknowledge?"

Pauley would have receipted without delay, but something nagged at him. "Can we discuss this, sir? Are they *quite* sure?"

Waites inclined his head at the order. "Justification's all there."

Pauley had considered Thun and checked everything about the Korean, the supremely bright son of an immigrant mother from Taegu and a Santa Barbara grocer. Investigated and *re*investigated by UNESA and COORDINT on his recruitment eight years ago—all, as the painstakingly detailed ER justification showed, toward his eventual cover assignment to a sensitive forward station like Limbo. Indoctrinated and with his Allied salary paid into a numbered Swiss account, Thun might wait years in minimal contact with his real employers, passing available information while on leave. The accompanying documents listed Allied contacts known to Pauley, drop sites, safe houses on Mars Station, bank account number, the lot. And yet . . .

"Nigel, you look at sixes and sevens," Waites noted kindly. "What seems to trouble you about this one?"

"I would have thought someone else."

"We all might." Waites spread his arms and let them slap against his ample hips. "Your usual thoroughness. We'd expect no less. Who?"

"Beaudry. Engineering replacement on our carrier."

"Ye-es," Waites admitted reflectively. "We considered him, some others like him. He's clean."

"But . . ." Normally Pauley would not have persisted. In the face of the evidence in his hand, he would have kept silent about his suspicions of Beaudry and consigned them to the shred-and-burn bag of memory. In this case, negating his own judgment could very possibly waste the wrong man. "That's my point, sir. He's more than clean. He's antiseptic. Like a metabolic scan exactly down the middle of acceptable tolerances."

Including a psych-profile that reflected the usual and expected variations but nothing seriously questionable. By comparison, Stoner was a sociopath, Roven a compulsive over-achiever compensating for lost parental approval, Tyne a borderline twitch fading into a mere vestigial facet of her job.

Even his own profile would not compare favorably to Beaudry's. The lieutenant was either the best balanced personality ever commissioned by UNESA or else a cleverly camouflaged pathology. Just the type to be recruited and used.

"And another thing. Thun's clearance was held up for a year because his uncle belonged to a radical group in Seoul. Hardesty's because his father belonged to a colony union that *might* have been greased with Corpse money. You remember Ed Reinecke? Clearance held up because, when he transferred to us, he was bedding a woman in Kansas who was once married to a Texas Mineral employee. Stoner? I tell you no lie. Not *only* because he was the Nicotine King of California, but he contributed to some fringe environmental group out to Save the Sand Lizard or God knows what. The group was sponsored by TM. D'you see what I mean? We went to such lengths to be sure of sensitive-access people. But Beaudry? Cleared to Top Secret in a few months. He must have lived under glass until the academy."

Waites held up a hand to forestall further argument. "Nigel, I respect your judgment, but this is a waste of time. Ever talk to Beaudry?"

Of course he had, by way of investigation, over coffee and casual conversation in the ward room.

"So have I," Waites concluded. "Rather a bore, isn't he? There are people like that. Not much chat beyond shop, hadn't done much before joining up. Less of a security risk than a want of liberal arts in his curriculum. Put your mind at rest." Colonel Waites' eyebrows raised. "Any further questions?"

Only one, considering the damning evidence in his hand. "Why didn't you chop Thun before this?"

"We're not omniscient. We didn't know, then we weren't sure. Do you think we'd ER before that?" Waites' tone went paternal, as if he were explaining a painful necessity to a favored son. "We're sure. I hate it, too. But. Well, come on, no more of that. Shall we brew some of that tea? Fetch the kettle and let it steep black, yes?"

That same day Search 528 came up with a vengeance. Enlisted Search ops worked around the clock copying the alien, while Stoner, Ellie and Hardesty endeavored to find the other end of the link. The volume of traffic was their second breakthrough, a large enough sample to give TANAL and CRYPT more material toward finding a lingual or cipher key. VOA digital readouts isolated ten or twelve distinctly different voices in the recordings. Matching consistent "chord" intervals in the double-voiced singing, cryptographers soon found them too limited as a lingual basis.

Charley Stoner disagreed, arguing with Pauley and the cryptographers gathered around a playback. "Look, these guys are ops just like us. They don't use all their language for chatter. How many of those chord intervals show consistent digital match?"

"So far about three hundred and fifty," Pauley said.

"Do we use more? Keep digging guys."

By far the weirdest aspect of the 528 recordings was the recovered human traffic that interspersed the singing, the most comical 528's attempt to reproduce human languages themselves. Though grotesquely mangled, French seemed easier for them to pronounce than the four other major tongues used in space. One French cryptographer submitted that as a possible clue to the alien anatomy.

"Russian, German and especially English are forward. They are formed with the lips and teeth in the front of the mouth, where French is throatier. They may not have the muscular articulation."

"Or evolved away from it," Pauley mused. "Hour after hour of this stuff, no change of freq to throw us off."

"Like they're worried?" Stoner put in. "They could blow us away with their household appliances. My kids have to hear this chatter. Might teach 'em to shut up on mission."

"Yes, sir. Speaking of which." The cryptographer changed microspools on the playback. "A hit song from the 528 top ten for Mister Stoner."

VENTURE 2 AND 3, CUT THE KLATSCH.

Stoner choked on his coffee. "What the hell—?"

. . . STILL LOOKING FOR 528. LET'S DO WHAT THEY UNDERPAY US FOR.

"Jesus, that's *me*."

"Local ops please copy," Pauley chuckled. "Disturbing, isn't it?"

Like hearing the eulogy at his own funeral. "But we were on scrambler."

Obviously no problem to 528. With an effort, Stoner moved beyond surprise to the ramifications. Inability to pronounce did not imply difficulty in comprehension. 528's concept of language might be as advanced as their technology. With a volume of human traffic, no telling how much of them these formidable creatures were reading.

Gunny Willington gave large thanks for small blessings since returning to Limbo. He and Jan were able to rest and there were real whole foods at mess. Pauley must be blackmailing the supply officer, or perhaps he bugged Dorfmann's quarters when the colonel was screwing someone in defiance of his own decree.

Both of them were scheduled for medical scan, Jan at 1300, Gunny an hour later. "See you tonight, your billet." There were things to talk over, decisions he and Jan had to make together.

She couldn't say for sure. "I never know now that the campfire girl's in with me."

One last inconvenience before their tours ended, though Gunny wondered at Jan's aversion to Roven. All right, the girl could be a cheerful, prattling nuisance, like too much sweetener in coffee, but she seemed to bug Jan beyond reason. Other facets of the downside were compulsory aerobics and the upcoming Proximity mission to hump when Gunny was marking off days on his FIGMO chart and looking forward to a predictable, ordinary job where boredom and an occasionally defective microwave or air filter were the worst life-threatening possibilities.

Captain Okeda of MED/SEC went over Gunny inside and out with more thoroughness than his own walk-around on his ship. He and Jan were redline already and so what, short as they were? Curiously, Jan was evasive about discharge and the future, if very direct about the results of her medical.

"M-syndrome. Metabolic deterioration, like that's news. Okeda says for twenty-eight I'm the healthiest forty year old he's ever examined. By the time I get straight, I'll be that old anyway. All that—and Roven."

The reassignment of quarters was a security measure like their isolation at mess, but a pain all around. Krug moved back in with Gunny and stoically made the best of it, Roven with Jan who didn't try at all. From comments by Charley and Frank, Gunny gathered the arrangement was hardest on Ellie Roven. She tiptoed around Jan and bent over backwards to keep her area tidy and her gear out of the way. Tried to be invisible.

Trying not to look too happy, I guess. Was that it? Gunny nudged at the question at first, then dug into it seriously. Sometimes when he and Jan had sex, he'd look at her flat, hard body with the detachment of familiarity and see clearly how the woman had become what she did, equipment that fitted into a Sparrow. Kissing her fingers with their torn cuticles and the lacerations where she picked nervously at fingertips, he felt there was too much of Jan still beyond him.

How do I reach her, take hold of her?

Only four years younger than Jan, Ellie was a hundred less in experience. But pretty and very feminine. Either that or just able to reflect happiness. Jan's features were too strong for prettiness. She could soften them with makeup and at such times she was striking. One night when she came to stay with him just before the IP, she'd put on a bit of lip gloss and done her eyes. Jan had blue-gray eyes, wide-set over prominent cheekbones and a nose and mouth stronger than most men would consider feminine. If Gunny were put to it, he'd say she just missed being beautiful, as if that mattered. She came to him that night with a need she couldn't express except with her body, and in their love-making she tore at him while Gunny lost himself in her.

Something else came to bother him over time, like a small pebble in his shoe. Jan always insisted he wear a condom, not that easy to come by since Dorfmann's holy war on human nature. No problem at first, but now that damned microscopic thickness of artificial membrane was a wall that kept him from touching her. He wanted Jan to have a baby. No way she could fly anymore with crits like hers, almost getting offed when that Corpse got a piece of her ship. Roven would never know how Jan flogged herself for that half second's delay in reaction time, or the nightmares it restimulated.

Gunny's own crits were ridiculous. Any doubts were removed by Dr. Okeda, the Japanese internist who ran the sonic scan twice and frowned deeply over the readouts.

"How do you feel generally, Lieutenant?"

"Rotten mostly."

"Local specifics?"

"All over."

"Regularity?"

"With all the laxatives? Forget it."

"I see," Okeda nodded. "And your stomach?"

"Not that good. Can't seem to digest the way I used to."

"I thought so. You are near the end of your present tour?"

"Amen," Gunny affirmed. "Real short and getting out."

"Yes, you are." It was a flat statement. "You may have serious problems. If you were replaceable, I would recommend to Major Pauley—"

"Hey, recommend," Gunny encouraged, closing up the Velcro on his coverall. "Talk to the man. Tell him I wet my bed, I'm suicidal, anything. Won't do a helluva lot of good, but I'd feel better. How about Jan? Tyne, I mean."

"Ask her." Okeda shook his head and made a notation on the form he was filling on his computer. "You may be one of the lucky ones, Willington. Go home, have a long life and the wisdom to value butterflies."

The reference sailed over Gunny's head. "Butterflies?"

"You do not know haiku? No matter."

"You said something about problems."

"There are growths in your colon. Just beginning and quite possibly benign. Quite common out here with prolonged low fiber diet. To be sure we'd have to do exploratory. Soon, I'd say."

Gunny understood. He looked away at the eye chart, the one test passed with flying colors. He made himself ask. "You mean cancer."

Okeda searched the pilot's battered face and seemed to like what he found there. "You have courage, Gunny. Most men could not ask so directly."

"Not like I wanted to."

"Where did you acquire such a nickname?"

"Flight training." He'd always led his class in gunnery, Jan a consistent close second and always out to beat him even then. "Well, there's only one more mission to hump."

"We can make sure when you come back to

process out," Okeda said. "I'll want Dr. Fuselli's opinion to back me up; in any case we'll save you the expense of a colony doctor."

Gunny decided not to tell Jan about the internal stuff yet; she had her own problems anyway. Still, the knowledge was a shadow over their future. They laughed a bit that evening over ward room cocoa and their general dilapidation, and Gunny recalled the doctor's reference to butterflies.

"Said the same thing to me," Jan remembered. "From a haiku. That's Japanese poetry, I think."

"Never read much poetry." Never did a lot of good things, Gunny realized.

"Okeda said it was Buddhist philosophy; like you can learn as much from the mole hill as the mountain." Jan pursed her lips quizzically. "That make sense?"

Yes, as Gunny saw it with new insight. In the essence of flight, the eagle soared no more proudly than the butterfly. "Or the bug."

Jan looked up at him, a light rime of chocolate on her upper lip. "Say again?"

"Nothing." Or the queen ant that sheds her wings after mating because she knows the time has come. To be what you can be and waste no lifetime on what you can't.

Yes.

Gunny pushed his cup away and got up. "Hang around, I'll be back. Want to talk to a man in PERS."

Rothberg's personal effects had been sent to his nearest of kin in his home colony, an aunt and uncle who had no desire for a condo on Mars Station. The price at sale time had been 100,000 endees, but Johnny R. had been paying it off since he was eighteen—no wonder the guy was always broke—so the place was two-thirds paid for now. UNESA would underwrite the note for the balance, but lapsed payments and interests would require seven thousand down.

No problem, Gunny accounted as he hurried back toward the ward room. His pay account in PERS, plus this month's pay came to about five thousand. With Jan kicking in, plus the thousand extra she got from the Corpse pilot—hell, they could make it in an easy glide. And there'd surely be a job for him at the flight training facility there. Should have started earlier, he realized. Like John: How many kids thought of retirement at eighteen? Smart man, Johnny R.

Smart and dead.

Don't think that way. Can't rig the odds, but you can help them. We'll do Hydri IV by the book, no unnecessary risks.

He was pleased to find Jan still at the table where he'd left her, absently cutting and recutting a worn deck of cards one-handed, the nearest she ever came to relaxation. Gunny strode down the compartment, calling hellos to Krug and other officers, to plunk himself down triumphantly across from Jan. He set the finance plan in front of her with something of a flourish. "Did it. This can be waiting when we get out. Our condo."

Jan gave him a sharp but uncomprehending glance, then ran her eyes over the first page. "Our—?"

"Johnny's condo. You liked it so much." In a rush Gunny told her how much was paid, how little to go, how he could swing most of the down payment if she could put in the rest. Jan only stared at the numbers like a foreign language. Her lack of enthusiasm began to deflate him. He thought she'd be happy, but she seemed offended.

"You just went ahead and did this without telling me?"

"Not, lady. For the last three months I've been telling you about it."

"I never said . . ." She trailed off.

"Jan, what's the matter?"

She picked at her already torn fingers, troubled. "What would we do in a colony? We don't even have jobs when we process out. And ten years is what? Quarter pension? Thought of that?"

"Sure I have. Got it all worked out. We get out and I put in for instructor in advanced tactics on Mars Station. We could both put in if you want."

She was not listening, just shaking her head. "I don't believe you just went and—"

"No, I didn't just. You sound pissed; what's the problem?"

"For starters?" she challenged. "Suppose you can't get an instructor's berth. What would you do for money?"

"I don't have to sweat that. They're screaming for people with our experience." He knew that for a fact, however grim. Most people with their experience had never reached twenty-five. "Classroom work, not flight. Or not much," he amended quickly, honestly put off by the thought of more flying even if he could pass the physical. "Home every night. *Bath* every night. Remember how we used to shower together on leave?"

When Jan didn't say anything, he hurried on in her silence. "Okay, so it might be a little thin at

first. 'Scuse me for not having all the answers. I
never did anything like this before."

"Maybe," Jan folded her hands, trying to look
composed. "Maybe I'm not getting out after all.
Did you think to ask about that?"

Gunny took a moment to assess the signals he
was receiving from her. Jan was backing down, trying to evade. "Are you kidding, Tyne? Stay in and
do what? We're redline. We wouldn't be flying
now if Pauley wasn't undermanned. It's over.
Never was a party, but now it is *over*, and because
we were real good and Jesus has the hots for us,
we're still alive. Not many from our class can say
that. Jan, look at me. Please." Gunny caught and
held her hands. "Talk to me, baby. What is it?"

She wouldn't meet his eyes. It confused him.
She'd never backed away from him personally before. They were too close for that.

"You didn't even ask me, Gunny."

His own exasperation began to boil over. "God
damn it!"

Two officers seated nearby glanced around as his
voice sharpened.

"I asked you every fucking *day*, Jan. One way or
another."

"Did you ask am I ready for this? If *I* want to
commit to a place for that long?"

"I guess that's it." He sat back, letting go of her
hands, suddenly feeling alone but very clear about
his own wants. "I guess that's the word. Commit.
Not just to a place but us."

Jan gulped the rest of her cocoa. Gunny thought
her hand was shaking as she set the cup down.
"And everything that goes with it, huh? You go

teach kids how not to get killed and I raise a hydroponic garden."

"I meant commit to something." Gunny wondered why it came out sounding so sad. Something he'd never seen in Jan before, or perhaps refused to see until now.

"Gunny, it's crazy."

"No. Anything else, that's crazy. Like you doing another tour. Like they'd let you stay in."

"I could find something," she snapped defiantly. "But all of a sudden it's a condo and kids."

"Makes sense to me."

"I have to go now. They're working on my ship. I should be there." Jan started to rise but Gunny stopped her with a hand on her wrist.

"This is weird, excuses like I'm hearing from you. Usually it's the guy with one foot out the door." Though he wanted children, that was one part of it he had never brought up. "I didn't say anything about kids."

"Kids!" she echoed bitterly. "I don't know if I can have kids. Years out here and everything that goes with it. I—"

Gunny held onto her. "Jan, I don't care. Years? Maybe. Out here we're old. Back in a normal life, we're young. We can't get those years back, but we don't have to throw away the rest. I'm trying to say I love you."

"Sure, Gunny. That changes everything, doesn't it? Like Roven and Hardesty."

God, couldn't he get anything right with this woman? "You are one flaming bitch sometimes."

"Why don't you ask what *I* want?"

"All right! What the hell *do* you want?"

Krug and another *Kennedy* pilot turned around

to stare at them. They didn't realize how their voices had risen.

Jan pulled away. "Let go of me, Gunny."

"Okay. What do you want?"

"I don't know right now. Can we talk about this later? I have to look at my ship."

Gunny gave it up for the moment. "Yeah, sure," he sighed. "Do that."

She left him staring at her empty cup, confused, asking himself how he'd screwed up. Did they ever understand each other and when did they fade out? No, Jan was scared. He knew her too well to misread that.

Gunny poured himself another cocoa he didn't really want, trying to psych out how to get them back on track. Trying *not* to factor in his medical problem. Lucky Okeda caught it. Growths on the colon; not much but starting.

I'm twenty-eight next month, he told himself surely. *There's still places where that can be young, and I'm going to live, Jan.*

Jan descended the ladder to the carrier hangar deck where her Sparrow was undergoing superstructure repair by two technicians. From the foot of their utility ladder, she called up. "Anyone working inside?"

"Negative, Lieutenant. Damage is almost all skin and second forward rib."

"Internal systems?"

"All green, sir."

"How'd you fix the tripod?"

"That was mechanical, sir. Must have been a glancing hit. Jammed part of the gear in the well. We got it."

Jan pulled herself up into the ship through the aft hatch, bumping her head against one of Roven's components. She sucked her breath in pain as the wave of unreasoning fury washed through her, wanting to tear at something with her bare hands. There'd be a scalp bruise, too tender and lingering too long as always. Never sturdy as Earthers' bones, her own were weaker than ever. Okeda called it premature osteoporosis. One hard fall in normal gravity, one bad turn of the ankle and Fracture City.

Since Gamma Three she couldn't remember the last time she felt good or slept well without verol or jayjay. Or wasn't running scared. She wasn't needed that much on hangar deck, just fled from Gunny because he was threatening her . . .

Jan writhed her thin body forward into the cockpit, switched on aux power and went through the motions of systems checkout. This was the last place where she could feel in control of anything, and that was needed when your body had fast-forwarded ten years while you weren't looking and the Japanese doctor got Oriental about butterflies.

Damn you, Gunny.

Scared, recognizing her fear and despising it, hating the sudden, huge bill somehow run up over ten years that she couldn't begin to pay. Assuming it was still possible with her fucked up insides, what if she did get pregnant again? Never mind intangibles like would she make a decent mother. Could she carry a child to term? What if she had a bad fall or miscarried naturally or—?

Or what? What am I afraid of?

Jan closed her eyes, peripherally aware of the

whine of machinery and the muffled voices of the tekkies working on the Sparrow's skin.

She'd been pure chickenshit with Gunny in the ward room. He'd talked about the place on Mars Station since Rothberg bought it, but today it suddenly seemed too close and real. She *had* to get away from him but still couldn't say why, always content to be with Gunny, happy enough when they made love, though sometimes unable to understand or accept his need for her. Distrustful of joy, afraid of letting go, afraid there'd be nothing inside when Gunny found the used-up place where she should be, used to be or never was. Used up, dried out, or was it ever there to begin with?

How much of her life had been jammed, strapped into a cockpit like this? Victories, medals, close calls, one too close. There was a time—stale joke, don't bother to laugh—when the oldtime leadbrains like Dorfmann sounded off in high-level hearings about the impossibility of allowing women in combat. Fifty years later, by erosion or evolution, the inadvisability—there was military progress for you—and then the fact rolled over their dogma. The traits were equal in both sexes. The more mature, settled ones, the female Willi Krugs, went into FTL. The younger, faster, meaner fuck-you kids were better for Shrikes, and like most of them, Jan had two early abortions. The first came before her original contra implant, the second when the implant didn't kick in right away. She didn't think twice about taking Liza Ross's blood money, because she might have been Ross herself. How much difference between them at twenty-one? Flying and drinking and living fast in between.

I could have had that first one with no problem.

That was by Fayad Whatsisface. Jan could never remember his last name except that he was Saudi and more in love with himself than any woman could ever hope to be. Fayad died of radiation burns when a Corpse hit ruptured his fusion shielding. Accidents, pregnancy and death alike. Tough, but that's how it goes—hey, somebody get Jan a drink . . .

The second was Jim Gilchrist who didn't know she was pregnant when he died with the rest of 18 Squadron in Gamma Three. Out of Wicklow, the son of a horse trainer. Jim always talked of going home to Ireland rich, but he never made one payday to the next without borrowing, and he died owing Jan five hundred and more to others. Great guy, Jim. God, could he throw the bullshit. Hey, that's how it goes, let's not have a fucking funeral. Where's the music? This round's on me—

Stop it!

Life would have been different with a baby, though Jan could never imagine how. In the last few days one odd thought kept reoccurring to her. Liza Ross, whose life had been shorter and better paid but otherwise the mirror of her own: Had she ever huddled inside her cockpit as a last refuge, trying to find something safe or at least sane, asking the same questions?

No. Jan wouldn't let herself soften with the thought. Ross died a greedy, stupid little cunt years before she grew the brains to ask anything. Like

Roven, too frigging dumb to read the odds rigged against her. God, you'd think Roven had never gone the route with a man before Hardesty came along, the little twit. Not just that but the effortless *tidiness* of the kid, the care she took with her appearance and how little it took to make her cheerful, chirping like a hypersensitive smoke detector.

Is that what bugs me, that she's happy? That she dares to be happy when I can't? Or that she refuses to be afraid?

The kid knew fear and showed it, terrified when the *Swift* almost got them. So was Jan but couldn't afford to lose control or express the fear with a ship and an extra life to account for. *And that costs, Roven.*

That...does damage, Gunny. Damn you, anyway!

ER at his discretion. Today as well as tomorrow. Get on with it.

"Kim?"

"One moment, sir." Sergeant Kim Thun methodically finished the word he was encyphering in a report and only then turned to acknowledge the IO. "Yes, sir?"

Pauley handed him a sealed Max/Sec envelope. "Please deliver these to Captain Satin and have him sign for them."

And while aboard the carrier, Thun was to hunt out ship's maintenance, someone in authority, and elicit a positive answer on better ventilation in the Search cubicle. "I don't care how long it takes. Find out what can be done and when."

That would keep Thun away long enough. Pauley saw the Korean to the airlock and then headed for the enlisted billet area.

Meticulous, prissy, compulsively neat little Thun whose single-speed efficiency no one could ruffle or accelerate. A plodder, a born clerk, faceless and invisible, perhaps someone Pauley himself would have recruited for a sleeper if needed. He was still uncomfortable about the ER, more for reasons of professional pride than anything else. He'd checked Thun out on the investigation; the man felt clean to Pauley's instincts, but the evidence was there. Why hadn't he been keen enough to peg the Korean before Waites did? Perhaps impressed with his own complex suspicions about Philip Beaudry, tripping over his own clever footwork.

Pauley paused to chat with the security guard posted between classified area access and the enlisted billets, casually mentioning that he was on a routine spot check of enlisted quarters to make sure no sensitive material had been inadvertently removed from Operations. And, of course, he'd root around for the usual contraband like cigarettes or drugs.

"They get a bit sloppy, these analysts. Something stuck in a pocket and forgotten."

Standard procedure. The guard passed him without question. Still in the man's sight, he entered the compartment next to Thun's knowing the occupants to be on duty, and remained a plausible time before moving onto Thun's quarters.

A man of inflexible habits, the sergeant had complained of his Polish billet mate, a cryptographer worlds neater than Charley Stoner, but Thun was a fanatically hygienic sort who would suspect a sterile dressing just unsealed. Pauley always imagined paradise for his immaculate sergeant would be, if possible, life in a vacuum where no air could carry germs. Thun attended more aerobic classes than required and never failed to take his vitamins. The outer limit of his debauchery was an occasional cup of warm *soju*, the clear rice wine from his mother's homeland.

Thun's area was squared away perfectly, not a thread or pin or mote of dust on the floor, not a wrinkle in the taut-tucked bed. Pauley moved to the wall cabinet above the small sink, its interior spotless, the contents of the two lower shelves (neatly labeled as Thun's) standing at attention as if already prepared for inspection. Toothbrush, floss, soap dish, aftershave and vitamins. From curiosity, Pauley sniffed the aftershave: more astringent than exotic. He might have guessed as much. He gave his attention to the vitamins. All the issue pills were there, augmented by others. Iron, B-stress, potassium and calcium supplements, citrus, lecithin, zinc lozenges, even vitamin K for which Pauley could remember no specific use. All personnel were reminded with tedious regularity how much of each to take each day. Kim Thun, who never mislaid a file or memo in the office, would not be negligent in his vitamin schedule.

Pauley opened the B-stress container and shook several of the saffron-colored tablets into his palm. The single capsule he added to them was the same size and of an almost identical shade. He poured the pills back into the container, closed it exactly as tight as before and replaced it as found, label forward.

He closed the billet hatch after him. So much for Thun, except for one niggling consideration unrelated to remorse. Excluding Max/Sec, Thun had access to the most sensitive data on Limbo, all of which must now be assumed compromised. Whatever disposition was effected, he should have been interrogated, pumped dry about everything he passed, when and where and to whom. This way was an outright waste. Tweedle must be losing his touch. Perversely, the notion rather pleased Nigel Pauley.

Returning to his office, he speculated idly on Tweedle's vitamin schedule. No point, but fun.

After a brief but luxurious hot shower, Stoner was planning to breakfast in his blues, but when the bitch box announced Sparrow mess a half hour earlier than usual, he sighed resignedly—*here it comes*—and changed into coveralls. The six of them filed past the single galley cook who handed each the familiar tray of low fiber concentrates, a small citrus drink and coffee with the sole virtue of being hot. Each tray came with a plastic bag of vitamins, diuretics and a powerful laxative pill.

Stoner sat down at the table beside Ellie and Frank. "My mama done told me. The honeymoon is over."

Gunny and Tyne took places opposite them with no eagerness about consuming what lay before them. "That time again," Gunny said.

Willi Krug joined the table, holding up the bag of pills. "Always the laxatives. I feel like a goose being fattened for his liver. Stuff it in, squeeze it out. They could maybe find a better way."

"You don't want to know it," Tyne mumbled, picking at her food.

"No, you don't," Stoner chimed in. "The option is Okeda's Okinawan nurse."

"*Sheis*. You mean enemas?"

Stoner gave him a gruesome smirk. "She's got a mean streak and a stroke like a bowling champ. Take the pills."

"Okay, so we're on mission clock again," Ellie chirped. "Dig in." She had bounced into the mess in freshly pressed blues and high spirits, refusing to be dampened by anything today, even added a touch of makeup for Frank's benefit. "Stoney, did you mean what you said about your house?"

Jan Tyne's eyes flicked up at her and down to the tray again. Her strong mouth tightened. Stoner tasted an exploratory half spoonful of the brown puree and forgot it. "Somewhere in Supply there's a friggin' sadist making a fortune on recycled food."

"Did you, Stoney?" Ellie persisted.

"The house? Sure, why not? It's just standing there empty. You'll have to sweep it out, open the windows, maybe chase out a few mice and lizards, but be my guest."

Ellie was visibly thrilled. "That is the best idea since the great stuff Ferrier served on the carrier. What did they call it, Frank, the salty fish eggs?"

"Caviar."

"That was super, but this is to die."

Frank tapped the edge of his tray with a fork. "Not this?"

"No, going Earthside. Finally doing it," she heralded to the table at large. "Going to celebrate Frank's birthday at Tahoe."

"By the lake," Frank said.

"By the lake," she echoed, tasting the sound of

it. "In Stoney's house. I figured it up. We've got *beaucoup* leave coming, and when we get back from prox, we put in." She invested the term with the hues of paradise. "Two whole months."

"Less travel time," Stoner reminded her.

"That's couple of weeks coldsleep there, same back. Leaves us almost a month by the lake. I never saw a real lake," Ellie breathed. "I am going to drink it with my eyes, smell, wallow in it and then paint it."

"In the sun," Frank dreamed. "It'll be summer back there, won't it, Stoney? February now, March when we go back. We'll be there in April or May. Off with the clothes and into a tan that doesn't come from a lamp."

"Sounds good," Gunny said. "Look, if you lay over on Mars Station, check out food prices. I'd really like to know."

"W'will," Ellie promised through a mouthful. "And Stoney says Reno's not that far for the big casinos, less than an hour. They still got quarter 'n half dollar slots. Be funny to have hard money in my pocket. Heavy. I'm gonna stock up on oil paints and real charcoal and—"

"Why not get married while you're there?"

Jan Tyne's sharp question had a cutting edge. No one at the table mistook the tone. It sneered. "I hear you can do it in half an hour in Reno. No waiting."

Frank put down his fork. "We weren't thinking that far ahead."

"I'll bet Roven is. Hell, why not get pregnant now?"

Gunny looked around at her. "For God's sake, Jan."

"I mean, if you're not already." She heard

Gunny but not the warning in his tone. A balance had been tipped. She leaned forward to Ellie. "Then they can't send you back here. You never could cut it anyway."

Ellie stiffened. Very slowly she laid down her fork. "You've been on my ass for months, haven't you? What is it, Tyne? Let's clear the air."

"Tell her the truth for once, Stoner. How it really is Earthside."

"Lieutenant Tyne," he said, keeping his eyes on his tray. "I think you could poison yourself on your own spit."

"No. *Tell* them."

None of them wanted to look at Tyne. She was ugly all of a sudden, a clenched fist inexplicably raised to threaten Ellie. "Give 'em the real word. They've never been there."

"Neither have you!" Ellie hurled back hotly.

"No, but I'm not fucking stupid. I don't live with my head up my ass like you. Suntan? Didn't Charley tell you about the ozone hole that'll fry anything not covered up? Like a whole new meaning for sunspot, little girl.

"And that lake, forget it. Any water not running fast and a lot that is, it's the color of the garbage dumped into it. You buy drinking water, it's twenty endees a gallon for anything safe, the last I heard. And food? Tell them, Stoner, you're the man with the word. Anything better than the crud on that tray costs a fortune if you can get black market. You won't be able to get back here fast enough."

Through this vicious outburst, more venomous and hurting than the disillusionment it conveyed, Ellie just stared at her older room mate. Always difficult and brittle, now the woman had gone ugly in front of her. The men were silent, embarrassed and unwilling to interfere, deferring instinctively to a primal female thing. Ellie rose from the table.

"Thanks a lot, Tyne. I'm leaving. I don't want to be around you, but I'm going to tell you something first." She crossed deliberately around the table to stand over Jan Tyne. "We know that. Stoney made it a pretty picture because he wanted to make me happy. Well, I am. We are, Frank and me, and I think that's more than you could ever manage."

Tense, coiled, Jan kept her gaze on her tray. "Don't crowd me, girl. Move."

"Sure," Ellie said with soft-spoken contempt. "Still moving is the only difference between you and that Corpse we took out of the pod."

Tyne slammed down her spoon so hard that it caromed off the table as she shot out of her seat, catching one foot on it. She stumbled, grabbing at Ellie, and took her over backwards. Before anyone could intervene, she was on top of Ellie, battering at her with both fists.

"Jan!" Gunny pulled her off Roven, Hardesty up now and planting himself between the women to shield Ellie, helping her to her feet.

"You're sick, Tyne," Ellie choked. "Just—"

Tyne twisted in Gunny's grip. "Let go of me!"

"Level out!" he ordered, just holding her more firmly. "Both of you knock it off."

"Tell that to Tyne," Hardesty glared at the pilot. "Who started this anyway?"

Gunny whirled on him fiercely. "I don't care. Get her out of here."

"Bullshit. You want to kick ass, start with your girlfriend."

"I said go, Frank."

Hardesty stood his ground, confused but loyal. He liked Gunny and they were no part of this, but suddenly they were. "Go to hell, Gunny."

"*Hold* it!" Stoner moved to intercede. For a dangerous instant he thought Gunny might deck the kid. No, he decided with relief. That violence wasn't in Willington. The moment passed. Gunny took Jan by the wrist and hauled her swiftly out of the mess compartment. In the tension hanging over them all, Stoner wished Ellie had belted Tyne one or two for good measure. The bitch needed it.

"*Genug*, all of you," Krug reminded them sternly. "You are officers. Enough of this. I am trying to eat."

"Damned right enough," Ellie trembled. "I won't fly with her. Fine me, bust me, but I *won't*.

"Okay, okay," Frank soothed. "You were in the right."

"*She didn't have to talk like that*," Ellie sobbed. "She didn't. Don't we live in enough shit already?"

Stoner warned Frank to silence with his eyes, letting Ellie press herself tight into the safety of him. Like a father, he thought. The notion squeezed at his own rarely used emotions. "There, there. It's okay. I'll fix it with Pauley. I'll fly with Tyne."

"W-will you, Stoney?"

"Sure. She's mean but I got the weight and reach on her. God! Will you look at *him*?"

Stolid as they came, unruffled by the flareup, Willi Krug had cleaned his tray and started on Tyne's.

"Are you reading this?" Stoner marveled. "He's going for seconds. How can you stand it?"

"Oh, it is not that bad." Willi's spoon scraped

bottom. He pulled Gunny's abandoned tray toward him. "I have in America eaten worse."

"*Where* in America?" Frank Hardesty's tension might have resolved in tears like Ellie, but here and now, blessedly, it turned aside in laughter at the sight of Willi's fork rising and falling like a piston. For all of them his methodical ingestion was suddenly and excruciatingly funny. They howled at it.

"If anyone . . . if any—oh, shit—if anyone gives a damn," Stoner spluttered when he found the breath, "tomorrow is St. Valentine's Day." He caught sight of the galley cook who'd witnessed the whole scene with fascination, and indicated Willi Krug with a flourish. "His compliments to the chef!"

Later the cook passed the gossip to his friends, how Tyne and Roven lost it and how the whole bugfuck Sparrow bunch first fought and then broke up over nothing at all. Nothing at all, because the cook couldn't hear the fear and desperation that wailed in that release.

Gunny pushed Jan into his own billet, clamping a lid on his own disgust while she huddled on the lower bunk, arms wrapped tight about her thin ribs. Shaking. This was too important for him to lose it now. This was where they got down to it. "Okay. What was that all about?"

"Stupid little . . ."

"I said what?"

"Stupid!"

Gunny leaned against the bulkhead, watching her. "I can't believe you did that to Roven. She wants to make a big thing of Earthside, what do you care?"

"Get off my six, Willington. You want me to leave, I'll leave."

"No. I want to hear you out." Now that the storm was past, Gunny imagined he began to understand the thing behind it. "Not about Roven at all, is it?"

"Gunny, I am wound very tight—"

"Is it?"

"—one more turn, that's all it'll take."

"I'm asking."

"Ask something I can answer."

"I'm trying. Stop being so damned . . . *hard*. It's a long way from strong; you're smart enough to know that." But she couldn't know how desperately he tried now to find the right words because they would never be more important. "Listen to me, Jan. Just sit there and listen. I'm not talking about Ellie. She just got in the way while you were running from me."

"You don't own me."

"No, but if I let you, you'd piss us both down the tubes. No thanks, I've been there. Roven doesn't bug you. She scares you to death with all that tomorrow talk. She does it because it's all she's got."

"A fucking *lie*."

"All they've got," he repeated patiently. Looking at her, a memory came to him, an image from an old book about a healthy tree growing out of a crack in dirty city cement, how hard it was to kill life unless you denied it and called it a lie. "All I've got, Jan."

Gunny shifted to sit beside her with slow, easy movements, nothing to set her in flight, because anything might now. He'd scared her with the condo thing, a woman who'd been running since Gamma Three. Maybe this was the wrong time, but they wouldn't hold the condo option open forever. *All I've got.* "You know where I'm going now? PERS. To close on that condo, get it any way I can."

Jan's voice was husky and low, barely discernible. "That's your choice, Gunny."

"How about you?" When she didn't answer, he thought: *in or out?* No, there was a better and gentler way to say it. "You love me, Jan."

"If you mean we're okay in bed—"

"More than that. I'm saying we need each other. I know that's scary to you, scared you every time you reached for me. Doesn't have to be, Jan. The times I've reached out for you—not just to get laid, but to take care of you, let you know I was there. You know something? I almost punched Frank out just now. But I knew I'd be hitting at something I want to be. Something I could lose. Just like you did."

And that was truth. He hoped the kids did get married in Reno and took reassignment. They had the guts for it. Trees flourished on nothing but hope, growing out of cement, but there had to be that. If the two of them were green and dumb, they were beautiful as well, or maybe just young enough not to have forgotten some things. Gunny gave Jan's taut shoulder a last squeeze and went to his locker. He counted the scrip out of his wallet into an envelope.

"This and what's on the credit record. Every last buck I've got. Like dice, Jan. Some points are hard to make, some easy, but first you have to put your money on the line. You want to play our number or bet we crap out?"

She just huddled there with her head ducked down.

"Jan?"

"Damn you, what gives you the right to come on like this? You take too much for granted."

"Because I love you. Why can't you take as much?"

"Leave me alone."

"No, this is too important. You run away from us, you better know why. Unless you're afraid of that too."

"Gunny—look at me." When she raised her head, her cheeks were streaming with tears, the awkward, homely pain of a proud woman living with her own kind of self-contempt. "*Look* at me, you son of a bitch. How much woman do you think is left? Okeda found a lot more than M-Syndrome."

As her head ducked down again, hiding away from him, Gunny flashed on another memory and, simultaneously, a fast-forward of merciless clarity, slamming part of truth at him before he knew the rest.

"Remember on leave, that bar where all the retired Shrike jocks hung out? How sad they were, the ones that didn't seem to have anything else, nowhere else to go? I don't want to push a beer belly up against that bar, talking about how it was in Gamma Three or someplace else, getting sloppy on three or four too many because there's nothing at home but walls and an old helmet. I don't want to be there because one night you'll show up to join the club, Jan. And I don't want to see that."

Jan wiped at her eyes. Her face was swollen. She hadn't cried since their leave. "What the hell are you talking about?"

"Jackie Carroll."

She looked away then and didn't see his eyes sweep over her in a caress and loving pity, as if pulling warm covers over a frightened child. Gunny tapped the envelope against his palm and folded it into a pocket. "You know what I think? Ozone hole, bad water, bad whatever, Ellie and Frank got it damned straight."

"And they sold you, huh?"

"No one sold me. I learned that in an E-pod." Gunny slid the hatch open. "Pauley needs me, I'm up in PERS buying a place to live. You want in, the offer's still open."

The hatch slid shut behind him.

Jan huddled on the bed, hugging herself tight as if to let go would leave the wound of her open only to be pierced again. She'd managed to say it finally, the hurting thing, but her cry for help had come out twisted and hard. *Look at me.* After all this time how much woman was left, or the youth like Roven's that she never had, or the courage against the scary time coming when she couldn't do anymore but still had to *be*?

Jackie Carroll. Jan hadn't remembered at first. When she did, the image was a delayed implosion. The bar on Mars Station near their leave quarters, the Debrief Room. Low lights, walls checkered with signed holo-pix of Shrike pilots, and the bartender Sid pointing out one of them with a proprietary flourish. A small, wiry woman lounging cockily against a cockpit ladder by her ship. Jan paid more attention to Gunny's appreciation of the woman than the picture itself. Pretty and *petite*, that was the old-fashioned word. The woman would look much better in Jan's new dress than she ever did, certainly more feminine. She had been Most Decorated something-or-other, and who cared?

Sid the bartender apparently cared very much. "Jackie? Oh, Jackie goes back. Way back. Never was a pilot like her, never will be again."

Twenty-five confirmed kills in the early days of the UNESA-Corpse conflict, one for each year of her life when the holo was snapped. Lifetime score, thirty-two.

Jan remembered; she and Gunny hit the bar early that day. There weren't many customers yet. "You mean Ghost Carroll?" Gunny recalled.

"That's her," Sid pointed reverently, setting a fresh Scotch before each of them. "They called her Ghost because no Corpse could ever target her long enough for a hit, and nobody ever got a second chance."

They had dinner in the bar and more drinks, a lot of them. They drank a lot that leave and especially that night, watching the regulars come in. You could tell the former Shrike jocks; there was a stamp on them: small-built men and a few women. When Jan caught their eye for a few seconds in passing, they still had what Pauley called the Lazarus look, but faded and blurred now with a kind of bafflement, and something indefinably sad about the way they kept looking around for familiar faces or just someone to talk to. One man kept trying to get credit with Sid who declined in a friendly and apologetic manner because the man's tab was already through the roof, and all evening he was trying to cadge from anyone who'd stand him one. A small man like the rest of them, his frame carrying a lot of alcohol fat that just hung on him.

Jan and Gunny hit the Scotch hard that night. That was the unspoken game plan for the leave: sex, whiskey and keep the party going. She was foggy when she went to the head and just faded out in one of the booths. Minutes or an hour later— who knew or cared?— she splashed her face and wobbled back to the bar. A grotesquely fat little woman had pulled her stool too close to Gunny, talking at him, rubbing her blubbery knees against his leg whenever she could. The white dress with black polka dot designs was a tent, and yet her body, swaddled in sagging folds of lard, might once have been lean and small-boned as Jan's.

Gunny looked embarrassed, then annoyed and finally harassed, but Jan had never had the feminine-social trick of letting another woman know she was trespassing, and anyway she would have rejected the idea as too permanent and possessive. Gunny introduced the woman to Jan who was too smashed to catch the name. The old bitch kept jabbering at him. Her complexion was blotched and unhealthy, with dark purplish circles under her eyes. Even in low lighting, her eyes looked cold and dead. She just said, "Hey" when Gunny presented Jan, and then ignored her, lighting cigarettes, butting them out half-smoked, picking them up again, each time waiting coyly for Gunny to light her.

Jan couldn't be jealous, it was too ridiculous. The pathetic old bitch was twice Gunny's age and looked more. Numb-drunk herself, Jan's hearing narrowed on the phlegmy, monotonous voice telling Gunny she had been known as the best fuck in four squadrons on some old carrier, which was maximum bullshit and Gunny would know that.

Nympho on a carrier? You got mean and irritable on flight diet, not horny, and if you were dumb enough to get a rep like that in a duty/combat situation, you'd be redlined out unfit, end of story.

Sid kept bringing the old bag double gins which she downed quickly and without any apparent pleasure, like medicine. When she spilled one on the tent dress, it only added to the ancient stains carried like watermarks.

"Those were the days. Un-fucking-believable days," she slurred wistfully, leaning close to suffering Gunny. "And I'm not through yet."

You are if you don't stop groping Gunny, Jan promised, murmuring in his ear, "Let's go home."

"Some've those guys are here tonight if y'don' believe me. Not through yet."

Meaning why didn't Gunny see for himself? Blitzed out as she was, Jan could still read desperation and begging in the sunken, shadowed eyes. Time to go home; she was still sober enough to ball like hell before she passed out, and she'd already given him the message loud and clear.

The bartender swept up the woman's empty glass. "One more time, Ghost?"

"Hell yes."

"And your tab? Pretty high."

"Ah, run it up, Sid. Let it ride." She stroked the bartender's cheek with a hand absurdly small and delicate for the fat-swaddled forearm. "Gimme 'nother. Who the fuck wants to go home? Hey"— as Gunny and Jan were finally making their escape—"don' go 'way . . ."

That was Jackie Carroll, thirty-two victories, best Shrike jock ever lived or ever would, the toast of four squadrons.

That was the future Gunny held up to her. Take a good look, lover.

No, that's not me. No way, Willington. Not me.

Cooled down, Jan recognized a gritty residue of shame toward Ellie Roven. Self-respect urged her to apologize but the shame held her back, so she did what she could manage, stopped riding Roven or complaining about personal items left by the billet sink. Roven kept an icy distance and ignored her.

At T minus forty-eight hours, the crews had the first of two mission briefings for Proximity. Gunny came in and took a seat next to Jan. She hadn't seen him since he walked out leaving her, and tried to read his mood now. "Well? You buy in?"

He took out his PDR, clearing it for fresh notes, barely glancing at her. "It's mine."

Mine. Not ours. "You don't even have a job to keep up the payments."

"How do I know I won't slip and break my neck on a cockpit ladder," Gunny countered easily. "It's a scary life, kid."

He didn't seem angry, just sure of himself. Then Pauley set down his tea and started the briefing and she didn't have time to think of anything else. They would be inserted in orbit around Hydri IV to nail a D/F fix on the surface transmitter and, if possible, traffic from the Jump ship.

Mister Roven would see Lieutenant Willington at the end of briefing.

Jan guessed at the reason for the Roven/Gunny huddle. Reassignment of flight station, Roven to switch with Stoner or Hardesty in her ship. Well, that figured. If she got Stoner, that would make her command pilot on the mission. She could handle that as well as Gunny anytime.

"Operators, make sure you're current on all 528 developments before jumpoff," Pauley concluded. "Tyne, report to Launch Control."

That would be Gosnell, the Launch tekky who also checked out post-repair integrity. On the hangar deck, as Jan approached her Sparrow, Gosnell skinned out of the cockpit and down the ladder to meet her, a bean-pole young man like Hardesty, with already thinning hair falling limply over his sallow forehead. Some people thought Goz was too serious, but Jan liked the kid. Give him a job, he got it done, no procrastinating or excuses. Serious eyes; he tried to *see* what he looked at even casually, and a way of turning his head slightly as you talked to him. Jan always thought he might be compensating for a slight hearing deficiency and didn't want the fact on his med/profile.

"Is she tight, Goz?"

"She's tight when you say, sir. You're taking her out."

Final checkout was her responsibility and her life, not to mention the operator's. Jan turned toward the ladder. "Okay, I'll check it out."

Something felt wrong as she swung toward the ladder and up the first steps. Not realizing the nervous energy in her momentum, her left arm slammed hard against the hand rail, hurting far more than it should.

Gosnell hovered close behind. "You okay?"

"Sure." She hauled herself through the hatch, switched on aux power and cockpit speakers. Gosnell would be talking from Launch Control. She started violently when his voice blurted suddenly out of the speaker.

"Copy, sir?"

Jan lowered the gain, quelling the vicious urge to scream at him. "Right. Sealing now."

Aft hatch read tight. She sealed the forward and cut in life support. "Pressurizing."

Normal pressure for small spacecraft was ten pounds psi, less than Earth sea level, but acceptable, better oxygen economy and what colony people were used to from birth. To check for integrity, standard procedure was to pressurize considerably higher. "Going to fourteen . . . sixteen."

Gosnell reported the pressure readings accurate. "Any leak should read now. Am I tight on your board?"

"Negative. Getting a slight emission in the repaired area."

There was no reason for the jolt of fear that lanced through Jan. "Specific?"

"Increase pressure, sir. Going to enhance."

At eighteen psi, Jan felt like a diver. On Gosnell's screen the emission would appear like a blob of colored steam. Waiting, Jan realized she was rigid, every muscle tensed against some threat—

"Got it!"

The sound of his voice was like an electrical shock. Her body jerked; Jan reacted from pure instinct, jabbing at her chest to unlock the seat harness that wasn't hooked, thrusting up like a swimmer to clear the cockpit and computer—freezing, cringing pitifully at the sight of the E-pod before regaining control. *What am I doing? Losing it on the hangar deck.*

She sank weakly back into the seat, eyes darting

wildly about the cockpit, the small space burying her, closing in—*don't tell me it isn't, I know this place*—shrinking, smothering her until she'd never—

"Lieutenant?"

—be able to get out in time—

"Lieutenant Tyne?"

—unless she clawed through the overhead before the coffin closed on her and—

She erupted from the hatch, head and torso, to find Gosnell's startled eyes only inches from her own.

"I found the leak, sir. You okay?"

She blinked at him. "What . . . ?"

"You cracked the hatch so fast, I could've lost some teeth."

"Sorry." Jan swung her legs clear and descended to the deck. "Aux is still on and I'm burning O^2. Switch off, will you?" She knew how lame she sounded; that was her job, but she couldn't go back inside now for anything. Could not make herself.

"Sure, sir." Gosnell knew she was out of it but didn't let it show. "Soon as she reads full integrity."

When Jan returned to her quarters, Ellie was there, folding underwear neatly into a compartment of her locker. After a hostile glance, she ignored Jan. Jan opened her own locker and took out her clean blues. She changed quickly, watching the other woman's back, doing up shirt and trousers before she could bring herself to speak. "Roven? Ellie?"

Ellie didn't turn around. "What?"

"I'm sorry I blew and hit you. I mean really sorry. I was dead wrong."

When Ellie turned around, Jan saw the purplish bruise darkening on her cheek. "I'm flying with Gunny from now on."

"I guess."

"That's the way it is."

Jan accepted that. "Can't blame you. I just wanted to say it was wrong all the way. Way out of line."

Ellie closed her locker and picked up her dress tunic. "When your tour's done, profile out. *That's* the way it is."

The truth stung but Jan took it.

"I respect you, Jan. You're a good pilot. Better than good, the best, same as Gunny. But Gunny knows it's done. When those Corpses blew a hole in us, you didn't lose it, not when it counted. I have you to thank for that, but you make it awfully hard to say. You don't have to be such a bitch."

Jan opened her wallet and checked the contents. "No, I didn't lose it with the *Swift*. I lost it a long time back and never found it again. For what it's worth, you and Frank have a good leave." She fingered the small bottle of cologne Ellie had left by the sink. "Look, this is a hell of a time to ask . . ."

"Oh, the cologne. Sorry I left it out. I'll learn."

"No, that's okay. I just wanted to ask if I could use a little of this tomorrow night. I'll be down with Gunny."

"Help yourself," Ellie offered, not hostile but still cool. "We might as well smell good while we can."

As Jan finished dressing, the loudspeakers came on, advising all personnel of an attitude adjustment in station orbit at 2300 the following day.

"Great," she grumbled. "One of these days

you'll get this place *finished*." She slammed her locker shut and left the compartment.

At T minus fourteen, their last night before jump off, Gunny put his delicate but earnest request to Willi Krug: would he shift down with Stoner for the night since Hardesty's bunk would be available?

Willi sighed, hating any change in his schedule.

"It's a lower," Gunny enticed.

"*Ja*, sure." Inconvenient but without admitting the fact, Willi had come to see his Sparrow mates as living in their own skewed, crazy kind of equilibrium. He grabbed his pajamas, stuffed toothbrush and paste into a pocket and a few moments later knocked on the hatch at A-27. "Surprise, Charley."

Stoner went on shuffling his deck of cards. "Hi, Willi."

"More surprise." Willi sniffed the air. "You are not smoking."

" 'Course not. It's illegal."

"Don't, yes?" Willi pleaded. "I am allergic."

Stoner raised his right hand. "Perish the thought."

Earlier that day a spot Maintenance inspection had caught him lighting up. As an officer he was politely relieved of his one remaining pack and requested to appear in PERS immediately to pay the fine. His last evening onstation and for uncounted more to come would be Spartan and smokeless. "Frank put fresh sheets on the bed. How about some blackjack, buck a hand?"

"A dollar! Five cents a hand."

The cards riffled swiftly through Stoner's fingers. "Nickel a *hand*?"

Quite reasonable to the frugal Willi who nurtured his retirement funds. "That is enough to make it interesting."

"Fifty cents?"

"Too much."

"How about a quarter?" Stoner cut and shuffled again. "Be a sport, Willi. You gotta die of *something*."

Lost in each other and the lovely moment, Ellie and Frank forgot the scheduled attitude adjustment. At T minus ten, wound around each other, they passed through a weird transition before floating gently up from the rumpled bed. They lost the mood completely.

"Ohmigod," Ellie panted. "What—?"

"Oh hell, it's the shift." Frank let go of her and grabbed for the bunk frame. "Hang on."

"Don't go 'way."

At the moment Frank's position made that difficult. "I got the frame."

Ellie scissored her legs tighter about his hips. "I got you, lover."

They drifted above the mattress like fish in a bowl. The moment was marred but they found laughter in it. "I love you," Frank whispered in her ear, "but this is ridiculous."

"Can you pull us down?"

"Interesting." Frank opened himself to the novelty, making a few exploratory moves with Ellie. They tended to roll like a round-bottomed boat. A few minutes later the adjustment completed and normal gravity returned, though they needed time to recapture their mood. Kissing Ellie's breasts, Frank speculated on the complete sexual experience in total weightlessness. "Stoney said it was great in a hot tub. I mean how would it feel when you come?"

Ellie teased his lips with hers. "Maybe you'd go."

They resolved to try it first chance after Tahoe. Dreaming about the lake and Stoney's house was fun and their major preoccupation now. They had plenty of money, and even if things weren't all that good Earthside, for that short a time they could live it up.

"We need to go home," Frank said. "Strange calling it home when we've never been there."

"No." Ellie slid her hand over his chest. His skin was smooth, not hairy except where it should be. "My folks from Quebec told me of the snow geese in Canada. No matter how far they migrated, they always came home. Even the old gods needed home," she remembered from mythology books. "Like Antaeus."

"Who's that?"

Ellie didn't remember much of Antaeus. When she mastered her own terminal in school, she accessed a spate of books from library central, anything about Earth, the more fabulous the more fascinating. Earth was a place where everything from sunlight and air, to flowers and colors were just *there* free for the loving, and that was magic to Ellie.

"Antaeus had to return and touch the earth once a day to retain his strength. Maybe it's a lesson to us. Bound to get out this far, bound to go on to the end of space, but we have to touch home sometimes, I guess, or fade out and die."

They made love again and then rested, talking sleepily of the house by the lake and the Sierra Nevadas Stoney told them about, the youngest mountains in the world, thrust up bare and strong, wearing snow on their peaks with the pride of that young strength. To see real snow . . . a place where they could hear the wind and breathe its sweetness into them. Their silences drew out longer and longer, and neither remembered falling asleep.

When Jan entered his compartment, she was in fresh-pressed blues and Gunny caught a pleasing whiff of cologne. By comparison he felt decidedly grungy. Jan turned about slowly, obviously waiting for approval.

"Well—damn."

Jan bridled. "What's wrong?"

"Nothing." Gunny could only grin at her. "You look great."

She had used makeup to soften her face and bring out her eyes. Gunny wished he'd thought to change his shirt at least and that he wasn't feeling so wiped out when she'd obviously expected to make love. "Better than great. Beautiful."

Jan undid her tunic and placed an envelope in his hand. "There."

"What's this?"

"Certified account statement. All PERS is holding for me. And all my scrip. Three thousand. What you wanted, right?"

He understood then, happy and off balance all at once. "Jan, I want you to be sure."

She hung her tunic in his locker. "Who's ever

sure? Bet the number, Gunny. Let's go for the condo."

He could only stare at the palpable decision in her hand. "Talk about . . . what happened? Judgment Day?"

"Just about." Beneath the subtle cosmetics—probably borrowed from Roven, he guessed—it was still Jan, but subdued and much more vulnerable. "Hey, don't ask dumb questions." She came into his arms.

"Your hair smells nice. Want a drink?"

"No." That she sounded very sure of. "No more jayjay, no more pills." Jan sat down on Gunny's bunk, unzipping her boots.

"You going to stay?"

"I guess."

He felt a quick spurt of irritation. Would it bust her butt to say she wanted to stay? "Don't do me any favors, Tyne."

When she answered, the old defensiveness was simply not there. "You know what I mean."

"Maybe I'd like to hear it from you once."

And maybe they should stop taking each other for granted. Whatever she thought the years had taken, there was plenty of hope for them. "Please stay, Jan. I need you to stay."

"I want to."

"I think for a while we have to spell it out for each other, what we need. Because outside of a cockpit, we're not the sharpest pair around."

"Not even in one anymore." Jan dropped her boot for punctuation. "That's the loving truth. Put out the lights."

In the darkness he watched her dim form as she stood up to undress. "You sound so tired."

"I am. Ever get to a point where you know—you *know* plain as a slap in the face—that whatever you were, you can't be that anymore?"

"You want war stories?" Gunny stayed her hand as she unsnapped the shirt. "Let me."

"I can do it."

"Come on. I get off unveiling you, it's exciting." He could feel the habitual tension in her body, but she allowed him to strip off her shirt and trousers. "Haven't seen you in a dress since leave."

"I still have the dress . . . Gunny?" she asked in a small voice, "is it all right if we don't do anything tonight?"

"Thanks." He laughed, honestly relieved. "I was wondering how to hint it without you thinking I was falling down on the job, but I'm out of it myself."

"Me too."

"Want something to help you sleep?"

"No, I'm off that. I don't care how long it takes to get to sleep."

"I'll just have to keep you company." Gunny turned down the bed.

"Awful tired . . ."

"Think we're getting old? I'll give you a rub." Gunny began gently to massage her thin back and hips, wanting, in a rush of pity and tenderness, to press all the fear and weariness out of Jan, to cover and protect her. That would take love and trust and time, but there would be all of those now.

Moving under the pressure of his hands, Jan murmured, "I lost it today in my ship. On the hangar deck. Just panicked."

She told him what happened, how she couldn't get out of the Sparrow fast enough, released the unreasoning pent up fear in shards that gradually softened to drowsiness partly muffled in the pillow. "Not a drop of milk on Limbo, did you know that? I asked."

Gunny had never drunk enough to know if he liked it or not. "So?"

"I used to love milk. Mama gave it to me on Christmas for a treat when there was any. Our colony had a dairy station until all the cows died. Poor cows couldn't cut it. Then there was beef stew for a while."

"Didn't know you liked milk."

He felt her soundless laugh beneath him. "With chocolate in it."

"We'll have milk in the house," he promised, wondering how much a liter cost now, powdered or, God forbid, fresh.

"Milk runs," Jan drowsed. "Remember you told me that's what they used to call easy missions? It's not going to be like that on Prox, is it?"

Gunny slipped down beside her, one arm over her back. The same picture had come into his mind when she mentioned milk. Maybe they were gradually moving closer enough now to finish each other's thoughts. People who trusted each other got that way. "Nothing you can't handle."

"Honest?"

"Scrunch over. Get comfortable."

"Honest, Gunny?" She twisted about to lean up over him. "We'll watch out for each other like we always did? Cover my ass, I'll cover yours."

"Like always."

"Nobody else to do it. Willi's okay but not that quick and—"

"Hey." Gunny slid his hands over her breasts,

cupping them, delighting in the tender luxury of loving the woman with no immediate need to make love to her. "We'll look out for each other."

"I got Stoney; that makes me command ship," she said. "Any deep shit, I have to call the plays, and after what happened today, I don't know if I can trust myself any—"

Gunny kissed her, tried to kiss the fear away. "Listen. You're a better pilot than Johnny was, better than me." That might be true; the rest certainly was. "And meaner than all of us. Can you cook too?"

Jan didn't know, never tried much, but that was better than thinking about Hydri IV. They talked easily about the condo and what they remembered of the floorplan. There was some of Johnny's furniture still there, and a good microwave and other appliances in the kitchen. Gunny was wryly amused at Jan's culinary innocence. You simply put the package in the 'wave or ate a sandwich.

"And first off," she yawned against his shoulder, "let's get a really huge bed. For a change."

"You got it," Gunny promised as his eyes closed.

Charley Stoner took Krug for twenty-five endees at blackjack because luck was running strong and cautious, methodical Willi always sandbagged at fifteen. Not sleepy at all, Stoner went back to Intercept with the midnight shift to listen for 528. The alien was still silent, but he knew the bastard was there somewhere.

He let his awareness drift with the auto-traverse receivers, up three kilohertz, down two, up three more, like the slow rocking of a boat on vast ocean billows of sound, sifting star noise and human signals from band to band. The solar flare was dying down. Faint Morse chirping dipped and rose in passing. Voice traffic, distant and distorted, the clean rhythm of a fast operator batting out thirty-five words per on an automatic key . . .

0100 hours. Stoner tuned manually to 100.4 megs. Thumb riding the vernier, he crawled back and forth across the frequency on the off chance of transmitter drift. Nothing but residual static from the fading solar flare, and star-scintillation crackle that had been perhaps a thousand years crossing the void to sputter in his ear for this one moment.

I know you're there, listening like me and wondering what kind of throat can make the sounds that come out of us. Trying to guess how close we'll dare to come. Come up now. I'm here, you fascinating son of a bitch. Talk to me.

He thought he heard something, a brief burst of unidentifiable sound, possibly the carrier wave of a transmitter being tuned . . . no. Gone now. Like a cat at a mousehole, Stoner let the crackling, whispering frequency become his entire world, knowing 528 was there.

Waiting.

At 0500, an hour before crew breakfast, Pauley was hailed to the station hospital and solemnly directed to a small operating room. The hatch was opened by Col. Dorfmann himself and locked behind the IO. There were four people in the compartment then, one of them partially zipped into a body bag on the operating table. Doctor Fuselli indicated the corpse. "One of yours, Major. Looks like suicide. Cyanide or some prussic derivative. Whatever, it was damned quick. Slammed his jaw falling down. His eyes were still open when they found him.''

They were closed now. Sergeant Thun looked prim and composed as in life.

Dorfmann turned massively on Pauley. "You got any clue about this?''

Pauley went convincingly incoherent, apparently at a loss for words. "No, I—no, sir.''

"He didn't bite the pill, he swallowed it," Fuselli said. "There's the outside possibility of murder.''

"Who'd want to kill a wimpy little gook like him?" Dorfmann glowered at the offending sight. "I'da said Thun was the steadiest head in your out-fit, Pauley; maybe the only one. My last tour and don't I have troubles enough? Gonna look bad on my final record, you know that? Not to mention all that next-of-kin paperwork. Jee-sus *shit*."

Dorfmann surged toward the hatch like a frus-trated sea lion, turning to accuse the IO one more time. "Ah told you that Search section ain't wired too tight, know what I mean? You better know what I mean. Fuselli's my witness. Pauley, you get back from mission, I want ev'y last one of those fruitcakes of yours psych-profiled, starting with Stoner. No, starting with you. Fuselli, you heard that. That's an order.''

Pauley nodded passively. "Understood, Colo-nel.''

"You first and that gaw-dam Stoner next. Son-vabitch, I caught him smoking *again*. One've these days I'll find where he gets them. Gotta be someone on the supply shuttle—then I'll have *all* their asses.''

Dorfmann peered at his Intelligence Officer and delivered himself of what he doubtlessly considered an acute observation. "Dam'f you don't look shook up, Nigel. Man'd think you never saw a stiff before."

For the paperwork on Thun's demise, Dorfmann's was simple compared to the process at COORDINT where, on occasions like this, the matter was a fine if shadowed art. Personnel clerks at UNESA closing Thun's file found a medical report documenting an early but serious drug problem, severe lack of self-esteem directly ascribed to substance abuse, and a tendency to depression. More attentive clerks might have wondered how he was cleared for sensitive material at a forward station, but none noticed the paper on which the report was printed seemed fresher than its indicated date. Meanwhile, administrative wheels turned in PERS to find Major Pauley a replacement. Dorfmann forwarded to COORDINT a doubtful assessment of the IO's judgment and abilities in choice and discipline of his subordinates, which Colonel Anthony Waites carefully round-filed.

At T minus one, the Sparrow crews filed into briefing with their flight bags and settled down with tea or coffee. They'd heard about Thun at breakfast, a downer but not their major worry at the moment as they cleared PDRs to record necessary data on the mission. No long days of good carrier food this time. *Kennedy* would go FTL to insert them around Hydri IV.

Stoner groaned at the prospect. "What's the rush? Not the going in, it's the coming out, deacceleration. Like sending your insides Western Union collect."

Pauley rode over the disgruntled snickers. "Listen up. Both ends of 528 have gone silent. Perhaps they've closed down on Hydri IV, we don't know. If not, we want to pinpoint that surface facility and finish the job for Ed Reinecke."

All things considered, rather an emotional appeal for Pauley, Stoner thought. *Don't make me cry. Just let's nail them before that Jump ship reads us.*

Pauley finished, dismissing them with a glance at his watch. "Hangar deck in fifteen minutes. First systems checkout and walkaround. Mister Stoner, please remain a moment."

When they were alone, Pauley invited his chief operator to the side table. "Real tea this morning. Want a cuppa?"

Stoner opted for another jolt of coffee. "That ship's out there, Nije."

Pauley refilled his tea. "I think we can cope this time. Here." He presented a cigarette to the incredulous Stoner. "Smoking lamp is lit."

Stoner touched his lighter to it and dragged deep. "Thanks. Some prick in PERS got my last pack."

"You ought to quit. This is expensive."

"Tell me about it. Where'd you get this?"

"From the prick's desk. If it's any consolation, Dorfmann's going mad trying to trace your connection."

"Thanks."

"He has his priorities. I have mine."

"Gives him something to do." Stoner inhaled deeply again. "Why does this feel like the last drag before a firing squad?"

"Come off it. You're just like Ed; you just complain more."

"Oh, yeah. I want 528 but . . ."

Pauley looked at him closely. "But?"

"I don't know," Stoner admitted quietly. "Things I never thought of before. Different somehow. I see Ellie and Frank making such a big deal out of going home. That broken down old house of mine, and I wish they were there now, not going to Prox. And then I think: Why not? Why shouldn't they go? They're the best and they got the pride of that, both of them. This ain't just what we do. It's what we are."

He sucked a last drag on the butt. "Where can I ditch this?"

Pauley offered the dregs of his tea. "In here. Let's give Dorfmann the Puritan thrill of discovery."

"I guess what I'm saying, I'm not a cowboy, Nije. Don't want to get anyone killed, especially me. Hell, I—I just wish Ed was here."

Stoner dropped his coffee cup into the recyc disposal, picked up his flight bag and lugged it out toward the airlock.

Pauley tucked away his few briefing notes. *I don't want to get anyone killed either. It's just the way things are.*

— IV —

GOING IN

The **Kennedy** took twenty-two hours to put the Sparrows in proximity to Beta Hydri IV. After deacceleration, the crews had two hours to rest and pop mild stimulants laced with B-1 and then had to prep their ships. Stoner was well into his pos checkout before Tyne skinned through the forward hatch. "Gimme com check, Stoney."

He complied with the lightweight headset and then his pressure helmet. "Read you."

"Thank you."

Stoner went on with his checklist before the thought occurred to him: the first time Tyne had not been in the ship before her op, nor could he recall her ever saying 'thank you' for anything. She hiked up over the computers, facing him.

"Goz wants to check the seal on that leak. You'll feel the pressure in your ears."

"Go ahead." Stoner noticed Ellie's St. Christopher medal hanging from a receiver vernier. He slipped it into a utility pocket, wishing Frank had a few extras. This time they'd need all the help they could get.

"Getting heavy in here," he commented as Tyne

pushed the interior pressure far beyond normal.

"Cutting now. Goz says we're tight."

Perhaps the B-1 stim made him feel better than usual, but Jan Tyne sounded downright pleasant today.

"I'm all green, Jan. You want to do pod check?"

Pleasant but reluctant. "No, you can handle that. You know the drill."

He started to say pod checkout was her job, but decided against it. "Okay, release the pod hatch."

"Do it manual. I've got to hit the medics. My stomach's gone weird." Tyne disappeared through the cockpit hatch. She could be a pain in the ass, but Stoner couldn't blame her for skipping this. He ducked his head down into the pod for a preliminary check before climbing into it. *Be it ever so humble.*

Before the 1200 briefing, Stoner spent half an hour in the cramped Ops cubicle, listening on 528's known frequencies. No signals, but a sense, stronger than ever, of someone waiting and listening on the other side of a door. Suited up except for helmet, the smell began to oppress him. As he swiveled about to crack the hatch, his arm brushed a microspool to the deck. Probably one of the standard blanks Pauley used for recording and retransmitting traffic to Limbo. Stoner read the label: SEARCH 528.

Nije was getting careless. Currently the most sensitive traffic coming through Search, and he left it where anyone might grab it? The retinal scan lock on the cubicle opened only for specific Max/Sec clearances, but security procedures always assumed any precaution could be circumvented.

Stoner slipped the spool into his mapcase with the new Hydri IV surface charts and clumped out to briefing.

Pauley was first there as usual. Stoner tucked the spool into his hand with a cluck of disapproval. "That's a no-no, Major. Shouldn't leave these lying around."

"Thank you, Stoney. I'll fine and flagellate myself."

"For a start."

Ellie and Frank came in, ungainly in pressure suits, then the pilots. Pauley allocated pilot/op callsigns and freqs. He was November. Bravo 1 for Tyne and Stoner in command ship, Bravo 2 for Willington and Roven, Bravo 3 for Krug and Hardesty. "If any reminder is still needed, all tix on scrambler and minimal—repeat minimal—chatter. Roven and Hardesty please note."

"Yes, sir," Ellie acknowledged gravely, with a sideways smile for Frank.

"You'll be spread out on this one," Pauley went on. "Stoner has worked out trajectories for optimum search coverage, so don't blame me if you come up zip. Kill the lights."

Stoner activated the holograph projector previously set up. A large, slowly rotating image of Hydri IV materialized, hanging in darkness as in space. Using a red dot cursor, Stoner traced flight paths for the three Sparrows. Willington/Roven would insert west to east along the equator, Krug/Hardesty pole to pole. Tyne/Stoner in Bravo 1 would turn the right-angle pattern of the others into an asterisk by moving transversely across them.

"Pilots note that launch velocity will be higher

than usual for faster orbit, but monitor your ODF anyway. Ops, this is our final shot. If 528 so much as sticks a whip antenna out of a gopher hole, we want to nail him."

"Lot of metal survey junk down there," Hardesty said. "False readings all over the place."

"So be sharp. That and other garbage will be registering on your sensors." The red dot streaked over the holo. "Here and there in the northern hemisphere, you got mountains with high iron and nickel content. Pilots, it'll light up on sensor like Christmas, but it ain't the pot of gold."

The cursor dipped south again. "You'll pick up clean metal readings about here . . . and here. These are marked on your charts, the stuff Frank mentioned. Dead survey transmitters. Diurnal rotation is eighteen-plus hours, but dayside is like twilight down there, so there's not much of a bandshift going nightside or coming out. Questions?"

Krug's thoughtful query came out of the gloom. "At least one of us will be blindside to the rest most of the time. How do we maintain com link?"

"November will maintain parallel course with Bravo 1, but farther out," Pauley put in. "We'll be able to maneuver quickly within com range of the blindside ship—"

He was interrupted raucously by the ship's hailer. "All duty Launch Control personnel report to hangar deck!"

"Lights please." When they came on, Stoner cut the holo and started to sit down, but added, "If I was one of those inspiring, natural-born leaders, I'd give you the old pre-game bullshit, but nobody would be fooled. Orbital velocity will be high as effective search can bear, but the plain fact is, whoever's blindside will be wishing like hell we had more backup out here."

Hardesty tucked his PDR into the map case. "I was just thinking that myself."

"We will have backup." The sound of hurrying footsteps clattered past outside the briefing compartment as Pauley stood up. "For security reasons we didn't tell you until now. *Langston* is enroute from Gamma Three with a full complement of Shrike squadrons, ETA about four hours. We thought we'd do it properly this time."

Ellie yipped: "Yay-y TEAM!"

"Wha-at?" Gunny was incredulous. "You mean we're going in with some muscle for once?"

They were all surprised and relieved at the disclosure. *Langston* was the newest UNESA carrier in the presidential class, with augmented nuclear and laser armament.

The hailer bellowed again. "Sparrow crews to hangar bay! Sparrow crews report to hangar bay!"

As the briefing broke up, Frank Hardesty squirmed his itching back futilely against the seat. "Hate these lousy skintights. I feel like a size ten foot in a nine shoe. Hey." He caught Ellie's gloved fingers in his own. "I know we can't talk much out there, but think Tahoe."

"House on the lake. Fresh fish to eat."

"Fresh anything," Frank yearned as they exited. "I could get horny over a plate of hash."

"For a whole month, nothing to do but eat and make out. Stay green, Frank. Green and cool." Ellie mouthed him a silent kiss.

"For you, Mister Roven—an all-green icicle."

Crossing the hangar deck to her ship, Tyne passed Gosnell who gave her a cheery thumbs up.

"I know it's classified, sir, but whatever you're after, good luck."

"After starbows, Goz."

"Say what?"

"This is where they all go down to a pot of gold."

The tekky didn't connect with that. "Yeah. Well, best of luck."

Tyne saw Stoner duck under the belly and through his hatch. As she climbed the ladder, someone called her name.

"Hey, Tyne!" Ellie Roven with a dazzling smile and middle finger raised aloft like a flag. "Do a diurnal on this."

Jan returned the salute with a grin. "Right. Rotate. Take care of Gunny."

"Will do. Don't let Stoney get food gunk all over my rig."

"Do my best." Tyne dropped into the cockpit, strapped in, twist-locked the helmet to her metal suit collar and activated her displays. "Launch, this is Bravo 1. Sealed and pressurizing."

She recognized Gosnell's crisp voice from Launch: "Copy, Bravo 1. Four minutes to drop . . . mark. Launch velocity 13,000 kays."

Good. No one would be blindside more than a half hour at that speed. Jan fed the factor to her system and flipped to pilot frequency. "Bravo 2 and 3, give me com check after launch. Factor is 13,000 kays."

She heard Willi's laconic retort and Gunny's tender support. "Yes, ma'am. You tell 'em, Boss."

She swept her eyes over the cockpit displays, reading status and condition in a quick, practiced glance. If this place was no longer safety, neither was there any more fear. Just a task mastered long ago and finished now with no regret. "Stoney, you sealed?"

"Secure." Strapped in his pos seat, Stoner slid the back erect to reach his receivers. All components could be operated from the seat arm controls but he preferred manual control whenever possible. An electronic command never felt as sure or direct as his own thumb on a vernier. "Bravo 2 and 3, com check as soon as you're launched. Sing out."

"Copy."

"Acknowledge."

"If 528's still here, he's tracking us right now. Don't make it easy for him." Stoner paused, wanting to say more to the kids. They deserved more, like *I love you and I'm proud of you both*. He'd had a hard time saying that to anyone and anyway they knew it already. "Stay sharp, you two."

He cut the tix and concentrated on recorder and D/F status.

At 1530 hours, circling the equator, Gunny Willington read Jan's ship and the carrier just reappearing in the northern hemisphere, edging southward. He wanted to talk to Jan but resisted the urge. He could find some legitimate excuse later, like his transmitter was doing hinky things or maybe that she read weird on his heat sensor. Jan would know what he meant. He pressed his com switch. "Ellie, we'll be nightside in about two minutes. How're you doing. Hear anything?"

"Negative, but I sure wish they built a head into this ship."

"Yeah, Jan always bitched about that. Didn't you go before we launched?"

"Sure did, but you're not a girl. Frank said you two bought into a place. Nice going."

"One of the terradomes on Mars Station. Look, I don't know if Jan said anything to you, but she's sorry about that punchout."

"She told me," Ellie said. "I know how it is. You going to get married?"

"Don't push my luck. It was major sweat just getting her to live with me."

"Monitor your surface scans, Gunny. I'm dropping down a band on manual search."

In Bravo 1, Tyne read Gunny on her P-scan and hoped he'd find some excuse to call. She wanted to hear the sound of his voice, but as command pilot had to enforce mission discipline. Her eyes narrowed on the surface scans. "Stoner, I'm getting a large metal concentration below. Humongous. Like a rash."

"Iron in the mountains." That and radio bandshift as they approached nightside were souping his receivers with natural interference.

A moment later Tyne spoke to him again. "November just advised. *Langston* just went sublight. In contact with our bridge on 150 megs, callsign Acorn." She flipped to pilot channel. "Bravo 2/3, did you read November?"

Krug responded laconically: of course he did. Gunny's tix came in aural hiccups. Jan smiled; he was jittering his transmit switch to sound like a malfunction.

"You're breaking up, Bravo 2," she sent. "You read me?"

"I definitely got you now," his voice caressed her ear. "Everything green?"

"Affirmative."

"You read funny on my heat sensors. You need a good walkaround and cockpit check."

"Just got to find the right tekky for the job."

"We'll work on that."

Jan was still smiling when Pauley broke into their moment. "Bravo, belt up for Christ's sake!"

For a short, abashed five seconds pilot channel went silent, then Gunny again in Sunday-sepulchral tones: "And the Lord spake, telling the world to belt up, and they by God did."

Above the southern pole, Willi Krug was first among the Sparrows to read *Langston*'s approach by sensor fluctuation: a spray of readings gradually steadying and confirmed by his perimeter scan. Through his forward view plates he saw, dimly illuminated by the distant sun, a streak of dull silver against darkness; only an instant, then the streak elongated as the carrier continued to deaccelerate in orbit around the planet.

Beautiful.

One day their own ships would match the mysteries of 528, make them commonplace as FTL, fold space like a circle of paper, half and quarter the illusion of vastness, tap the poetry of physical existence in the soul of matter, even as German artists had mined romanticism from the human spirit. "Perfect flight is being there," said the old book. True enough. The writer had been a German-American mystic, a flyer himself from the transitional age of combustion to jet.

Hardesty broke into his meditation. "Got the *Langston* hailing on 150. Willi, you there?"

"I know," the pilot answered softly. "I saw her."

The incoming carrier's ident beacon on 150 megs was followed by a brief voice hail from its bridge.

"Chelsea" requested permission to board *Kennedy* by shuttle craft. Another high-level staffer, Hardesty thought, getting his kicks and making a status thing out of codenames. Hardesty took a navigational fix from Willi, noted it on his surface chart and went on listening for 528, watching for the double-voice visuals on his matrixed screen. 75 megs was one of the known 528 frequencies. He prowled manually back and forth across the channel like a shark around a lifeboat. A few seconds past, one of his auto-traverse receivers had registered a visual blip on 75.1, which might have been a short burst of transmitter wave. The sound came again like a heavy drop of water falling into a pool.

He switched one receiver to oscillator and heard the faint whistle of a definite wave dip and rise, then tuned a second receiver to 100.4 megs and activated his D/F. "Bravo 1 from 3. Possible on 75.1 measured, over."

Stoner came back instantly. "Copy, tuning to back you up."

"Bravo 3: Is 2 blindside now?"

"Affirmative. Get pilot pos check. Same here when I make the slice."

"Copy, 3 out. Willi, I need another pos check on surface."

Krug obliged with precise latitude/longitude to the second. "You have something?"

Before answering, Hardesty interpolated their velocity and the time factor into his D/F cut, knowing Stoner would do the same. "We got Christmas, Willi! Stand by."

Once more the moaning carrier wave from 528. A few seconds later, Stoner reported crisply.

"Bravo 3, I got him. We got a slice. November, November, did you read?"

"Read and heed," Pauley snapped back. "Send coordinates."

Hardesty fed his readings, then Stoner his. Even with interpolation not an exact match but close enough when they brought Ellie in to nail. Hardesty volunteered a diagnosis.

"He sounds like he's having transmitter trouble."

Pauley requested he specify.

"Any technology can develop bugs, even these guys from over the rainbow. My guess is he's trying to call the Jump ship but something's wrong. Transmitter glitch."

"November here. Acknowledge. Stand by."

In Bravo 1, Tyne gave quick sit/rep to Stoner. "November's altering course to recall Bravo 2 for a fix. He says good on you."

"Could be a winner," Stoner sang out jubilantly. "Advise when you scan Bravo 2—and look, don't get pissed if I open a tube. I'm hungry."

"Get it all in your mouth, Stoney, not on the Velcro."

No use to warn; Jan knew there'd be a blob of gunk here or there. A few minutes later she heard November's recall to Gunny: Break off his pattern to join the other ships. Jan waited for his blip to reappear on P-scan. *Careful and by the book, Gunny. Stay close to me. It's a milk run after all.*

With Roven moving in for a fix, Pauley marked the D/F slice on his surface chart. Good results so far, all profit and no loss. The Jump ship, if it appeared, would almost surely have to reenter normal space to transmit, giving their two carriers marginal warning. Downside was the unexpected presence of "Chelsea." What the hell was Waites doing out here now? Checking up on him? Didn't trust him to get the job done? Paranoia being the occupational disease of intelligence gathering, Pauley tried to fathom Waites' motives before the perennially cheerful, moon-faced little man lit up the Ops cubicle with his upper class Home Counties charm, which the IO knew to be purely epidermal. Was there a change of plan? He hoped there might be for the sake of the three Sparrows on his radar plot. He could recall his people, go home and forget the whole dirty business.

Someone buzzed outside the cubicle. Irritably, Pauley slammed the entry button, admitting Colonel Waites who stepped into the small space and secured the hatch behind him in a quick, surprisingly graceful movement for a soft-looking little man one would imagine to have the reflexes of a tree sloth.

"Hel-*lo*, Nigel!"

"Good to see you, sir," Pauley prevaricated cordially, clasping the offered hand. "To what do we owe the honor?"

"Oh, I get tired of hearing it all second hand. Since *Langston* was joining the party, on a whim I thought I'd like to come along, be here when you . . . nail 528? Nail, isn't that what they call a positive D/F?"

"Right." Pauley tried to read behind the man's opaque good humor. "Any change in plan?"

"None," Waites assured him pleasantly. "What's happening with you fellows? Fill me in."

Pauley demonstrated the situation on his two in-use screens. One, an enhanced section of planet surface, showed two converging green lines, the D/F pie slice from Stoner and Hardesty. The other screen as radar plot showed three red dots against a sphere, two close together, the third nearing them. "That's Ellie Roven moving in to complete the fix."

"And baby makes three?"

"That's how it's done."

Waites rubbed his palms together. "What sort of traffic?"

"None. Just intermittent carrier wave."

Waites looked dubious. "D/F on nothing but bits of wave? That's dicey."

"No, sir. That's Stoner, Roven and Hardesty. They're the best." Pauley enlarged the compliment with a pride that surprised him. "Better than best. They're bloody mystic."

"Indeed? Interesting."

Quite, if Waites could appreciate the Zen point at which mastery melded with instinct. *Like mine that tells me something has changed.* "Roven will nail 528 when he comes up."

"If he comes up."

"He's trying. Frank thinks he's got a glitch."

"Frank?"

"Hardesty. My newest *wunderkind.*"

Waites leaned toward the screen where three dot-ships were aligning neatly along the same south latitude. "Nigel, you've not got too close to your people, have you? Happens to the best of us."

Pauley kept his eyes on the screen. *God damn you, Tony.* "You know better of me, Colonel. I didn't get that close to my wife, which is why the dear girl very sensibly divorced me."

"And Adrienne?"

Not much of a surprise. Discreet as they'd been, Waites would still know about Adrienne and not give a damn unless she were a security risk to his white-haired boy.

"Sorry," his superior added in tactful apology. "That was awkward."

"Past history, sir." As the bastard would know, probably to the precise day it ended.

"Lovely woman."

"Yes. Excuse me." Pauley called Stoner on ops channel. "Bravo 1, advise sit/rep."

The reply crackled across speaker hiss. "Negative tix, November. Wave fluctuates, keeps dropping off. Hang in, we're on it."

"Copy. November out." Pauley turned to Waites. "Nothing but to wait them out. We'll have some warning if the Jump ship becomes a factor."

"When they become a factor," Waites corrected with delicate emphasis. "You're quite clear on your orders? The tractor beam?"

"Neutralized," Pauley told him. "I used the Burglar on the primary and backup system. Ate them both."

"Suppose they line-check in Launch Control?"

"That will take more time than Satin will have."

"Good." Waites clapped the younger man on the shoulder. "Now, with the captain's permission, I'd like to tour your engine department. Damned things fascinate me, probably because I'm a dead bloody loss on a bicycle. Anything you need, Nigel?"

"Yes, actually. This compartment could use better ventilation. I've complained but nothing gets done. Think you might pull a few strings?"

"Certainly I'll try," Waites sniffed. "The need is blatant."

When the hatch slid shut behind him, Pauley took a deep breath, then loaded the microspool of Search 528 traffic into his transmitter deck.

If the IO thought of his people as mystic in their talents, Tony Waites equally valued his own knack for finding the right man for any slot. Pauley himself was one, Lt. Philip Beaudry of the engineering department another. As Waites eased his rotund bulk down a ladder, he mused on their differences: radical but bent to one purpose. Nigel had a core of cold, unemotional courage, Beaudry of resentment and over-compensation.

That Pauley's wife had left him years ago was an occupational commonplace. He would always be a solitary man who kept others at a distance, but with a marvelous grasp of the game in which they would now initiate a decisive series of events. Maintenance or destabilization of any balance presented its own imperatives which Pauley, by training and nature, saw as abstractions and little else. As such he evolved directly from the first Cromwell through the old CIA and MI-5 to COORDINT.

In a temporary but crucial role, Philip Beaudry would now come into play, selected, groomed and placed by Waites through key flaws rather than strengths: colony-born to a dissolute mother with a menial job and no husband, placed in a school as a welfare case. Some colony children became self-reliant, even driven over-achievers. Others turned negative. In Beaudry's case, talented in physics but tending to grandiose emotional fantasy, afraid of authority and resenting it, the young man lacked the requisite stability to take him up the fast track of FTL command. He won his commission in engineering, mediocre in class standing, and waited impatiently for the opportunity that would somehow vindicate his starved self-esteem.

Long before *Moyers* and *Condor* were lost, COORDINT realized UNESA could not control private corporations effectively or develop the potential of Beta Hydri IV without a planned scenario, an "effected resolution," as the working euphemism went. For this Waites required the specific insertion of a certain agent in a particular position with no orders but to be industrious in his low-profile cover capacity and to wait, possibly for years with no need of employing him at all.

Beaudry was perfect for Waites' purposes, attracted to the secret importance of the mission which would enlarge his own. To this end Waites kept their liaison one-to-one, carefully preserving the fiction that a mere key handful knew the identity of the Mystery Man who would ultimately justify the means he must use. When fatherly Tony Waites gave the word, the young man would obey eagerly for the greater if dimly comprehended good. Later Beaudry would relocate with promotion and his already laundered record. Scenario pristine thus far, but later it got sticky. Before all details had been finalized, the question arose at COORDINT: Was Pauley to be briefed or not? When the evolved plan dictated otherwise, COORDINT had already alerted him to the suspected sleeper on Limbo. With the plot finalized, Waites had to rescind the suspicions or provide a suspect. Farewell Kim Bok Thun.

Nevertheless, Tony Waites made a mental note

that future operations of this nature be better conceived before implementation.

Pauley's function would end when he transmitted the 528 microspool at maximum power, which the Jump ship or surface listening station would surely intercept. If Waites had any scruples about Pauley's termination along with all the other expendables, they faltered with Nigel's suspicion of Beaudry's too-median-bland profile and died when he saw the man's face bent over the cubicle screens, lit by something more than their pale glow. Emotionally involved with his people, judged them "mystic," wangled them extra luxuries and considerations, indulged them on Limbo. Took needless personal risk in salvaging sensitive data from *Condor*. The man had grown careless, even self-destructive. Like one too long without sleep who droops insensibly though still aware of purpose, Nigel Pauley had lost his objectivity where his people were concerned. Possibly—probably—he would sacrifice what he must, but Colonel Anthony Waites couldn't gamble on variables within a political equation designed to profit every UNESA nation, even if few of their decision makers were aware of it. They would be presented with the *fait accompli* profitable all around.

Pauley had to go with the rest, already marked for it, but Waites now rested easier in his decision. For what it might be worth, he would much rather sacrifice Beaudry.

You were too good, Nigel. You smelled out Beaudry where no one else ever could. I am sorry.

Beaudry awaited him at the secure hatch to the drive compartment. Waites always thought him too good-looking for a man: black hair in tight curls, high coloring, a bit smarmy in his manner, too eager to please in order to manipulate others, a mouth that hinted of petulance. Thoroughly unexceptional, a man to be trusted only in his flaws.

"Good evening, sir!"

"Philip, my boy! Hope I haven't kept you waiting long."

"Not at *all*, Colonel," Beaudry denied too heartily. His eyes flicked to Waites' locked attaché case. "Ready for the tour?"

"By all means, Phil."

Beaudry presented himself for the hatch's retinal scan and stood aside for Waites when it slid open. He introduced the colonel to the duty watch officer, pointing out various components and how they functioned and tied in to bridge commands, shields and pile, bringing Waites eventually to the separate, FTL compartment housing the tachyon drive complex.

"That's what I really wanted to see," Waites enthused innocently for the duty officer's benefit. "Difficult to comprehend matter that moves faster than light by itself. Have to take it on faith, I suppose."

Beaudry ushered Waites ahead of him into the smaller compartment where a single tek in coveralls monitored a complicated bank of displays. The space was given mostly to components and the acceleration pads for duty crew.

Beaudry presented the slim enlisted man. "Specialist First Class Molyneux, sir. Colonel Waites from COORDINT."

Molyneux looked a bright sort to Waites, if no more than twenty. "Did you want a look around, sir? Not much to see when we're not engaged, not much more when we are."

"I'm giving Colonel Waites the grand tour," Beaudry said. "Go take yourself a break, Molyneux."

The tekky declined respectfully. "Alert status until we leave Hydri IV, sir. Can't leave station for any reason."

"Of course you can't," Waites agreed smoothly. "Wouldn't want to get you in trouble. Tell me, Mollynoo: this apparatus here . . ."

Waites guided the tek to a bank of glowing green tubes behind a polarized view plate. "Is this part of the tachyon drive?"

"The guts of it, sir. Those tubes—"

He broke off with a startled grunt as Beaudry pinned his arms from behind. Waites' left hand clamped over Molyneux's mouth. The small syringe in his right pressed against the young man's throat over the carotid artery. Molyneux went limp.

"Quick, Phil. Put him on one of the accel pads."

They laid the body out. The eyes were still wide open in the last surprise and shock. Waites closed them. "Wish he had gone for coffee. That's the worst of it, Phil. So expensive."

Beaudry stared at the body. "Are you sure . . . ?"

"Quite. He'll be brain dead in twenty seconds. Steady on, boy. We've only a minute or two."

In minor shock, Beaudry swallowed hard at the killing but more at the casual efficiency of this cheery little Earther who killed a man like a kindly uncle pausing in the middle of a bedtime story to twist the head off his nephew. Beaudry touched the side of the housing for the computer tie-in to the bridge. "I'll need your component here, sir."

From his attaché case Waites took a black rectangular object the size of a small jewel case, activating a tiny red light on one surface. He pressed one side to the housing where magnets held it firmly in place, waiting until the red light turned green. "Ready."

"Is that what they call a Burglar?"

"No, a little more devious. A Jumper. Some call it Fibber. It overrides any malfunction or intruder alarm here or on the bridge. You could reprogram to tootle Chopin and no one would suspect."

"Tootle?" The whimsical term was lost on Beaudry. "What's a Chopin?"

Waites regarded him with an amused pity. "Oh, brave new world that yet is so deprived. Never mind, it's working. Let's get on."

Beaudry's fingers danced over the terminal keyboard for about thirty seconds. "That's it. We're reprogrammed. Detach."

Waites removed the Jumper and tucked it back in his case, extracting now a plastic package about two inches square fitted with two small magnetic plates. Beaudry lifted the view shield over the tachyon tubes and clapped the package against the casing well out of sight. "Done, sir."

"Yes." Waites glanced at his watch. "Now tell me exactly what will happen and when."

Beaudry glanced nervously at Molyneux's body. "Bridge will do the job for us, sir."

"How? No frills, just cut to the chase."

When Satin initiated standard engagement sequences for FTL, the controls would be following Beaudry's new program which could not be overridden now. No unusual readings would display on the bridge. The final sequence from normal space to trans-light would detonate the sabotage charge, obliterating the entire compartment.

"And to think I have trouble with my microwave," Waites admired. "Well, then." He rubbed his palms together briskly and gave his stunned attention to the body on the accel pad. "My God! The man simply collapsed a second ago. We must do something."

Waites opened the hatch, calling raggedly for someone to for God's sake get a doctor.

Doctor Fuselli could diagnose nothing on the spot beyond an apparent stroke, possibly cerebral hemorrhage. Since *Langston* had more facilities and a ranking doctor, Molyneux's body was bagged for shuttle back to the larger carrier with Waites who requested Beaudry accompany him for the purpose of witness statement. The shuttle had a small closed passenger compartment that divided them from the bored pilot who took no more note of the bagged body than he would a sack of laundry. Beaudry sat facing Waites with the body between them. From his recruitment by Waites, the young man had been guided through many covert techniques toward specific ends, but never told why. The enormity of the last few minutes staggered him. At the moment, to him, this single murder was the whole reality, not the crippling of an entire ship.

"Why, Colonel?"

Waites glanced up sanguinely. "Hm?"

"There's no need for me to know, but I can't help wondering why."

"Don't, laddy."

Beaudry couldn't help it, now that the results were real and dead in front of him. "What is so big it's worth this?"

"Phil," Waites soothed in the fatherly way he'd cultivated the young man from the beginning. "I don't know all the whys myself, nor do all of my own superiors. That's the frustrating aspect of our work, that we never see its end result as a cook or carpenter can. The game will be worth the candle. Best not labor to understand all of it just now."

"Yes, sir." Beaudry looked away to avoid the nearness of the body. "If you say so. I trust you."

Waites despised him with a smile. *I do say, you biddable little man. You won't know fuck-all ever, except you survive a disaster through circumstance to get a nice soft berth somewhere else. Our choice, of course, because you're ours from here out. You don't travel or work where we can't reach and control you, or even marry unless we approve the silly bitch. When we whistle, you'll come running. If we need you to assume the position like Molyneux here, you'll pass out neatly as he did and without undue notice.*

"Today was rough for you," he observed with gentle solicitude. "But you came through; you carried the can, Phil. You've got good stuff. Loyalty is valuable. You'll be near the top of the promotion list always. That end result I *can* promise."

Not too near or too quickly; that might stir suspicion in certain quarters despite altered reports, but higher than the sod could have ordinarily hoped for. Beaudry was petty cash.

You ask why? Waites reflected acidly while bathing his protege in the warmth of paternal confidence. *Because I have to change history today. That inevitably requires as many plumbers as statesmen. I'm here to create a dramatic disaster and commence an inter-species conflict sufficiently alarming back home to give us the backing and budget we need. What would you say to that, you mediocre little shit?*

The Sparrows cruised back and forth along the south latitude target line. On the barren surface of Hydri IV poisonous winds stirred huge dust clouds as the target area grayed into the feeble light of dayside.

In Bravo 2, Ellie scratched furiously at her itching scalp, listening. The slice formed by Frank and Stoner's D/F readings had narrowed the search area to an incomplete triangle of about eight kilometers. Her own fix would pinpoint to less than a third of that. 528's last burst of wave was too brief to yield more than a directional approximate. Ellie checked her D/F array. Functioning perfectly, locked on 75.1 megs with zero drift.

No signals. She pressed her com switch. "Gunny, read anything good on surface scan?"

"Nothing definite. Scattered magnetic trace minerals, that's it."

The installation had to be subterranean, Ellie concluded, with a retractable antenna system. Glitched or not, any permanent surface array would read on sensors. *Come up and let me nail you. If I don't get to a head in the next hour, bad things are going to happen.*

She snapped alert at another blurt of transmitter wave on 75.1. Stronger this time, strong as she'd ever read it, and then the familiar double voice sang in her ears. Ellie wiped her screen to D/F alone. Stoner and Frank would be duplicating, but she carried the ball now. Her screen showed surface simulation with a solid green line between her Sparrow and the target signal. In the upper left hand corner, the coordinates fluttered and stilled to a firm reading.

"Bravo 1 from 2. We have a fix!"

While the alto duet wailed, Pauley came on. "Bravo, Bravo. Well done! Your fix is a two-kay area. You lot could find a dime down there. Thanks and God bless. November out."

The triangle was closed. Frank and Ellie whooped their victory over ops channel until Stoner cut in. "Knock it off! *Listen*."

Something in the tone of his command silenced them like an electronic circuit cut off. "Listen," he said again. "He's different."

After all this time Stoner could have reproduced 528's typical intervals on a piano or synthesizer. What they heard now was not typical, the intervals smaller and dissonant with a ragged impurity of tone and far more rapid fluctuation.

The insight was like a slap in the face to Stoner. *Emotion. Panic. Sounds like he's scared to death. Losing it.*

At November, Pauley signaled himself ready to record. Pre-set on three auxiliary frequencies the 528 transmission flowed from the Sparrows to their carrier. With the fix nailed, Stoner relaxed a little, aware that his back itched under the skintight. He writhed against the padded seat back for the minimal relief that afforded. "Bravo 2 and 3, we're not finished. Listen for the Jump ship on 100.4 and other known freqs. Auto-traverse on one receiver in case he's shifted band."

Stoner tuned his own rig, matrixing his screen for frequency visuals. As the auto-traverse slid across 95 megs, the corresponding square on his screen leaped to life with the familiar dancing snakes. Before Stoner could signal his ops, Frank was in his ear, excited.

"Bravo 1 from 3. 95 megs! Five-by, booming in. Got to be the other end."

And then Ellie: "I have 528 on 110 and 120 megs. Chill down, Bravo 3, that's just November boosting traffic to Limbo."

The hell it was. No way. "Negative, negative," Stoner denied. "Those are not the assigned booster freqs and"—his ears knew surely before his mind—"that's not what we tixed just now. Different."

"Bravo 3." Ellie's light voice squeaked higher with disbelief. "He's on 130 and 140 megs. He's all over!"

"Activate D/F again, 2 and 3. Try for a new slice. Stand by." Stoner flipped back to com. "Tyne, can you read anything big beside our carriers?"

"Negative," she reported. "Nobody but us happy campers. You got something?"

"You know it." Stoner cut in his own D/F. "Sounds like he's sending from our own E-pod."

"Nothing on perimeter scan. Just the carriers."

Stoner's fingers danced on the seat arm while the directional indicators on his screen fluttered only an instant before the green line firmed. Impossible. Stoner had no time to understand before Ellie came on again.

"Bravo 2 here. I have directional. It's crazy."

The signal emanated from their carrier. Pauley's search cubicle. Hardesty confirmed. Stoner had to believe the evidence of his instruments. Not the assigned booster frequencies to Limbo, not the tightly directional signal that required, but an omnidirectional broadcast wave with all the power at Pauley's command. Nor was it the jarring, agitated alien voice they'd heard minutes ago.

"That's old traffic," Hardesty said. "I remember that. Gotta be a recording. What the hell is going on?"

Stoner tried to think clearly. "Advise your pilots and stay on it. Don't transmit. November, November from Bravo 1, over."

Nothing but channel hiss. *What are you doing, Nije?*

"Stoner, seal," Tyne snapped suddenly over com. "Got a bogey. Extreme range. 70,000-plus kays and closing. Gunny and Krug confirm. Just there all of a sudden. Has to be the Jump ship. Button up, it's getting crowded out here."

"Right." Stoner locked the helmet to his collar. "November, come in. November, if you read, your bridge is registering the bogey. Request recall now. Acknowledge."

Still no answer. Stoner's gloved finger shook over the com switch. This was what he'd always feared about Sparrows, what happened to Ed, what was happening to him now. "Tyne, I can't raise Pauley. How about you?"

"No, I tried on command. Worked Jane's on the bogey. Pretty long range, but nothing like a match. 65,000 and closing. We get recall now or Satin won't have time to beam us in."

"I'll keep trying. November . . ." The voice died in his throat as Stoner remembered. What and how but not why. The hell with procedure now. "God damn you, Pauley. I know you can hear me. I saw that 528 spool you're sending. We remember that traffic. I don't know what you're doing, but recall. Recall! Get us the fuck *out* of here. Acknowledge or we'll take action on our own."

When Pauley responded, a man issuing a probable death sentence, his voice didn't falter with any nuance of regret. "November here. There's a bogey closing and total disable on tractor beam. We are going to battle stations. Cannot recall. November out."

Stoner stared helplessly at nothing. November out. Bye-bye, end of message. He couldn't believe what he was thinking. "You hear that, Tyne?"

"Yeah."

"Can we run for the carrier?"

"With no beam, we're just three more targets. Bravo 2 and 3, stay on station."

Stoner felt he ought to say something to his kids, but Frank beat him to it. "Bravo 2 from 3. Stay green, love."

"We're chilled out," she jittered slightly, "but I wish I'd worn a diaper."

In Bravo 1, Stoner appealed to his pilot. "Can you figure this, Jan?"

"No, but you know how it stacks up."

They all did. Even if Launch had the beam operational in the next few minutes, their margin for recall was running out now. Satin could not maneuver tactically and align for them at the same time. Why was secondary to the fact on Tyne's sensors. While Satin responded to the alien threat, *Langston* was withdrawing rapidly with no sign of launching fighters. As command Sparrow, Jan Tyne felt suddenly and terribly alone. "See that, guys?"

"Bravo 3 armed," Krug reported. "I did not forget this time. Where is *Langston* going?"

"What's the difference?" Gunny answered him. "That's all she wrote. Bravo 2 armed."

"Bravo 1 armed."

But for the actual dying, they were already dead. Whatever had happened, no one could blame Alexi Satin for a glitched T-beam or abandoning six for the sake of two hundred. As Jan followed *Langston* dwindling on her image screen, Gunny reminded her gently, "Your call, Jan."

"Yeah. I'm not much on this glorious leader stuff, but both of you close up on me."

Frank Hardesty's tix was a naked, bitter indictment. "Pauley wanted that Jump ship to hear him. No other way to read it."

"Stow that and listen up." Stoner tried to wet his lips with a tongue gone dry. "Monitor on pilot channel. Tyne's got the ball now." And maybe God if that helped, and that was the end of the news. Goodnight, world. With a bleak glance at the E-pod, he tightened his harness and sent a last message to November. "Pauley? I know you hear me. I don't know why you did this, but I hope 528 gets you first, and the odds on that are real good. Bravo 1 out."

In the Search cubicle Pauley heard the gallows valedictory of Charley Stoner who knew he and his people had been purposefully thrown away. For himself, Pauley was surprised only by the evacuation of the *Langston*. That was not the plan. Lure the Jump ship in, sacrifice the Sparrows while both carriers valiantly engaged the enemy long enough to create a traumatic incident, but not—

The serpentine logic of his profession supplied

part of the answer. Waites. Somehow. For Waites' reasons which he was not to know.

Pauley sent: "I hear you, Charley." He switched off and left the cubicle.

In a few minutes Captain Alexi Satin had lived years through a commander's nightmare. His immediate order on the appearance of the bogey was to prepare T-beam for retrieval, his second to align for pickup. His exec officer reported the beam not functioning.

"What? Who is on watch? Let me speak to—" Satin spat the question on hailer. "Launch Control: Who is this?"

"Specialist Gosnell, sir. Something—I don't know. I can't enable."

"Backup?"

"Negative, sir. Something's just fried the whole system. We're working on it, but it's like someone did it deliberately."

Eyes darting from the screen with the nearing Jump ship to the radar plot with its cluster of three dots to whom he could offer no hope, Satin begrudged his few seconds of confusion. As his orders read, if engagement were imminent, *Langston* was to engage the attacker while Satin retrieved his ES-craft. But his status officer had reported Captain Mbutu's carrier gone FTL and off the scans.

"Armament, report when online. Helm, continue evasive action."

"They're firing, sir. 30,000 kays. Still pretty wide but not much diffusion. Some kind of plasma."

Energy plasma with minimal diffusion at 30,000 kilometers. *Kennedy* had nothing to match it. Launch suspected sabotage; he smelled larger treachery. Satin spun away from the hailer toward the communication pos, noticing Pauley as the IO appeared on the bridge.

"Sir, we have *Langston* calling. They're out of FTL."

Satin wasted no time on courtesies. "Mbutu, what are you doing? Why did you withdraw?"

The answer came after twenty-five seconds in a rich west African timbre. "This is Mbutu. Withdrew per my orders. Why did you not? Advise your situation."

"Advise?" Satin would have cursed were there time for that. "Alien at . . . 28,000, firing on us. I am evading. Rejoin immediately."

Again the maddening, unaffordable delay. He snapped the question at Helm and Navigation. "Status?"

"26,000 kays, sir. Still firing."

The forlorn, lost image of three Sparrows flashed once more and finally through Satin's mind. "Match *Langston* course. Continue evasion. Prepare for FTL."

Mbutu's response came after a longer lag. "Negative rejoin. My orders from UNESA Fleet Command, and yours as well, specifically order withdrawal. Will you comply? Over."

"Fleet Command . . ." Satin shot an uncomprehending glance across the bridge at Pauley. "My orders are not from Fleet but COORDINT, Captain. Cannot account for the discrepancy and have no time to debate. Withdrawing on your course. Thanks *so* much for enlightenment."

As he swung away in disgust, the bridge rocked and shuddered under Satin. He stumbled and caught himself. "Damage Control, where are we hit?"

A glancing burst had grazed them aft, but skin integrity was not compromised. Seething, Satin stabbed at the hailer button on his seat arm. "Drive, this is the Captain."

"Drive, aye."

"Initiate FTL sequencing, advise each phase when complete. Pauley, you are COORDINT. Can you explain why Mbutu has one set of orders and I another?"

Nigel Pauley could have elucidated much but not all, answering questions for himself even as he posed them. Waites must have encrypted different fleet orders into Mbutu's computer system, easy enough for a master plumber like Tony. That was as far as his own logic took him as he strapped onto the accel-pad. If Pauley's mind could not yet connect with the dark-logic end of it, he would in time.

Another hit rocked the carrier, more severe this time. Pauley pitied Satin and cursed Waites as Damage Control reported a breach in the ward room/mess area. Three fatalities. Satin ordered the bodies secured.

"No bodies, sir." The DC tek sounded badly shaken. "Just sucked out of the breach. Two . . . two crewmen and the mess officer, Captain Ferrier. We sealed the compartment off."

Oh Christ, not Adrienne. Pauley winced against the impact of her loss. *You did this, Waites, but I helped.*

The fact came to that in his merciless estimation. He was to be the Judas goat leading the others to sacrifice. *But not Adrienne, that's too expensive. You haven't won yet, Tweedle. Someone will know before Judas dangles.*

Drive reported standing by for final FTL sequence. Satin made sure all personnel were secured. "Helm, coordinates locked in?"

"Locked."

"Initiate."

In those last seconds, Pauley's mind, the disciplined synapses of a master of complex deceptions, flooded with a surge of cognition that perceived the endgame and the series of moves concluding it. Waites wanting to tour the drive compartment . . . sudden cerebral hemorrhage in a healthy young crewman. Beaudry just happening to be on hand, accompanying Waites and the body as a witness to the other carrier.

And still there.

Beaudry—

The Sparrow crews listened on pilot channel for each other, for anything. Blind at his position, Stoner asked sit/rep from Jan.

"Satin's taking hits, trying to accelerate. 528 closing."

Nothing else to say. Tyne brought herself back to their own grave situation: orbital decay factor still low but creeping higher with a corresponding increase in skin temperature. Maneuvering for the D/F fix had cost them much in velocity. "We're not dead yet, Bravo. Let's get upstairs. Stay on my six until you read zero ODF. Full thrusters now."

Afterburners streaks of light, the Sparrows shot up and away from Hydri IV. As ODF and temperature fell again, Willi Krug noted philosophically, "*Machts nicht* now, but there goes my place on the promotion list."

Gunny had to laugh. "I don't believe it, guys. Listen to the thirty-year man."

"Lieutenant Krug," Jan offered ceremonially. "As command pilot, I promote you very temporary full colonel for distinguished flying. Just stay on my tail, *Herr Colonel*."

"*Danke*. Not that we're going anywhere."

"That's Willi," Gunny observed. "Even now he has to be German. Could be worse, fella. 528 could be coming for us."

And probably would but no one wanted to think of that now. At 8,000 kilometers from planet surface, Tyne cut thrusters and directed the two others to coast on her port and starboard. They could still read their carrier's condition on scans: intact but badly damaged, bleeding heat trails as the alien inexorably closed.

Stoner unstrapped and floated forward to read the action on Tyne's screens. "What's happening?"

"They were working toward trans-light, but something's wrong. Shouldn't take so—"

The words froze as her screen image of *Kennedy* sprouted a huge blister filled with a spray of tiny firefly heat traces that flickered and faded rapidly. Stoner looked away. *That's people.*

"That was not a hit," Krug informed them from experience. "An internal explosion. She is finished."

With such damage the carrier would never take the stress of transition to FTL.

"Stoner, tell your ops to shut down their sys-

tems," Tyne ordered. "Pilots need all power for
the ship now."

He levered himself back to his position, securing the harness, and relayed the command to Ellie and Frank. "Monitor on pilot channel. Don't
answer, just do it. Don't worry, kids. *Langston* or
somebody will pick us up."

They'd know there wasn't much chance of that.
Stoner wished he could find the right thing to say
to them, more to do so they wouldn't just sit
helpless and waiting to die. He tried to think
through his own leaden fear and the grim facts.
There was some chance. If 528 left them alone,
they could last a good while in the ships and for
days in the pods. Maybe someone would hear
their beacons in time.

He'd been off channel for the few moments of
his cold-sweat calculation. Tyne broke in on com.
"Stoney? Get on pilot channel. It's Pauley."

Pauley closed the cubicle hatch behind him.
The crippled ship was dying. After the explosion
in the FTL compartment, Satin had tried to turn
on the alien, ordering Pauley back to his own station in Ops. The bridge took the first direct hit
seconds after he left, and then another just beyond Operations, cutting Pauley off from the pod
bay where the first survivors were ejecting now.

The fissure in the Operations bulkhead length-
ened as he watched, life support hissing out in a
sibilant coda to his own swan song. The bridge
was gone, the carrier a disintegrating hulk, much
of its skin gone brittle from the effect of the 528
weaponry. The bulkhead rift just beyond his cubicle would rend, then gape wide . . .

His screens glowed feebly on auxiliary power cut in automatically when the main died. On one screen the horseshoe crab shape of the Jump ship loomed hugely. He swept radar to find his Sparrows. Farther out and close together, coasting away from Hydri IV toward nothing.

Pauley slid down into the pos seat, pressing his tix switch. "November to Bravo. Don't know if you read me. I'm on aux power."

He opened a drawer and extracted a half pint bottle of cognac, a gift from Adrienne on her last leave in Paris. Almost empty. "Going on the last of my life support. Cheers."

Lifting his right arm hurt; he'd fallen on it hard when the bridge was hit just behind him. He swallowed half the remaining liquor in one slug. "Bravo, any of you. If you hear me, Krug's theory of their weapons was correct. Complete molecular disruption of a wide area around the actual wound, a kind of metal fatigue like gangrene. Very effective."

Beyond the hatch, the hiss of escaping oxygen had deepened to a rush. Pauley heard the discordant shriek of rotted metal ripping like cloth.

"You can see what's happening. I won't last long and don't imagine anyone will weep for that, since I Burglared the T-beam, but I want you to know why at least. You deserve that much—as much as I know, in all events. Proximity was just a cover, Stoney. The real object was to lure 528 out and provide an incident, start a war so UNESA would be justified in coming in with a major assault and takeover of the planet before one of the Corpses did. With dramatically horrifying sacrifices, you understand. After *Swift* and *Condor*, we were certain of what we'd suspected for years. We can't do much against all of them but fight a delaying action. We have to scare the governments into voting us the money to go all out. It's all budget, people. Imperative action against available funds. We can't just deter. We have to pre-empt."

Pauley raised the bottle again, letting the last cognac burn down his throat in a fiery benediction.

"You were to be the slaughtered heroes, the well-publicized moral outrage. Considering the swiftness with which news goes to holo-TV now, I wouldn't be surprised if we were all martyred in a mini-series. I don't know how to call it, but I do know Waites. Colonel Anthony Waites of COORDINT. Anyone gets out, remember the name. He must have felt three Sparrows weren't sufficient horror. Somewhere along the gameplan, Waites factored this ship and me into the equation. He switched orders on *Langston*; that's why they withdrew. Poor sod Mbutu, they'll probably break him just to make it look good. That's all I can assume just now. Forgive me; I'm not too mentally agile at the moment."

No more air hiss beyond the hatch, only the barely audible whisper of atmosphere seeping from his cubicle.

"You people have more of a chance than I do. Bridge activated distress calls. Maybe *Langston* will come back. If you get out, tell them what happened. Tell what I did. Tell them why Waites sent us all up the spout. Christ, am I a ghost already? Stoner? Anyone? Do you copy?"

"This is Stoner," the dry voice came over his speakers. "We all read you."

"Good. Pretty lonely in here. Not much air left. A few minutes and that's it. Bloody well knit myself up, didn't I? Talk to me, Stoney."

Stoner was amazed to find some atom of pity for the poor inhuman bastard. "So that's why you canceled the request for more pilots."

"With the new orders they would have been redundant. There's a line in *Henry V* that says it nicely, but I'll spare you poetry."

"Thanks. We don't feel very poetic now." Stoner paused over his own feelings. More like terminal empathy. They were all going the same route. "Talk to him, Jan. He knows he's had it."

She came back on ship's com. "What do I say to someone who killed me and Gunny? You wave goodbye if you want. Fuck him."

Stoner would talk to him. He'd say goodbye whether or not it was more than Pauley deserved. "November, you still there?"

". . . read you weak but clear. Not much power left."

"We're all listening. This is for all of us. How long have you known we had to go down?"

"The orders came before IP," Pauley said. "Why do you think I was drunk for three days? Trying to live with what I had to do. *Had* to do. Like wasting Thun."

Had to . . . waste. Over the hissing ether, the professional effecter of resolutions spoke of murders while some renegade human regret loaded the terrible *had to* with a plea for understanding if not forgiveness.

"Was it worth all this, Nije?"

The answer was fainter as the last of the auxiliary power faltered. "Yes, you'd ask that, you old Earther. Irrelevant as it is. They fingered Thun to cover up the real sleeper agent. Beaudry—I knew it was Beaudry, had to be. Anyone gets out, remember him along with Waites. Philip Beaudry. If I'd guessed I was for it too, I'd have stayed drunk longer."

"Major, this is Frank Hardesty." The condemnation knifed across the widening gulf between doomed Sparrows and a dead carrier. "Too damned bad about you. Don't ask me to understand, you son of a bitch. Don't say nothing personal and all that. Ellie and I found a life. You knew that; every fucking day you knew it and still planned to off us. And you could stand up at briefings and look us in the eye."

"I'm sorry, Frank."

"You're sorry! I'm talking about a life, something you'd never understand. That's not easy to find nowadays, not out here. And you killed it. My only payback is knowing you'll go first, and that helps. Jesus and Saint John forgive me, but I'm glad."

"This is me, Pauley. Ellie Roven. Frank said it for me. Damn you forever."

"Okay, cut the overkill," Stoner checked them. "He's right. We have more chance than he does." He paused with the pathetic absurdity of confession and condemnation alike now, the dead impotently cursing the dead at their own funeral. There was a weird embarrassment in bidding goodbye to his own assassin. "I don't know what to say to you, Nije."

"I'll take a shot," Gunny volunteered. "Got no

pity for you, Major, but don't wait until you can't breathe in there. Go cleaner than that, you copy?"

"Clear, Willington." Fainter still. Pauley's power was almost gone. "This position doesn't have the options of an E-pod. No pill, no sidearm. Worst of all, no more cognac. Had a passing urge for a cigarette, Stoney. Looked around to see if you hadn't squirreled one away somewhere."

"Sorry. Dorfmann got the last."

"Pity. Well, the silly bastard's got a smoke-free station now. It was the ambition of his declining years to psych out where you got them. Always wondered myself."

"It ain't too hard when you bet queens against a shuttle pilot who trusts God to fill inside straights."

Pauley's laugh was a mere ghost whisper now, but Stoner read it. "You know I'll never tell. Getting stuffy in here. Air's very thin. Cold, too. Goodbye, Stoney. I'm going for a walk. November out."

The channel whispered in their ears. No one spoke. Beyond Pauley's cubicle there was no oxygen at all, Ops compartment breached and open to space. When Pauley cracked the hatch, the last of his air would rush past him into Kelvin zero void. His lungs would rupture and perhaps his blood freeze before Pauley drowned in it, unconscious in seconds, frozen brittle hard in a few more. November out.

"This is Bravo 1," Jan Tyne sent to all of them. "Operators switch to command channel. We should all be on one freq now. And no chatter. Pilots have priority. Stoner, I'm setting the same course as *Langston*. Send a distress. Tell 'em where we are."

"Will do. Where's the bogey?"

After a moment, Tyne answered flatly, "Close as you'll ever want. They've seen us."

"Calling distress now. Ellie, Frank, you heard the order. Get on pilot channel and stay quiet. And—" Pauley used to sign off that way out of habit, but Stoner passionately meant it now. "God bless, kids."

He tuned one receiver to standard distress frequency before thinking about it and wished he hadn't. The channel howled with the banshee wail of multiple pods, survivors from the carrier. A dozen or more of them, beacons blurring together, lagging, separating into syncopation, then arhythmic . . .

Stoner spun the vernier to wipe their cries from his ears and mind, tuning his main transmitter to 150 megs, the hailing frequency used by *Langston*, fingers stabbing directional adjustment into antenna controls.

"*Langston*. Carrier *Langston* or any vessel copying. This is Bravo 1 requesting assistance. Three Sparrow ES-craft off carrier *Kennedy*. Carrier down, repeat down. *Langston*, we are on your last known course, full thruster capability but we are being pursued by alien Jump ship. Any vessel copying, if you read go to sensors for wreckage, image for pods if possible. Listen on distress for pods. There are survivors from the carrier, vicinity Hydri IV."

Helpless rage exploded in Charley Stoner. "You people out there listen to me. And you, Colonel Waites. Pauley gave us the word on you. You wanted a fucking outrage? You got one, so make the most of it because I sure hate dying for nothing. *Langston, Langston*, any vessel copying. Bravo 1 sending distress, request assistance. Approximately 9000 kays out from Hydri IV on *Langston's* last known course."

The alien ship loomed huge as an amber full moon on the pilots' perimeter scan. At 75 kilometers they read the small craft emerging like wasps from a hive.

"Seven, eight," Gunny counted. "I read ten."

Coming on, attacking in a swarm, no formation at all. With no time or margin for error, Jan Tyne drew on experience and instinct. "Pilots, get your ops into the pods. Stoney, I've released the pod hatch. Get in. Advise when sealed."

"Sealed?" He didn't understand at first. "What about you?"

"Look, we don't have many options—Willi! You're too tight on me! Angle out." Jan's voice came over Stoner's helmet phones, sure of herself and admitting no argument. "We can't outrun or outgun, and I couldn't even face pod drill, remember? Sorry, I've been there. Seal and pressurize."

He understood then but couldn't accept. "Goddammit, girl, you can't—"

"Yes, I can, Mr. Stoner. I've got a chance in a fight. In a pod I'll die. Go on. That's an order."

"Crazy . . ." Stoner slammed at the harness release, hauling himself up and toward the open pod hatch.

"God, they are fast," Willi Krug marveled over pilot channel. "I read them already at only 50 kays."

"Ellie going into the pod," Gunny reported. His screens imaged the alien fighters in detail as they approached: fat delta shapes less than a third of a Sparrow's length and not more than two meters dorsal to belly. "What are they, Munchkins?"

In Bravo 1, Stoner closed the pod hatch after him. "Sealed and pressurizing." The pod's status board read green, eject doors open. He heard the pop! as Tyne blew the explosive bolts. "Pressure 10 psi, all green. Jan, you sure you want it this way?"

"I can't do it, Stoney."

"Good luck, lady."

"*Vaya con Dios*. And listen, you walking accident. We ever crew again, you better be housebroken."

Jan blew Stoner clear of the Sparrow, statusing Gunny, Willi and the incoming hostiles at a glance. "Going tac now. VR helmets. Turn on me. Gunny, you're my number two. Willi, you're cover shooter. Now."

The three Sparrows arced up to gain elevation over the 528 swarm, Willi several hundred meters higher and behind as they came out of the turn, Gunny behind Jan at four o'clock. In the precise simulation of her VR, Jan saw with disbelief that the cluster of hostiles didn't deploy in response as experienced fighters would.

"See 'em? They're nothing on tackem, guys. Let's go, Gunny. Willi, cover our six."

They lanced down through the surprised delta craft, firing forward and then after lasers as they broke out into open space, Willi holding his high position.

"I hit one!" he exulted. "Hardesty is prepping pod for—"

Even as he spoke, Jan's VR registered the three incredibly swift dots rising toward Willi like the growth of some graceful, deadly flower on time-lapse film, *"Willi! Low on your six—"*

The blue-white lines shot out, carving Willi's ship into three sections from which smaller fragments crumbled away. On heat sensors, two red and yellow blobs flared and paled quickly as warmth bled from breached pressure suits.

I hope Roven didn't see that, Jan prayed. She'd know anyway if she lived that long. "Stay with me, Gunny. They're meatballs; got nothing but speed. How's Roven?"

"In the pod and prepping."

"Blow her and let's do it again, fore and aft, copy?"

"Go, girl."

They shot across the last intervening distance, forward lasers firing in a converging pattern. As they broke through the ragged group of 528s, their after weaponry searched and found targets.

"Way to go, Jan! Smoke the little—"

Gunny's voice broke off with his tix switch still open. Jan heard the other sound, then blank hiss over the channel. On her helmet display, Gunny's ship yawed, then recovered. "Gunny, you're hit. Turn on me, I'll cover. Talk to me." She pushed the Sparrow forward of his in the turn, burning ATs to waggle and present less of a target as the deadly blue-white lances streaked about her. They hit Gunny but no way would they kill him. Jan set the Sparrow on a long, converging course with his as they closed again on the delta fighters. "Target with me. Acknowledge."

Gunny's response was flat, leached of its usual vitality. Shocked. "Got you . . ."

"Are you hurt?"

"Negative. Targeting lead ship. We can't miss."

"Kill'm," Jan snarled. "Kill'm. Fire on my mark—now."

In this moment, she was pure predator, what all her life had shaped her to be, watching the lead ship lurch under their concerted fire and sheer into another, both caroming out of the swarm. "Talk to me, Gunny."

"Still with you, Jan."

She squeezed her eyes shut, wrapping her soul around the sound of him. "Where are you hit?"

"Bad. In the pod, I blew the bolts. Little slow on eject. Just a little slow. The hit must've . . . right through the eject doors. Wide open back there. I had to scrub VR and seal before I froze in here."

"Stay on me. They're doing something."

The hell with VR. Jan stripped it off and locked on her pressure helmet as she read the change in the alien formation boring in on them, dividing into two groups. Getting smart at last. "Armament status?"

"Ninety-eight percent, still big and bad, but the skin breach . . . getting redline stress readings."

"Wide turn. Ease her around."

They looped high, sacrificing speed for position, and plummeted again toward their enemy. Jan cradled one delta in her HUD targeting and fired. The 528 ship blossomed on her heat sensor, bleeding heat and atmosphere. In perfect unison, she and Gunny knifed between the two ragged groups, rear lasers slashing.

I wish that was Pauley, Jan prayed darkly, turning wide again, trying to cover Gunny but reading the hull stress that would fragment his ship any moment. *But it's us, Gunny, you and me, and these meatballs never saw and never were anything good as us.*

Her ship rocked as the plasma burst tore through her dorsal skin. The target veered out of her imaging, then settled again as she fired and saw the delta craft spin out of control. *Getting cold in here. Seconds, that's all we have, Gunny. But it's okay. I'm not afraid anymore, not even to live.*

And then his voice soothed in her ear as if they were lying close together, sharing one pillow the way they did at the end of their leave. "I saw that hit. You okay, Jan?"

"Yeah, but I think this is the last dance."

"Me too. Breaking up. Can't maneuver much. She won't take any more stress."

"I know." Jan read the falling temperature in her cockpit. Outside the frail barrier of her suit and helmet, there was killing cold. "Ever see an open log fire on a real hearth?"

"In pictures. I'll build you one," Gunny promised. "Let's go for the condo, Jan."

"Let's." Jan watched the nearest attacking ship creep the right way down her HUD targeting. "Firing—now."

A moment of gravity as the pod spurted from the Sparrow's belly, then weightless in his straps with the beacon bleeping lustily from the tiny speaker. Stoner checked the power level on the beacon transmitter and lowered the oxygen regulator to conserve, glad he'd done the pod drill himself. Everything checked out except distilled water. For some reason the gallon container had been half empty; he'd filled it. Sidearm clamped to its magnetic panel and, just above that, the small fliptop plastic box—but forget that. No way was Mrs. Stoner's only son going to bite the Big O. He'd go easy on food and water.

His harness was too loose; he floated in it. Stoner tightened down. No gravity or sense of movement. For a while, until he dared, he avoided peering from the view plates. Space revolved around the motionless center of him. The pod was still spinning with its original impetus, a small planet with a population of one.

On the next revolution he could see moving points of light darting furiously against a backdrop of stars, a swarm of fireflies surging after two others, lasers lancing at their targets.

The distant battle revolved beyond view again while the beacon piped monotonously. Stoner glared at the small digital clock racking up seconds into minutes. From the instant Tyne blew him clear, his life expectancy was bleeding from that clock.

The firefly battle swam back into view, fainter and more distant, the needle bursts of weaponry thin as spiderwebs against black space, the swarm closing on one remaining target visible only by forward laser and afterburners ablaze in its savage attack against the hostile lights. The picture slid away and when the universe rolled once more, the remaining swarm receded in a loose formation, their business quite finished.

Stoner lay back and closed his eyes. He guessed

the last ship was Tyne. In a Shrike she would have taken more of them with her.

"Is that all? All of us?" he challenged the pod beacon sending its futile call. "Is this how we go out?"

Stoner broke out one of the C-bars. The vitamin-enriched chocolate gave his taste buds an immediate rush. He hadn't eaten anything since breakfast and a quick slurp out of a tube. He chewed in slow rhythm with his tired thoughts. *Pauley's last stand.*

Nije asked for it, went looking for the Indians and damned well found them. If the whole miserable mission was a calculated outrage, the movers and shakers Earthside better get real mad and come with everything they had, because a few carriers weren't going to cut it against 528. And when he got here, Custer better get smart and listen good while 528 did the talking. That was going to bust some balls in the cavalry. Stoner would love to be there, especially with the news Pauley laid on him. That wasn't likely now, but one thing was.

Whoever they are, 528 knows we'll keep coming. We have to. Not that much left at home. We'll come with the same old bullshit: peace, friends. Love, honor and obey us! And here's Charley Stoner, the black little period at the bottom of the exclamation point. Must be the oxygen, because I'm thinking cool and clear now. He tried to estimate how long before the sidearm became a serious choice. Tyne had said they weren't dead yet, and opted to turn and fight. And here he was with everything he feared already gone down, and still alive. When the worst happened, his fear hadn't paralyzed him. He'd handled it better than he thought he would.

Stoner tucked away the remainder of the C-bar, took a small sip of water and tried to get comfortable. Behind his closed eyelids exhaustion sucked him down toward sleep. The picture of Ellie and Frank floated into his slowing mind. He hoped they got out, one of them at least. Better them than himself. On the carrier, scared to death, he'd asked *why me*? Still a good question. Somehow random luck and second chances weren't good enough, not for his kids. You made luck into religion because behind the faith in luck were hard numbers, and every choice you made out here shifted those figures toward survival or death. Stoner thought of the clock dealing out his redundant leftover life like cards from a deck.

His eyes shot open. He'd dreamed he was falling and his arms went out reflexively to steady him. Something physical had jarred him awake. Elapsed time on the pod clock read 1:10:27 since eject. But something was different. His beacon signal was fuzzy with interference. For a bad moment Stoner thought the damned thing was crapping out on him. Then he felt the gravity as his pod lifted in the pull of a tractor beam. He twisted in his straps, pressing his face to the overhead plate. *Langston* came back for him. Jesus, he always had more dumb luck than anyone except Ed—

Not *Langston*, not that endless dark surface of unknown configuration sliding majestically by his overhead view. His pod was being drawn along it toward a reddish glare that hurt his eyes. In a surge of animal panic, Stoner grabbed for the sidearm—then tittered weakly. *Get real, Custer*.

If this was 528, the silly weapon wouldn't impress them beyond killing him quick, but somehow it all worked out even. Reinecke heard them first. He would meet them first. The reality hurricaned into Stoner's mind and gut in a riot of fear, excitement and naked curiosity. He unlocked the harness. A last atom of common sense made him stuff all the C-bars into utility pockets.

The pod settled on a solid surface with a muffled bump. Stoner reached for his helmet. The whole rear third of it carried compressed oxygen and the pod's reserve cannisters could be attached if needed. He was securing them when he heard the familiar alto duet. Something brushed against the pod's outer skin.

528 looked in at him.

The lighting beyond his plates was dim. Stoner stared back into enormous eyes like flawless sapphires and imagined he read humanity there.

He reached for the hatch lever—*might as well, can't dance anymore*—popped it open and stood up, rising halfway out of the pod into a vast chamber, lowlit and bare except for three frail humanoid creatures no more than four and a half feet in height. One of them crooned at him, making tentative gestures with spindly arms raised up and down close to its neck. Stoner recognized the standard intervals of thirds and fourths in the voice. The creature gestured again, delicate hands at neck level. They wanted him to remove his helmet.

His common sense said: eventually, so why not now? Natural reluctance urged him to stay inside it, but exhaustion had eroded the long fear with everything else. Stoner unlocked the helmet and pulled it off to a weird accompaniment of six fluting, twittering tones. Timorously, like a mouse venturing into a room known for its cats, Stoner breathed in the soupy, miasmic atmosphere that struck his skin like the humidity of New Orleans in August, containing oxygen but something else that rasped his lungs like a file. In the soft, reddish glow his captors were slender, delicate little beings with bodies undefined as those of pre-pubescent girls and with near-translucent skin. Their big-eyed, red-veined faces were framed in sparse, silky-fine hair the color of bleached linen. Their garments seemed a composite of some sort of fiber laced with circuitry. Stoner wondered if the suits were a form of MUX interface.

One of them held up a fragile, transparent apparatus and flowed gracefully toward him. It pressed the mask to its own face, then held it out to Stoner in fingers fragile as plant tendrils. The canned life support held a mixture more compatible but still irritated his throat and lungs.

The sextet sang to each other through lipless mouths, only now and then discordant; then a kind of cooing which might have been curiosity equal to his own. Standing half in, half out of the pod, awkward and frightened, clutching the mask to his face, Stoner raised one hand in surrender. He didn't expect the I Come in Peace approach would impress them by now.

"Uh, hi. I don't know if you read me, but none of this mess was my idea."

They fell back a little as he climbed out of the pod and stepped onto the deck of the vast blood-hued chamber. What mechanical features he could distinguish had no recognizable function. Vast and bare—and his head was swimming. The mixture in the breathing mask . . . he felt dizzy, his throat aching.

One of the little creatures came forward and reached out. Stoner touched his gauntlet to the absurdly delicate hand. There was barely any pressure in the alien's touch. Stoner pointed to the mask, lungs laboring. "Not right . . ."

"Ooooo."

"I can't breathe!"

"Ooowwee uhllissen—"

Stoner tore the mask away as he went light-headed, groping for his own helmet. He fell back against the pod as the last strength left him, but the little man/woman/whatever still tried to communicate. It seemed very important that Stoner understand.

"Ooooweee lissen eeyoo."

Stoner's hands didn't work right and seemed terribly far away. He dropped the helmet, gasping for breath. But he understood.

"Yeah. We listen you too. I can't—"

The deck came up to meet him. Before blacking out, Stoner felt those impossibly slim fingers fitting the mask to his face again, fiddling with some kind of adjustment. He wondered if he was dying.

He couldn't be dead, not with such dreams.

Stoner came up out of a sleep stained with violent colors and ghost faces he knew, gradually aware of light beyond his eyelids and a trembling throughout his body. Adrenaline hangover; he'd run on nerves and fear since the Sparrow launched. Now the springs were winding down.

He lay on a pallet of some material that seemed to caress and invite his pummeled body to melt into it. Stoner opened his eyes, roving them about in low, indirect light, still too exhausted to move his head. A bare chamber much smaller than the first. He yawned, realizing that he breathed with no difficulty or any artificial support, not the heavy gunk of the other chamber but a mixture close in pressure and composition to space standard 10 psi.

Stoner breathed deep. He didn't feel physically ambitious; any movement right now ought to be considered carefully and avoided if possible. He took more deep, sighing breaths, then groggily turned his head far enough to see his helmet lying on the deck beside the pallet. He closed his eyes again—

"Hey, Stoney."

—so wiped out he had to remind himself that someone had spoken his name, a voice he ought to remember: gravelly but gentle and humorous.

"Wake up, clown."

It came from somewhere behind him. With a terminal effort, Stoner raised himself on one elbow, twisting around. Six feet away, an emaciated scarecrow in a soiled pressure suit sat on another cot set against a bulkhead, chewing ravenously at one of Stoner's C-bars. Stoner blinked at the grimy wraith with its overgrown hair and scraggly beard. His lips moved but the sound came out a disbelieving whisper.

"Ed . . . ?"

The scarecrow grinned at him, swallowing the last of the C-bar. "In the flesh."

What was left of the flesh. Ed Reinecke had lost at least sixty pounds. When he pushed his skeletal frame off the bed to come sit by Stoner, he showed no more substance than a coat hanger. The heavy pressure suit rustled and fell in about the nothing of him. The skin hung loose on facial bones, not shrunken yet to adjust to the rapid loss of supporting flesh.

"Glad you stocked up." Ed groped Stoner's utility pocket for another C-bar, carefully broke off half and replaced the rest.

"Ed, is it really—?" Stoner felt for the old solidity of his friend under the suit's material. "Christ, where *are* you?"

Reinecke waved listlessly at a shallow bowl on the deck by his bed, containing the remains of a substance like purple cat food. "They synthesize it for me, like the atmosphere in this room. Keeps you alive, that's about all."

He bit gratefully into the human concentrate. "Never thought this miserable shit would taste so good. You look awful. Can you sit up?"

He shifted stiffly out of the way as Stoner swung his legs onto the deck. "Did you get my last tix from Hydri IV? Things got hairy. Had to go on Morse and hope someone copied."

"I copied you." Stoner rubbed at his eyes. They felt gritty. "We wrote you off for dead."

"Man, how long ago was that?" Reinecke's once-hearty voice was now reedy and insubstantial as his flesh. "I lost track."

"Months—but you're one beautiful sight, Ed."

"Once they got the *Moyers*, didn't take long to zap us. One burst. Cut the Sparrow in half. I guess Johnny went quick . . . hope he did. Lucky I was sealed. That's a real naked feeling ejecting from half a Sparrow." Reinecke finished the last of the food. His eyes went hungrily to the utility pocket where the rest lay, but he made himself look away. "Who'd you fly with?"

"Tyne."

"Hey, Superbitch. Did she make it?"

"No." Stoner tried to stand but his legs were unreliable under him. He sagged back onto the bed. "Never felt so old in my life."

"That'll pass. They're pretty good about regulating gravity and atmosphere in here. Sampled the life support in my helmet and pod and reproduced it. Probably wonder how anyone can breathe atmosphere thin as ours."

"No, it's everything else. Everyone else." Stoner held his head in his hands. "All gone, Ed."

Reinecke's sunken eyes remembered a meaning for that. "Ellie too?"

His friend's answer was no more than a slight movement of his head. They sat in silence. After a time, Stoner mumbled, "They give you anything to drink?"

"They brought your water from the pod." With the stiff, strengthless movements of an arthritic old man, Reinecke fetched the container. They both drank from it. When Stoner said he felt better, his friend brought him the dish of purple food and an oval bowl containing a warm liquid of an emerald green hue. The solid food had a consistency somewhere between flaked meat and sand, and smelled like wet cement. Stoner put it aside. "What do they call that?"

"I don't know. I could sing it for you if I was built like them. Get used to it; that's all there is. Try the green soup. Best thing on the menu, sort of like chicken broth."

Stoner took an experimental sip. Chicken it was

not, but he felt an instant, nourishing lift. He struggled past the taste and finished the bowl.

"You look bad, Stoney. What happened out
there?"

Stoner didn't want to remember. "Not pretty.
Two hundred and five people, and that's just the
beginning."

Reinecke looked down at the paper-dry skin on
his hands. "God. I could've told them."

"Listen to me, Ed. Case you make it out and I
don't." Stoner clutched at the emaciated arm under
Reinecke's sleeve. "Someone has to remember."

He told Ed all he knew: what Pauley confessed
before he went, what UNESA tried to do and
planned to do. His friend only shook his head
gravely.

"They can't, Stoney. No way. These people, I
read enough of their sound-meanings to know
happy from sad and normal from pissed off or
scared, and they are very scared of us."

"So am I now," Stoner grated. Something white
hot rose from his gorge, too savage to be checked
much longer. "People like Pauley and Waites. All
we are to them is disposable tissues. I had to listen to Ellie and Frank when Pauley gave us the
word. When they knew they were dead already,
but still wouldn't break . . . brave kids. They
damned him."

"Easy, boy." Reinecke's stick of an arm encircled
his friend's shoulders. He used to be a bull but now
the embrace had no strength left. Stoner tried to
follow what Ed told him, that no one had a prayer
against these people, not now nor for years to
come.

"Way ahead of us in some ways, smart and

gutsy, but not much stamina and a long way from home like us.''

The ship was big only because they needed it for atmosphere. What equipment Reinecke had seen was fantastically miniaturized, but Jump must be a recent development because all the bugs weren't worked out yet. They'd received a transmission from their people on Hydri IV about a large, un-identified craft in the vicinity and sent two ships to intercept. The other ship never came out of Jump. Still in there, Reinecke surmised. Actually nowhere.

"It was that Corpse ship *Condor*. They voice-hailed and sent tone signals. I was sweating that it wasn't you guys.''

"Next one was us,'' Stoner mumbled. "They came out of Jump . . .''

"That's what I'm saying. When you don't come out just right, it's a nightmare.''

"I scoped them coming in. We didn't have a chance. Then they just stopped. Willi Krug figured a bad reentry.''

"Bad? You need a new word for hell,'' Reinecke said, his voice feeble as an old man's. "Think I'm this weak just from malnutrition? Total disorien-tation. Outside space and time, then slammed back in ass backwards. Some died, the commander par-alyzed. Some went insane, making sounds like you never want to hear again, sounds you couldn't be-lieve any living thing could make. Had to be mercy-killed.''

Reinecke himself experienced doppelganger in vision and personality, near-total physical collapse and the lingering, exquisite torture of every organ in his body, every apse in his brain drifting apart in different time zones for lack of any cohesion.

"Pitiful: I'd think to look at my watch and a minute later wonder why my arm was up, think my
name was Ed and forget the last one. Afterward,
two of them rolled in here in a sort of high-tech
wheelchair, so wiped out they couldn't move. They
thought I'd be dead. Blew them away when they
saw me stand up. They're not tough enough to be
out here and it ain't like they want to be."

Reinecke couldn't psych their thought processes
at all, except they seemed more emotional than
Earthers, if that was the word. Maybe not exploring
outward like humans, but going back, retreating as
humans came on.

"But they're great ops, Stoney. They've monitored us since our first probes got beyond the home
system, and they don't like what they read."

"Neither do I," Stoner husked wearily.

"But talk about *rigs*! Compared to them we're
Marconi sending a buzzy spark from big vacuum
tubes. And their receivers—well, look. This you
will not believe."

Reinecke fumbled ineffectually at the opening to
his utility pocket. Stoner could see that his hand
movements were severely uncoordinated. He finally got it open, bringing out a small object in the
palm of his hand. "See this?"

Stoner would have gasped if he had that much
energy left. Like the miracle of Ed being here, he
couldn't be that lucky.

"Full spectrum receivers, transmitters and recorders no bigger than this. You'll see."

Stoner took the package from his friend's hand
like a holy relic. There was a God somewhere; it
still contained at least ten cigarettes. He put one

between dry, trembling lips. "You ... you got a light?"

Reinecke snapped his lighter to the cigarette. "Last of the packs you paid me with, remember? They think it's part of my diet."

Stoner took a deep, end of the world drag, held the smoke and exhaled luxuriously. "Thanks, Ed. Just I'm not very tough either, I guess. Been scared shitless so long and so tired."

"Go easy." Reinecke borrowed a drag and butted the cigarette carefully on the deck. "Got to make these last with the C-bars."

"Don't know what for. I don't figure we'll last long enough for them to be a health hazard."

"Ah, who knows?" Reinecke tried to grin; a pinched effort. "Maybe like us they got a zoo for rare and dangerous species." He broke off, listening. Stoner caught a humming sound that grew louder as something approached their compartment. "They're coming. Listen, just before they blew us away, I got a clean cut on the surface transmitter. How about you?"

Did that matter now? It did, yes, for his own reasons. Stoner wobbled to his feet, still sick with the loss of his people, still terrified and knowing he'd be more so when 528 started on him. "Cut, slice and fix. Ellie and Frank and me, we nailed him."

"I was betting you would. You're the boss hot rock, Stoney. You could teach their ops something."

Damn right he was and damn right he just might. For Ellie and Frank that would be some part of winning and help make it clear to the Corpses

and the Pauleys that they couldn't just walk in anymore.

Reinecke tried to get up but somehow couldn't
make it just yet. He held out a hand. "Help me up?
I get awful weak sometimes. This food has no
nourishment for humans."

They stood together, Reinecke leaning on Stoner's arm like his great-grandfather as the door
parted up and down soundlessly. A wizened little
528 creature huddled in a device that floated forward inches above the deck. Two others flanked
him respectfully, all of them wearing the transparent breathing masks against the chamber's thin human atmosphere.

Stoner asked out of the side of his mouth,
"Who's this? A him or a her?"

"Can't tell. None of them do much for you that
way. This is the commander. Can't walk since the
bad Jump."

The great sapphire eyes searched Stoner's face.
The lipless mouth warbled a series of tone intervals.

Reinecke translated. "Question sound. Wants to
know about you."

"How much do they understand?"

"More than we do of them; just speaking is a
problem. They have a wider range of hearing, so
keep it low, slow and clear."

Gazing down at the shriveled form in its carrier,
Stoner gleaned an impression of advanced age
from the papery, wrinkled texture of the thin skin
and a clouded milkiness in the eyes. And a dignity:
wounded and crippled but still in command.
"Sure, I'll sing for him."

He began softly, drawing out the sounds, but

something emotional was rising from his stomach. "My name is Charles Stoner, warrant officer, UNESA serial ident 0-696534 . . ."

He faltered. A strong gust of the alien atmosphere had rushed in with the aliens to sear his lungs again. He choked and coughed; as if that tripped some release, the held-in thing spilled out of Stoner, no more to be denied. He began to cry, holding onto Ed as the wracking, painful grief tore out of him for what had been done to people he loved.

The sounds startled the aliens. They covered their delicate ears, high-squealing their unease.

"Stoney, chill down, get a grip. It hurts their ears."

He couldn't stop if he wanted to but had to weep for the betrayal that brought them all to this; for the blind waste of his kids and the futile courage of Tyne, Gunny and Krug. For the necessity that would bring more like them as monsters to be feared by these aliens as humans dreaded poisonous snakes or rabid dogs. For all those who would die before the smarter ones learned they couldn't win for centuries, maybe never, as if that would stop them. With the gut emotion went the last of Stoner's strength. He sank down on the edge of his cot, wiping clumsily at his tears.

The old commander began to speak/sing in low intervals like two wood flutes, rising harmoniously in fourths and fifths.

"What's he saying, do you know?"

"They're more emotional than us," Reinecke interpreted. "And they have tear ducts; they can cry. Close as I read, now they know you're human, civilized. They feel sorry for you."

Human. Perhaps a vastly more complex defini-
tion of the concept. "It's a good thing they didn't
haul in Tyne," Stoner husked through the last of
his tears. "If she couldn't get to Pauley, she'd beat
the hell out of them."

Ed sat down beside him with a wheezy grunt
while the three aliens conferred musically. The old
one's chair floated closer to the bed. Behind the
transparent breathing mask, the mouth shaped into
an oval.

"I think you're in," Reinecke figured. "That's the
way they smile."

The commander made several attempts before
the word came out at all recognizable. "Sssoo-
nuh?"

"That's me." His voice was a dry whisper now,
all he could manage. "Charley Stoner."

He formed his lips into an approximation of the
alien's smile, reaching for the offered hand.

AVONOVA PRESENTS
AWARD-WINNING NOVELS
FROM MASTERS OF SCIENCE FICTION

WULFSYARN
by Phillip Mann   71717-4/ $4.99 US

MIRROR TO THE SKY
by Mark S. Geston   71703-4/ $4.99 US/ $5.99 Can

THE DESTINY MAKERS
by George Turner   71887-1/ $4.99 US/ $5.99 Can

A DEEPER SEA
by Alexander Jablokov   71709-3/ $4.99 US/ $5.99 Can

BEGGARS IN SPAIN
by Nancy Kress   71877-4/ $4.99 US/ $5.99 Can

FLYING TO VALHALLA
by Charles Pellegrino   71881-2/ $4.99 US/ $5.99 Can

ETERNAL LIGHT
by Paul J. McAuley   76623-X/ $4.99 US/ $5.99 Can
